THE NOMINEE
A Novel

MICHAEL KINNAMON

chalice
stories

Print: 9780827225374
EPUB: 9780827225381
EPDF: 9780827225398

ChalicePress.com

Printed in the United States of America

This book is dedicated to The Disciples LGBTQ+ Alliance (formerly Gay Lesbian and Affirming Disciples [GLAD]), for its inspiring witness to the wholeness of the church,

and to

Rev. Dr. John O. Humbert, for modeling gracious leadership.

CONTENTS

PROLOGUE

Later, people would ask, "Was it worth it?" and Matthew would answer with a qualified yes. He had learned much about himself during those eight months, grown thicker skin, seen people at their best as well as their worst, discovered it is possible to speak about reconciliation too easily and too quickly. Abigail also claimed that the whole business had given him a few gray hairs, although he couldn't see what she was talking about. "If I have gray hairs," he told his daughter, "it's probably because of you!"

There was no doubt, however, that the nomination had taken a toll on Margaret. Not on their marriage, which had proved more durable than any threats, and maybe not on her faith, but certainly on the way she felt about the church. She still participated in their congregation in Lexington, at least occasionally, but when a friend casually referred to the church as a "safe haven," Margaret openly scoffed. The church, she declared, is no more safe than Congress is civil! Her husband might continue to teach that the church is the body of Christ, still insist he had been part of an important church-wide dialogue, but his nomination had allowed her to see that, at best, that was only part of the story. As far as she was concerned, he had dodged a bullet in more ways than one.

Matthew saw it differently. He would tell anyone who asked that the story of his nomination wasn't just about the church but about society as a whole. Any politician would recognize the challenges he had faced, any aspiring leader would understand the issues. Even those who never set foot in a sanctuary.

Neither Matthew nor Margaret could have foreseen any of this in the spring of 1991. It was the year of Operation Desert Storm, the year the Soviet Union fragmented and the Cold War ended, the year of the deadliest mass shooting by a lone gunman (to that point) in

U.S. history, and the year the "culture wars" fracturing U.S. society were given a name. James Davison Hunter's book was titled, *Culture Wars: The Struggle to Define America*, but Matthew told students that the subtitle could just as well have been The Struggle to Define the Church. They went hand in hand.

CHAPTER ONE

It had been a challenging week at Disciples Theological Seminary. Matthew's major headache of the moment was dealing with a congregation that was unhappy with its student minister.

"It's not because she's a woman," one of the church's elders had assured him, "although this is the second one in a row you've sent us. It's that she wants to change the worship service when people here—at least most of us—like it the way it is. Change is okay, we're not against changing things sometimes, but not when you first walk in the door."

This was much on his mind as he drove through mid-day traffic in Indianapolis. He could picture himself forcefully reminding the disingenuous elder that Stephanie had been the student minister at Tall Oak Christian Church since September, so it was hardly hasty to suggest a worship change in February. And let's cut to the chase: Would the church have raised the same objections if the student had been male? If Tall Oak wanted student ministers better than they deserved, they should *insist* on having women, because the majority of the seminary's best students were female. But, in fact, what he had said to the elder was, "I'll speak with her, see if we can't work something out, find some common ground." Some battles, he told himself, just aren't worth the effort. Better to maintain good relations with the congregation, which would be there long after particular students were gone.

Then last Thursday, two students—Heather and Lisa—announced during a school-wide convocation that they were more than just good friends. Why, he asked himself over and over, had they felt compelled to make such a public declaration of something that was hardly news to anyone who spent any time on campus?

Carter thought they might lose a couple of trustees if word got out, which it probably would because there was at least one trustee at the convocation. "Betsy was all smiles afterward," Carter reported in his southern drawl, "but that doesn't mean much. In Kentucky, the knives are sugarcoated."

Margaret had tried to help Matthew put the whole matter in perspective. "Carter," she reminded him, "always blows things out of proportion. Besides, it's not on your plate. You're just the dean. It's his job as president to worry about trustees."

As it turned out, Carter heard nothing from the trustees about the convocation, but Matthew got a call the next day from an irate alumnus, an old one from the sound of his voice, demanding to know if the students had been dismissed. And if not, why not? "That's the last thing we need in the church unless your plan is to kill it!" It was one call, Margaret pointed out, but three days later Matthew still couldn't get the man's words, the sheer rage in them, out of his head.

Enough of this! he told himself as he turned into the parking lot, past the sign that read "Disciples of Christ–National Headquarters." Concentrate on the meeting at hand. Why had Duane Porter, the head of the denomination, asked him to come for "a quick conversation"? But the elder and Stephanie, the irate alumnus and Heather and Lisa were not easily dismissed. As Margaret often observed, it was his nature to stew over problems, especially when they included anger at him. "You don't like not being liked."

And the seminary wasn't the only thing on his mind. On Monday, Abigail had been reprimanded by her fourth-grade teacher—with a note sent to her parents—for wearing a T-shirt that said "Stop the War" across the front, the hand-written letters made of gold and silver glitter. Matthew found it hard to be upset about this, but Margaret, a teacher herself, pointed out that schools have dress codes for a reason. She could only imagine the messages her ninth graders would display if such things were allowed in the district. Not to mention that their daughter, without asking, had smeared Elmer's Glue all over the front of a new piece of clothing and scattered glitter all over her room.

"*You* want to stop the war," Abigail said to her father when he tried to talk to her about it. "I hear Mom and you say that all the time."

"Yes, but ..."

"So, what's the big deal about saying so at school?"

"Nothing, but when you put it on your T-shirt ..."

"Andy, that's Andrea but we call her Andy, had on a T-shirt with Bart Simpson on the front, and nobody told her she couldn't wear it."

"That's different. Your shirt was saying something that not everybody agrees with. So, the school is trying to avoid controversial things."

"Well, that's silly," Abigail snorted. "We studied the American Revolution, and it was controversial to somebody, I bet."

While Matthew was trying to decide how best to answer that, she added, "What if it said 'Win the War'? Would I still have got yelled at?"

The memory made him smile as he locked the car and left the parking lot. Matthew had told Duane's secretary he would be there around one but, true to form, it was closer to twelve thirty when he entered the headquarters building. For several minutes, he wandered past portraits and other paintings that lined the wide, dimly lit hallways, greeting two or three people whose names he managed to remember. Finally, at twelve forty-five, he approached the secretary's desk in the office marked "General Minister and President" and, to his surprise, was immediately ushered in.

Duane greeted him with an awkward hug. "You know my deputies, Isabel and Marvin, the people whose job is to keep me from doing stupid things. I told them you'd be early." Duane laughed loudly, which, in Matthew's experience, he did much of the time.

As they were shaking hands, Isabel asked, "What was your speech about? Duane said you were in town speaking at a conference."

Now it was Matthew who smiled. "It was an event for academic types, so. ... Well, the title was "The Understanding of Sanctification in Protestant and Catholic Theologies of Baptism: Implications for Ecumenical Convergence."

"I'm into churchy things," said Marvin, "and that sounds boring even to me." This time they all laughed.

Duane grasped Matthew's elbow and guided him toward the oval conference table that filled one end of the large office. "I was just showing Marvin and Isabel a few of the pictures I took at the World Council of Churches' assembly in Australia. Our assemblies are bigger, if you can believe it, but this was still pretty impressive."

He took a seat at the middle of the table, Isabel sitting to his left, Marvin and Matthew peering over his shoulders. "I just got back on Sunday," he said, looking up at Matthew, "but our folks in communications developed these in a hurry."

The first picture in the stack of photographs showed Duane standing next to a man he identified as a Greek Orthodox bishop. The bishop wore a tall, black head covering, complete with flowing veil down the back, a black cassock buttoned to the neck below his beard, and an ornate pectoral medallion of the Madonna and Child; Duane wore rumpled khakis and a polo shirt. "I wonder," said Marvin, "if a visitor to the assembly could tell which one is a religious leader." More laughter.

"Duane," said Isabel, "you ought to at least wear a suit, like Matthew." She looked over her shoulder. "I've never seen you in anything but a suit. Give Duane here some pointers, will you? So he doesn't embarrass us every time he goes to one of these big assemblies."

Duane laughed along, but Matthew noticed he hurried past a picture of him with a bishop from India who was wearing a peach-colored robe and a head covering festooned with crosses. The next one showed a group holding signs: "World Council of Churches Supports Terrorists," "Prayer not Politics," "Not all diversity is approved by God."

"Those people were outside the convention center every day," said Duane, shaking his head. "It rained a couple of days, but there they were. Every single day."

He slipped that picture to the bottom of the stack, revealing one of a man—sweating profusely in the Australian summer—holding a sign that read, "WCC says Jesus isn't Lord!"

"I tried to talk to *this* guy, tell him his sign isn't true. Not a bit. Well, what I told him is that it's idiotic nonsense, but that just made him yell louder. He had his convictions, so he sure didn't want to hear any testimony from me."

"Maybe we should pay people to come protest at our assembly," said Marvin. "That might get us some press coverage for a change." Three of them chuckled while Duane laughed out loud.

He started to uncover the next photo, but Isabel stopped him. "Marvin and I have a one o'clock meeting and, in any case, we need to let you two talk. But give us your thumbnail assessment of the assembly."

Duane leaned back in his chair. "To tell the truth, it was disappointing. Very disappointing. It's good to see friends, go to a few workshops, hear what's going on in other churches, but overall. ... If you'd asked me last fall, I would have predicted this assembly would be one big celebration: the Berlin Wall coming down, Mandela being released. The churches had a role in these things, a big role. We should celebrate that."

"And then," said Marvin, "came the war."

"Yeah, then came the war. I guess there was even some talk of postponing the assembly, although it's almost impossible to turn a ship like that around after all the preparation."

He and Isabel stood up.

"Did you hear about all the trouble they had electing presidents?"

Since Duane now seemed to be looking at him, Matthew shook his head.

"You would think electing presidents would be pretty straightforward because WCC presidents don't do much. Mainly symbolic. But some of the Africans didn't like the African who was nominated. Then the youth demanded we have a president who's under thirty. Then ... I don't know what. Not enough of the nominees were left-handed or something." Duane laughed, but Matthew could tell it wasn't because he thought what he was saying was funny. "The war colored the whole assembly, that's what it felt like to me. They fought about everything. Everything! In the end, they—I guess I should say we—hardly could agree on how many presidents to elect, let alone who to elect. It was a mess."

As he and Isabel reached the doorway, Marvin turned back. "You didn't say anything, Duane, about the bomb. I read in a press release that there was some kind of explosion during the closing worship. What was that about?"

"It didn't amount to much," Duane told them, still smiling. "Not much. Some fool threw something at the platform up front. It sounded like a loud firecracker from where I was sitting, but there was a lot of smoke, a whole lot of smoke, and I guess one person was hurt." He shook his head. "I asked somebody on the staff if they'd expected trouble, and she just said it's hard to prepare for every kind of threat."

Once the deputies were gone, Duane invited Matthew to join him in the chairs set in front of the large, mahogany desk. He also offered a cup of coffee from the pot on a table behind the desk, which Matthew accepted, thinking of his drive back to Lexington.

"It seems impossible," said Duane, once he had settled in his chair, "but I graduated from DTS almost forty years ago, maybe before you were born. How are things there from your perspective?" So, Matthew gave a short report, quickly mentioning Stephanie and the elder, Heather and Lisa, and, finally, the phone call from the alumnus.

"Just one call?" said Duane, smiling. "You're lucky."

"You sound like Margaret."

"Several gave me an earful after my letter to the church on the war in the Gulf. Whoa, boy! Four or five were rah, rah America, said I needed to be more supportive of the troops, that kind of thing. The others said I didn't go far enough, that I should have totally condemned it. I told them that Disciples for Peace is bringing an anti-war resolution to the General Assembly, so they should get behind that."

Matthew started to say *but that's eight months from now* when the phone buzzed on Duane's desk. After listening for a few seconds, he put his hand over the receiver and said, "I need to take this, but it won't be long so just stay here."

While Duane spoke, Matthew surveyed the bookshelves that ran along one wall, smiling at how the titles revealed when Duane went to seminary. Would someone, he wondered, be able to tell when he graduated from Yale just by looking at his books? Placed among the volumes were baseballs autographed by the '65 Dodgers, the '68 Cardinals, and Ted Williams. Matthew looked at Duane, and they both smiled as Matthew pretended to stick this last one in the pocket of his suit coat.

On the opposite wall, between tall windows, were pictures of Duane in various church settings. Matthew was studying one he guessed was taken in Zaire, the Disciples largest mission field, when Duane hung up. "It looks like I need to go sooner than I thought," he announced. "There's always something that somebody thinks is a crisis. Anyway, you're probably anxious to get on the road. But we've got a few more minutes." He walked back around the desk. "How's that daughter of yours? One of my favorite kids!"

Matthew answered by pulling out an envelope Abigail had slipped into his suitcase. "She read somewhere about a girl who put notes in her dad's luggage whenever he leaves town, so now she does that." It was one of his father's business envelopes, but "Frank's Hardware and Lumber, Oak Grove, Iowa" had been crossed out, and in its place "Miss Abigail McCoy, Lexington, Kentucky" was written in bright red ink. Inside was a picture of Abigail, wearing a Cubs baseball cap over her long, brown hair, which made her head look big on top of her thin neck and shoulders. The picture was supposed to be of both children, but it cut off half of her three-year-old brother, Zachary. Duane laughed even harder after Matthew turned the picture over to where Abigail had written in red ink, "So you won't forget what we look like," even though her father was only going to be gone two nights.

Duane stood up and retrieved a paper bag from behind his desk. "Well, I have something for her. I remember you saying Abigail likes to collect pens and note pads and lapel buttons and whatever from the display tables at our assemblies, so I picked up a few things for her at the one in Australia."

He pulled a kangaroo-shaped refrigerator magnet from the bag with obvious satisfaction. "I bet she won't find anything like this at our assembly in Tulsa!"

Matthew managed to say "That's very thoughtful ..." before Duane quickly continued. "Actually, these display areas are getting out of hand. The assembly bookstore, tables with stuff from all our ministries, exhibits from the universities and seminaries, booths for selling stoles and communion sets and I don't know what all else. In Tulsa, it will take up half the convention center! That's one of the things the planning committee has got to talk about when it meets next week. There are so many loose ends eight months out, but we always manage to pull it together somehow. They come every two years, whether we're ready or not."

Duane drained his coffee cup and sat forward in his chair. "Of course, the big item of business is the election of a new General Minister and President, so I can retire and go to spring training next year." He reached out and put his hand on Matthew's arm. "And that's why I asked you to stop by. I think you know the search committee is meeting in the next couple of days. They keep me out of it, of course, but I know they're whittling down the list to a final three candidates. So don't be surprised, don't be surprised, if you get a call early next week."

"Maybe," said Matthew, "you should just be nominated for another term. Save the church a lot of hassle." He meant it tongue in cheek, but Duane seemed to take the remark seriously.

"I feel good about what I've done, most of it, but I'm not the guy for this time in the life of the church. One six-year term is enough, don't you think? At least for me. People see me as part of what was, not what's coming." Matthew could sense the emotion just below the surface.

"It would be nice … gratifying to be one of the three invited for an interview," Matthew admitted, "but I doubt very much …"

"This church needs a leader of your generation. And we definitely need somebody with your ability to see both sides of an argument." Duane's smile was now back in place. "I have to be neutral, that's what they tell me, but that doesn't mean I can't encourage the right person. Anyway, don't be surprised, that's all I'm saying, don't be surprised if you get a call. And when you get it, say yes! After that, we'll leave it to the church to make the right decision."

It was after one thirty when Matthew left the headquarters building, which meant he wasn't home until late afternoon. During the drive, he tried to focus on other things—the class he would teach on Tuesday, Stephanie and her congregation, possible fallout from Heather and Lisa—but his mind kept coming back to the conversation with Duane. That's what he wanted to talk about with Margaret, but it seemed to take forever before they could sit down, glass of wine in hand, and talk about anything.

First, she had to pick up Zachary at daycare while he retrieved Abigail from the neighbors, where she often went after school. Then, since the kids were clamoring for food, they warmed up a left-over casserole and ate a hastily prepared dinner, during which Abigail railed about a class project that was, in her words, "too stupid for words. They act like we're in the third grade!" Matthew started to say, *Well, you are only in the fourth*, but thought better of it. Margaret, however, asked "Who's 'they?'" which prolonged the complaint.

After dinner Matthew pulled out the bag from Duane, which Abigail took her time looking through, commenting on the quality of each item, even deigning to share a couple with her brother. She also told them what she knew about where kangaroos keep their babies and that it was now summer—well, almost fall—in Australia because they are upside down. "Dad, if you lived there in the winter—our winter, that is—you could watch baseball all year." He started to say, *Except that they don't play baseball in Australia*, but decided against it.

Finally, Zachary followed his sister down the stairs in their split-level home, leaving the adults alone in the living room. Before they had even settled in their usual chairs, however, Margaret let out a long sigh and said, "This is the last year I'll try teaching *Grapes of Wrath* to ninth graders." Matthew did as expected and asked why, which led to a lament he had heard from her before. "They just don't have the maturity to feel someone else's problems. And this is really the wrong book because these kids are so busy rebelling against their parents they can't appreciate how important family is, how hard you have to fight to protect it."

By the time she asked how the meeting went, what had seemed like a big deal now felt far less significant. "Duane thinks I may be one of the final three candidates for GMP," he told her. "But he's not on the inside of that process, and I don't think it's very likely."

The call from the chairman of the search committee came at the beginning of the following week—Monday, March 4—while Matthew was in a meeting. He returned it the minute he was free, only to be told that Reverend Wilkins—who, in addition to his committee responsibility, was pastor of a large congregation in Memphis—wasn't available. When they finally connected, the chairman offered a quick word of congratulations and then was all business.

"I assume you know the process, but I'll run through it just in case. Interview with the Executive Committee a week from Friday—

that is, the fifteenth—in Indy. They choose one of the three of you to be the nominee for General Minister and President." He used the familiar abbreviation: GMP. "The nominee speaks to the General Board in July. Assuming two-thirds of the Board vote in favor, the nomination goes to the General Assembly for a final vote in October."

Matthew told him that sounded fine, if a little overwhelming, Reverend Wilkins made no response, and that was that.

Fifteen minutes later, he got a second call, this one from Duane. Matthew knew from various church meetings that Duane's voice got higher when he was excited, and right now it was very high. "I told you to expect a call, didn't I?!"

Duane's enthusiasm made Matthew smile. "It means a lot to me that you would be in touch." He paused. "Especially since Ralph Wilkins didn't seem—how should I say it?—very happy about talking with me. Maybe he was just trying to sound neutral."

"Don't pay any attention to him," said Duane. "There will be a few who think you're too young, as if there's some rule says the GMP needs to be over forty. Of course, people my age think being young is a great qualification." He laughed before adding, "The other two they're recommending are also friends of mine, but. ... And there may be a few who want someone with experience leading a congregation, but that's just until they get to know you and see what you've learned from being dean of a seminary. Anyway, I just wanted to say congratulations. I don't think it violates the process—do you?—for me to offer a word of encouragement." Matthew could hear the emotion in Duane's voice, and he found it endearing, especially when Duane added, "God be with you."

The rest of the day was packed, so Matthew was eager to talk about the calls with Margaret, who, it turned out, was excited by his news but maybe not as much as he had hoped. "You expected this," she said after a congratulatory kiss. "Didn't you?" And she was predictably cautious. "This would mean you'd be gone from the kids even more than you are now."

They had, of course, been over this same ground as he met with the search committee. Then, however, it was a theoretical possibility; now it was an increasingly real one. "I'm just interviewing," he told her. "I can always say no."

"No, you can't. It's already too late for that. I'm happy for you, Matthew, because I think you want this, and you would be *good* at it. But if you're chosen, it will take a toll on the family, that's all I'm saying." She paused and smiled, slightly. "Of course, I'm proud of you. It's an honor to get this far, regardless of what happens. I'm sure you'll be the youngest one they interview ... and the best dressed."

Matthew had class the next morning, so it wasn't until he was back in his office that he allowed himself the luxury of thinking about the nomination. Margaret was right: He had half expected to be invited for this interview, or at least could imagine it. He was, after all, well respected in the church as an educator and as an advocate for Christian unity, which Disciples had historically seen as their church's special mission. Hadn't Duane said the church needs a reconciler, someone who can bring people together by seeing both sides of a conflict?

On the other hand, he would be giving up a lot. He loved teaching, although as dean he didn't get to do as much of it as he would like. Maybe there was almost as much teaching as General Minister and President, if you did it the right way. But why was it that each step professionally took him farther away from what he loved?

They would have to move to Indianapolis, and that would mean uprooting Abigail, who liked her school in Lexington. But Abigail was outgoing, made friends easily—more like her mother than like him in that regard. He had no problem in front of classes or crowds (or interview committees), and he liked one-on-one conversations, most of the time, but schmoozing at parties or informal gatherings where you had to make small talk with lots of people drove him crazy. He could picture Duane skating from one cluster of people to another, making them all laugh with some comment or corny joke. The very thought of it made Matthew tired. That, he mentally noted, could be a drawback.

Then the question: Should he mention the interview to the faculty? He had already spoken with Carter, because if he *was* the nominee, it would have a significant impact on the seminary. But what if he talked to others and then wasn't chosen? And wasn't that the more likely outcome? As Duane had pointed out, indirectly, he hadn't been the pastor of a congregation. Duane hadn't told him who the other two candidates were, but they were almost certainly older pastors or regional ministers, men who had years of experience in the decision-making structures of the denomination. The Executive Committee would say nice things about how articulate he was but tell him, in effect, that he hadn't yet paid his dues. Or they would carry on about how he could serve the church better where he was. So, all this imagining was pretty pointless, even a little silly.

Whenever he felt burdened, Matthew's usual practice was to have lunch at The Sizzling Griddle, just four blocks from Disciples Theological Seminary but in a part of town where seminary types generally didn't venture. It gave him a chance to get away from the same conversations with the same people. He didn't like sitting at a table by himself, so he always sat on a stool at the faded green counter with its aluminum trim, facing the glass-doored cabinet full of pies. Besides, what he really liked about the café was talking with Edgar, the owner. Edgar had a gift of saying a lot without many words. Today seemed like a day he could use Edgar's wisdom.

"Looks like you got something on your mind," Edgar said, once Matthew had settled on his favorite stool, "and I can't tell if it's something good or something bad."

"I'm not sure either. It's a decision I have to make. Actually, not a decision *I* have to make, at least not yet." He leaned closer. "This is just between us … ?"

Edgar rolled his eyes and walked down the counter to pour coffee for another customer. When he returned, he asked, "Who am I gonna talk to about you … the pies?" They both smiled.

"I'm being considered for another job, a big leadership position—*the* big leadership position—in my church. It would mean moving, and Margaret's not wild about the idea."

"How about you? Is it the right job for you?" Before Matthew could answer, Edgar was called away again, leaving him to ponder the question. When he was with church people, he wanted to be thought of as a scholar. But, in truth, he was often uncomfortable in purely academic settings. His natural habitat was the church—wasn't it? —but as an academic. When this reverie ended, he saw that Edgar was standing in front of him.

"Would the church be better off if you got the job?" When Matthew hesitated, Edgar added, "Sounds to me like you need to talk to God some more about this."

As soon as he finished his piece of pecan pie, Matthew headed for the seminary chapel, a long, narrow sanctuary with blond oak pews, reflecting its construction in the 1950s. He walked slowly down the center aisle before taking a seat in a front pew near the piano. Ahead of him, above the chancel and communion table, was the round, stained-glass window of a dove, and he concentrated on that until thoughts began to come unbidden. He could pray to be free of pride, but didn't he get to be a little proud, at least for a week and a half? He started to pray for the strength to speak truly about the church during the interview, but that felt too self-centered. *Dear God, help* me *do well.*

He got up and walked to the communion table, where he prayed for the other two candidates, whoever they were, and that seemed right. Would the church be better off if he was GMP? He prayed for the Disciples that, whatever choice was made, the church would be built up in love. He liked that phrase from Paul's letters. He then prayed for the wider church, including Christians in Iraq who were suffering as a result of the U.S. invasion. That felt even better, although his mental picture of Iraqi Christians was pretty abstract. And what about Muslims in Iraq? He prayed for them, too, including Saddam Hussein. Love your enemies, after all.

Finally, his prayer came back to himself. He gave thanks that others saw gifts of leadership in him, although he found it almost consoling to realize that he wasn't likely to be the one selected.

But he was. On the first ballot. The moderator of the church, Raymond Crawford, the man whose main tasks were to the chair the Executive Committee and preside at the next General Assembly, told him the vote was unanimous; but Matthew wondered if that was because those who were opposed changed their votes once the outcome was decided. He had been part of such technically unifying procedures.

Duane seemed positively giddy, but Matthew, although surprised and pleased, tried not to show it, at least too much. He had felt in control of the interview from the outset. This kind of format—questions and answers, as if teaching—was what he did best.

The office of GMP, he'd told the committee, was not a place where programs were initiated. Its most important function was to hold the different parts of the church together.

"We have liberal congregations in Ann Arbor and New York and conservative ones in Huntsville and Tulsa, and they all need to be respected, to feel that they are part of one church." He could see members of the committee nodding as he said it. "I feel well equipped to carry out this task," he added, "because I deal with students who come from inner-city Chicago and from Appalachia, from Alabama and Oregon and Germany and India." There was no need to spell this out further. They were obviously confident in his capacity as a reconciler.

Beyond that, he'd said, his background meant he would place emphasis on revitalizing Christian education. To be more specific, he would set goals for the church: Half of all adult Disciples in regular Bible study (which he would like to do, if only his schedule permitted); a commitment from parents to read the Bible with their children every week (which reminded him that he needed to do this more often with Abigail and Zachary); and a commitment to reach out to at least one unchurched family or person each month (which he and Margaret intended to do once they had a bit more time).

Some of the members later told him that this took them by surprise. They had expected him to be academic, whatever they meant by that, but Matthew had thought about this carefully. They knew he was a scholar, so he could be very practical. They knew he was involved in the global church (at least somewhat), so he could focus on congregational life. They knew he dealt with other churches (sort of), so he could talk about recovering their identity as Disciples.

He did mention his opposition to the Gulf War and how Disciples had a heritage of working for peace. But while somewhat edgier, this was still low-hanging fruit, as national committees were always more liberal than most people in the pews. Someone talked about supporting the troops and giving thanks that the fighting was pretty much over, and everyone agreed on that.

Finally, a member of the committee asked him the question he thought of as his most vulnerable point: "How good are you at administration?"

"Well, it's not what I think about when I'm standing in the shower." Laughter, always a good sign. "But I sure do a lot of it as dean of a seminary. As an administrator, I may not always do things right; but as a leader, I will always try to do the right things." And that was that. Within minutes, Raymond invited him back into the room where the committee was meeting, and informed him that he was the nominee.

After the committee adjourned with prayer, Duane invited Matthew to come to his office. "Your future office," he told him, "so I won't put any more holes in the wall." They admired the old photos of Ebbets Field, the Polo Grounds, and Connie Mack Stadium that filled one wall of the office and talked about seeing a baseball game together. They stood for a while looking out a window at the trees that were beginning to bud on the grounds of the Disciples headquarters. They talked about the desk that had been left there by Duane's predecessor and then about what a good leader he had been, without specifying what they meant by that.

As Matthew was getting ready to leave, Duane said, "I love this church. Love this church! You know, I was a member of the committee that restructured the Disciples in the 1960s. Funny how that all happened. I was just a local minister in Pennsylvania, and I guess the committee didn't have enough local ministers or people from Pennsylvania, or maybe enough people under forty, so there I was. And if that hadn't happened, I wouldn't be here. Do you think God is in things like that?"

Matthew decided the question was rhetorical and, after a pause, Duane continued, "Of course, we were already starting to lose members way back then. I think you're the one to get us back on track, help us get in step with the times."

Matthew returned home, the familiar drive from Indianapolis to Lexington, where he and Margaret celebrated by taking Abigail and Zachary to McDonalds. He wished she had asked him more about the interview—what he'd said to the committee, the kinds of questions they'd put to him—but she also wanted to share the struggles of ninth graders to understand Robert Frost. And, in any case, eating dinner with a three-year-old and a nine-year-old in a fast-food restaurant was hardly conducive to serious conversation. They apparently said enough, however, that when the family got home Abigail asked, "What were you and Mom talking about? A minister who's a general?" He tried to tell her about being General Minister and President without going into all the implications, like having to move. "Does this mean you'll be famous? Will you be like the Pope and dress in white clothes?" He reminded her of their friend Duane, who had brought her the trinkets from Australia (smiling as he thought of the picture of Duane next to the Orthodox bishop), but she couldn't remember what Duane looked like and certainly not what he wore.

On Sunday, he begged off going to church. The congregation wouldn't know he was back, and he just wasn't ready to talk to everyone about being the nominee. He could envision it: over and over, the same questions—*How's it feel to be the big cheese? When you thinking of moving?*—and the same jokes—*Can't you just leave Margaret and the kids?* Abigail and Zachary weren't at all upset by the decision to skip worship, which worried him a little.

He knew there would be a pile of memos waiting for him at the seminary, but since he didn't have a class to teach until Tuesday, and he didn't feel like dealing with administrative things, he decided to use Monday to fill out the "Meet the Nominee" questionnaire given him by the Executive Committee. He had completed one of these onerous exercises for the search committee, but this one—which was longer!—was intended, he supposed, for the General Board at its meeting with him in July.

"Reflect on your personal lifestyle, including family relationships, your involvement in a local congregation, and whether or not you tithe." Did they really need to get so personal? He toyed with giving a one-line response—*My lifestyle and relationships are fine!*—but then wrote that he and his family lived modestly in a middle-class area of Lexington. As he wrote, he could picture Margaret, legs tucked beneath her in her favorite dark green and cranberry-colored armchair. "I drive a Chevette, although this may not show the wisdom requisite for church leadership." A little humor, he decided, would be well received.

What else would be good to tell them? He and Margaret, especially Margaret, spent a lot of time shuttling from school to preschool to violin practice. They ate out too much, liked to spend an occasional evening with close friends, and so were grateful to have Beth—a student at the seminary—who helped with child care. He loved baseball and classical music, especially opera, but much of their recreation involved things that appealed to three- and nine-year-olds. His favorite exercise was running, which he struggled to do somewhat regularly, especially when he was on the road. They were members of a small, middle-class congregation, although his various speaking engagements meant he was a sporadic attender. Between their pledge and special offerings, their giving amounted to around ten percent of their salaries, "after taxes." He took out the last two words, then put them back. He didn't add that they also gave a bit to the local Catholic parish where Margaret occasionally attended Mass.

There were expected questions about his "hopes and dreams" for the Disciples of Christ as the church moved into the twenty-first century—a question apparently designed to make sure he knew how the denomination worked—and a question about his administrative skills, which he acknowledged as his area of "greatest weakness" before changing it to "the area I have worked hardest to improve," although that was a bit of a stretch. Why, he wondered, hadn't he asked Duane more about how he spent his days?

"Discuss your style of conflict management, along with tensions you see within the Disciples of Christ." His answer to this one took longer than he had expected, mainly because he wanted to challenge the idea of "managing" conflict. "Conflict," he wrote, "can be a sign of health in the church." He started to back this up with a quotation from a well-known scholar, but then decided the whole answer sounded too academic. Instead, he wrote, "Like most people, I don't enjoy conflict, but I know it's part of the job. And I have certainly had experience dealing with it." He followed this with a couple of examples from the seminary, including his recent experience with Stephanie and the elder. He mentioned that he was a member of the board of the local Conflict Resolution Center but then took it out, since he hadn't been able to attend a meeting in four months. Instead, he finished the answer by emphasizing that there *were* real sources of conflict within the Disciples: among different racial-ethnic constituencies, between the local and national church, and between members of different generations. As GMP, his role would be to help all parties think in terms of the whole church, not just a particular caucus.

He answered a question about the "unique gifts that equip you to be the next General Minister and President" by first saying, "I don't know that I am the person best equipped for this position," before talking at some length about his gifts as a teacher, his ability to communicate effectively, his knowledge of the church and its tradition, and his apparent gift of leadership. "At the seminary," he wrote, "people see me as someone who knows how to be in charge" ... which was true, although there were times when he didn't feel in charge. "As the father of small children, I am open to surprises, an important trait for any leader."

He sat for ten minutes staring at the question, "Is there anything else the church should know about you as it prepares to vote on your nomination?" Should he tell them he had been in psychotherapy? That he had once needed to take a week away from the office when things got overwhelming? That he tended to get a bit obsessive when he got anxious? But had any of this truly hindered his performance as dean and professor? And, in any case, was this really the business of the whole General Board? He wrote "No."

Then there was a question Matthew answered in two brief paragraphs, revising them to say more about his work with African American students and his efforts to make things easier for students with disabilities: "Reflect on your experience of working with and supporting groups that our contemporary society might describe as 'different.'"

CHAPTER TWO

Disciples Theological Seminary is a cluster of stately, red-brick buildings in the Georgian colonial style across Limestone Avenue from the University of Kentucky. As one faces the campus, student apartments are on the right; the chapel and the library, with its columned portico, in the center; and the two-story classroom and office building on the left, all behind a beautiful, sloping lawn and a U-shaped drive. A suite with offices of the dean and president is the first door visitors come to after entering the classroom building, but Matthew didn't worry about drop-in traffic because Lucinda, secretary for the president and dean, was very protective. Just inside the entrance is a guestbook, which includes an entry from ABIGAIL MCAVOY, DEANS DAUGHTER in red pen and capital letters. In the space for comments, she had written, "a good place to hang out but can be boring."

Matthew knew that other evaluations of DTS were as mixed as Abigail's. To some people in the church, this was a leading seminary, where a number of Disciples leaders had studied, including Duane. To others, however, it was a second-rate school with ever-precarious finances. Both perceptions, he realized, could be plausibly defended. Like perceptions of the church as a whole.

Because a high percentage of students lived on campus, it was easy to gather for a special convocation to discuss the big news: the impending departure of their dean. The poster advertising the convocation—scheduled for Thursday, April 4—spoke of their "beloved Dean," but Matthew knew that was a stretch. He wasn't outgoing enough or down-home enough to be "beloved." But he was clearly respected and generally well liked. He knew that, in a curious way, his reserve made him more attractive to some of the students, as if they needed the approval of one who didn't give it lightly. He prided himself in being fair-minded with student complaints and in being present for community events, which students seemed to appreciate, especially when Abigail and Zachary came along. When Matthew was honest with himself, he had to admit he had favorites, which is why some students thought of him as pastoral, while others would never have used that word to describe him. *Did the Executive Committee think of me as pastoral?* he wondered. *Is it now up to me to let others see this side of my personality?*

On the day of the convocation, there was a buzz in the room, a feeling of nervous energy, part celebration, part anxiety about what this all might mean. At least that's how Matthew interpreted the atmosphere as he walked to the front of the long fellowship hall, lined with windows on one side and posters from art museums on the other. There was a raised platform at one end of the room, but Matthew urged Carter to keep the microphone on the floor, close to the front row of round tables. DTS was not a large seminary, just over a hundred full-time students preparing for various types of ministry, but the room was filled. In addition to students, Matthew could see alums who lived in the area, and he was pleased to see that not only the faculty but most of the custodial and secretarial staff were there, several of them leaning against the back wall. Had Carter sent around a memo he hadn't seen, or had they come out of genuine interest?

In his opening words, Carter warmly congratulated Matthew, joked about all the influence the seminary would now have in Indianapolis (apparently forgetting that Duane was also a graduate of the school), and set forth the process of the nomination, including the timeline until the final vote in the General Assembly. When Matthew stood up, to loud applause, he thanked everyone for being there and then reminded them that this was not yet a done deal. "So if you're one who's counting on a new dean, don't get your hopes too high just yet." After laughter, he said, "None of us needs another speech. So let's just make this a conversation among friends who care about the church."

The first question, however, caught him off guard: "What do you think of what's happened with Rodney King?"

This was so unexpected that Matthew almost laughed, although he knew this wasn't the right response. "That all happened right as I was interviewing, so I haven't had time to follow the story as closely as I would like. What do you think about it?"

The student, a third-year African American woman named Reena, didn't take the bait. "I don't hear our denomination saying *anything* about it. And when a black man gets beat up like that by the police, somebody ought to be saying *something*"—the last word said emphatically. "This is my question: Once you're General Minister—is that what they call it?, the head guy—will you have more guts than the current one? Or will you say like everybody else, 'Why can't we all just get along?'" There was laughter, but muted, here and there in the hall.

Matthew couldn't resist. "Who *is* the current General Minister and President?" The student shrugged her shoulders, so Matthew asked, "Who can tell me?" There was a brief pause before several voices called out "Duane Porter," although one person called him Duane Proctor.

"How many here know that he sent a letter to all of the congregations, a year or so ago, talking about racism?" Fewer than a dozen hands went up, and those, it seemed to him, without much conviction. "A letter may not be the strongest thing we can do, but it's something, a way of inviting conversation in the church. I don't know whether Reverend Porter has said anything about Rodney King specifically. I hope he has. I hope I would. But part of the problem is communication. Our leaders in the church don't always communicate effectively, and we don't always pay enough attention when they do."

"Communication is the answer," said Reena, "only if you have something to say."

The next several questions had to do with the future of the seminary: What difference will this make for us? He tried to assure them that the seminary would be in good hands, but they all knew that the ecumenical character of the school owed a lot to him. A leader, he reflected soberly while taking a sip of water, should do a better job of trying to be replaceable.

At one point, Lisa and Heather stood up together and, instead of asking a question, said how nice it was that, for a change, *they* weren't the big news on campus. *As if they hadn't asked to be*, Matthew thought to himself. Their comment, said in a slightly campy way, arms around one another, got a round of applause, although Matthew noticed that not everyone was clapping, not even all the students.

The conversation went a different direction when an alumnus wanted to know about the World Council of Churches assembly. "You're involved with that council, so do you know any more about the bombing? It sounded to me from the news reports I read that they were really trying to downplay it, but I suspect there's more to the story."

Why, Matthew wondered, did people focus on the one moment of publicized turmoil instead of all the other things the council was doing? "I've only been part of a couple of working groups on baptism, but Reverend Porter was at the assembly and he says it wasn't a big deal, not really a 'bombing' but some kind of small explosion. That's all I know."

"It's a good thing they weren't meeting in this country," a student called out, "or the protesters would have been armed!" And again, he saw that the laughter and applause were by no means universal.

The next question came from a student who was serving as the associate at a church in Lexington. "We were talking earlier about one of Reverend Porter's letters to congregations. I just happened to see his recent letter about the war, and all he said, basically, was that Disciples have different opinions and need to talk about it without tearing the church apart. Is that really all the guidance we can get from the General Minister and President?"

Matthew nodded. "It's a fair question. I wish he could have said more, but he's pastor to the whole denomination, hawks as well as doves. It's hard ..."

"So, you won't say more when you are General Minister?" When Matthew was slow to respond, the student added, "Our senior minister—you know him, Reverend Knight—didn't share the letter with the congregation. He said it was like telling kids not to fight over who gets to use the hose first when the house is on fire." There was tittering in the hall.

"I understand where you and Reverend Knight are coming from," said Matthew, "and you have heard me speak here at DTS against the war. I'm a member of Disciples for Peace because the church should advocate for peace in the world. But what about peace in the church? Isn't that also important? Duane was calling for civil dialogue. Isn't modeling that part of our witness?" He cleared his throat. "I don't really want to promise now what I will say or do on any particular issue, but I take your point."

The tone changed when Greg, a member of the morning prayer group—which Matthew attended whenever he was in town and didn't need to manage the kids and was ready for whatever was on his morning agenda—asked how prayer had figured in his decision making. Matthew smiled. Greg was too polite to ask directly, "Have you taken this to the Lord in prayer?" but that, of course, is what he really wanted to know.

"I have prayed about it," he said, thinking especially of the time in the seminary chapel. "But you all know that decision making is complex. How did you decide to come to seminary, to quit whatever you were doing and enter ministry? It's no longer such a popular thing to do, so how did you make that decision?" Greg actually started to answer, but Matthew didn't let him. "Like you, I suspect, I have tried to examine my own gifts. What do I do well? How does that match with what it takes to be General Minister and President? When I let my name go to the search committee, it was because I thought I might have those gifts, and then," he paused for a minute to choose the right words, "I trusted the discernment of others in the church. And, yes, I believe God is in this whole process ... somewhere."

Finally, Beth, the student who often stayed with Abigail and Zachary when Matthew and Margaret went out for the evening, asked, "Are you excited about being our GMP?"

Was he excited? There was a bit of apprehension (perhaps more than a bit), a good bit of pride, a bit of sadness that comes with departures—and, yes, he decided, quite a bit of excitement. "I suppose it hasn't fully sunk in yet," he told her. "I like challenges, and this is certainly a challenging time to be in church leadership. But I will miss all of you. Well, most of you." More laughter, the kind that comes when something is close to the truth.

After the convocation, Carter told Matthew he would like him to speak with Heather and Lisa, urge them to be a little less public with their affection. Matthew was still thinking about how—gracefully—to say, "Tone it down," when Lucinda ushered them into his office the following Monday. He invited the two young women to have a seat at his round, wooden table, covered with rings left by decades of coffee cups and Coke bottles. He started to speak, but Lisa beat him to it. "Have you ever been to a gay pride parade?" Matthew smiled and shook his head.

Heather leaned forward, arms on the table. "How about a worship service for the gay community?"

"No," said Matthew, "but I bet you have some recommendations."

Rather than offer them, Heather added, "You must know we aren't the only LGBT students at DTS." She laughed, perhaps at the string of initials, but then turned serious. "We, Lisa and me, feel pretty comfortable with you, but some others aren't so sure."

"So," said Lisa, "we think you ought to experience a parade—June 30th, in Chicago."

"They expect a hundred thousand people, maybe more," said Heather. "Mayor Daley, for God's sake, was there a couple of years ago. Your theology's in the right place, but you need to meet more gay people, not just us."

"It's hard with the kids to get away for one more thing," he told them, "but I'll think about it. Just keep in mind that change is slower here in Lexington than it is in Chicago."

Soon after learning he was the nominee, Matthew had suggested to Margaret that they celebrate by getting away for a weekend, just the two of them. They could ask Beth to stay with the kids, get a little romance back in their lives. That's when she reminded him that they had promised to take Abigail and Zachary to a state park once spring arrived. They could still make it romantic, just not as much.

It so happened that there was a full moon the weekend of April 13–14, which meant that if the sky was clear there would be a moonbow at Cumberland Falls. They managed to reserve the last available two-bedroom cabin and, once school was out on Friday the 12th, they headed a hundred miles south to their favorite state park.

Saturday was a fun day but exhausting, especially for Matthew. The four of them set out on what sounded in the park's brochure like a relatively short hike, past wildflowers and budding dogwoods. But Zachary was too small to walk very far or very fast, so Matthew ended up carrying all thirty-four pounds of him in the child carrier that fit on his back. Who, he muttered, thought three and a half miles was short, particularly when the trail seemed to go more uphill than down and was more uneven than not? His morning jog wasn't much farther than that, and it was usually on level ground without a kid on his back! This was followed by swimming and a lengthy game of tag with Abigail and Zachary, who now had boundless energy.

So Matthew, feeling less than romantic, was ready for an early dinner. They reserved a table for six o'clock at the restaurant in the lodge, its large windows overlooking the Cumberland River, but, at Matthew's urging, were at the lodge by five forty-five.

"As usual," Abigail said as she plopped in a chair. "Hurry up and then wait." The chair was big enough for Zachary to wiggle in beside her while their mother smiled.

"I shouldn't have to defend being a couple of minutes early. Spend the time looking around this great room." He pointed to the massive stone fireplace and knotty pine paneling.

"At least," said Abigail, "you can't wear a tie this weekend, especially when you're carrying Zachary. He might grab it, and then ..." She made a hanging motion, her tongue hanging out, which made Zachary laugh.

Once they were seated and had ordered, Abigail wanted to know if her dad would be at the fourth-grade open house. Matthew glanced at Margaret. "Remind me what day it is."

"It's on Thursday, Dad. I showed you and Mom the note about it last week."

"I'm sorry, Abigail, but I've got to be out of town on Thursday and Friday. I'll be ..."

"Speaking at some church meeting."

Matthew nodded and pursed his lips.

"I'll be there," said Margaret.

"That's right, and Mom can tell me all about it. Besides, I'm sure you are doing great, like you always do."

Abigail fiddled with her water glass, looking at the table. "It's probably better you're not there anyway."

"Why do you say that?"

"Because Mrs. Jesperson will probably make a big deal of how she yelled at me for wearing the shirt against the war."

"I'm sure she didn't yell at you," said Margaret. "She was just telling you it was against the rules. She had to say that, same as I would with my students."

Abigail raised her eyebrows. "It felt like yelling to me." For a second, it looked as if she might cry. "How are you supposed to know when something is really serious and when it isn't?"

"My meeting is in Chicago," Matthew told her, trying to change the subject, "so I'm certain I can pick up some postcards for your collection."

Their food was delivered, and once Zachary had plenty of ketchup for his French fries, Margaret spoke directly to Matthew. "You're not the only one who's making presentations. Your daughter gave a book report to her whole class on Thursday."

Guilt. Why hadn't he remembered this? He turned to Abigail. "How'd it go?"

"It wasn't so scary," she said between bites of hamburger. "I remembered how you told me to think of the other kids as heads of cabbage when I talk to them." She giggled and Zachary, though he wasn't sure what had been said, laughed out loud.

"Tell your father what you talked about."

"Well, everybody has to make a book report. So, I told Mrs. Jesperson that I was going to make mine on *The Diary of Anne Frank.* Anne with an e. She pretended to write the name in the air with her finger. "But she wouldn't let me."

Matthew glanced again at Margaret. "What did she say?"

"Well, I said I wanted to report on that book because it's against war, and she said 'No, it's not.' She said it's too old for me, but how can it be too old for me when I've already read it?" She took a bite of hamburger.

"Tell him what you ended up doing," said Margaret.

"Well, she told me to do it on a Judy Blume book, which I used to like but that was last year. So, I said if that's what she wants I'll do my report on the whole 'Fudge' series. And then she said to just pick one book because the class will like it better if I don't tell them everything I know. So that's what I did." Matthew couldn't help but smile, and he saw that Margaret was smiling as well.

An hour or so after finishing dinner, the four of them joined the crowd at a spot with a good view of the sixty-foot falls. Zachary sat on his dad's shoulders as they watched the shimmering white bow appear below the falls soon after dark. Margaret put her arms around her husband and daughter, and they stood in silent appreciation until Zachary began to slump.

When the kids were in bed, the adults poured a glass of wine and pulled the two wooden chairs on the cabin's porch close together. Light from the full moon cast intricate shadows from the hemlock trees that grew near the cabin, and they sat quietly watching until Matthew cleared his throat. "I only remember going on two family vacations when my mother was alive—I think I told you this before—and one of them was here. I'm pretty sure we stayed in the lodge."

"I can't remember if you said she had a special connection to Kentucky."

Matthew shrugged. "I have no idea, but then there's a lot I don't know about her." He paused. "But I've told you that before too."

Margaret took a sip of wine, leaned on the arm of her chair, and took his hand. "Are you ready for the next few months?"

It was several seconds before he answered. "To be honest, I'm not sure what I can do to get ready. I'm supposed to make some kind of presentation to the General Board in July, but I think that's pretty much a formality. I need to meet with Duane a time or two to get up to speed, see what parts of the administrative work can be palmed off on someone else."

"While you're at it," she said, "see if you can find somebody who does laundry and cooks dinner." They both smiled, and she squeezed his hand. The cool wind had picked up, shadows from the hemlocks dancing near the cabin. Margaret pulled her sweater tighter.

"I know you're still working and have a lot on your to-do list," she said, "but there are a thousand things we need to do as a family to get ready, and I can't do all of them by myself. Eventually, we'll have to sell our house, look for one in Indianapolis, check out Abigail's new school, find a preschool for Zachary, and see if I can find a teaching position. Having the assembly in October really complicates matters. Do the kids and I stay in Lexington until the end of the year? Do we assume the nomination will go smoothly and go ahead and move before school starts in the fall? This is all making me very anxious."

She drained what was left of her wine. "It seems premature since you haven't been elected yet—sorry, I know it's not an election—you haven't been confirmed yet, but I suppose I should begin submitting applications to various schools."

She looked at him, and even in the dark he could see she was smiling as she said, "And then, the biggest thing of all, I still have to wrap my head around being the wife of the Disciples General Minister and President. That's quite a leap for a good Catholic girl."

On the Monday after their weekend at Cumberland Falls, two weeks after his nomination was officially announced, Matthew called his father. He had intended to call him soon after he received word of the nomination, but things seemed to get in the way. They had never talked very often, but this delay, he realized, was pretty inexcusable. He started by asking about his younger sister, Karen, who lived near their father in Oak Grove. "Call and ask her," said Frank. "Still has a phone, last I checked."

That, he guessed, was as good a transition as any. "Dad, I have some news."

"Reverend Wainwright announced it in church on Sunday, a week ago Sunday, actually. Made a pretty big deal of it, really did. I'll say that for him. Beverly said after church that she never could imagine how you became a minister. Honest to God, I don't know what gets into her! I could've thumped her one! But the others seemed real pleased."

"Thanks, Dad."

"Of course, I told 'em this might mean they'll have to kiss your ring." He laughed at his own joke.

"No ring kissing in the Disciples," said Matthew. "In fact, there's not a whole lot of power in the position." Pause. "I hope *you* feel good about it, Dad."

"That's what Ned says."

"Ned who? Says about what?"

"Our congressman! You haven't been gone that long, have you? Lives right here in Oak Grove. You must have met him twenty ..."

"Yes, I know who Ned what's his name the congressman is. What's this ..."

"He says people in Congress don't have near as much power as you'd think. Of course, I don't think he amounts to much, far as I can tell. Doesn't seem to do much harm, I suppose, and occasionally he gets farmers this or that. But I never could tell what he stands for. For himself, I guess. People keep voting for him because they're afraid they'll get somebody worse, I suppose."

Matthew could feel himself growing defensive. He pictured his father sitting in his office, in the same wooden swivel chair he'd had for thirty years, fiddling with the Frank Thomas bobblehead Matthew had given him. "Dad, you're not saying I'm like that." He realized it was more of a question than an assertion. In any case, Frank ignored him.

"I hate to think what your mother would've thought of him. Will you have to move somewhere? Indianapolis, I suppose."

"Yes, you know the headquarters is there. You'll have to come for a visit, and I can show you all the church offices, where your offering money goes."

"So this is a full-time job?" It was half question, half tentative statement.

"Dad! This is the top position in the church. Of course it's full-time, if you consider sixty hours a week full-time."

"How's that going to work with the kids? You've got to think about them, you know."

As Matthew got off the call, Duane came to his mind. Duane and his father were the same generation, even had the same passion for baseball, but it was the differences that stood out as he thought about them. Speaking with Frank was often a trial, completely unlike his times with Duane. So, he was pleased when Lucinda told him the following morning, not long before his scheduled class, that Duane was on the line.

"You must have known I needed a call from you." But even as Duane went through the pleasantries—"How's Margaret? How's my favorite girl?"—Matthew could feel that his tone was nothing like the exuberance of previous conversations.

"Matthew, I have … Something has come up we need to discuss, something we need to discuss now, if you have a minute."

"Sure. I've got about ten before I have to go to class. What's up?" A question about his schedule? Something about Iraq? Rodney King?

Duane cleared his throat, twice. "A layman in the Farmington, Indiana, congregation—a man named Harold Judkins—is trying to make a big flap about one of your answers in the 'Meet the Nominee' profile."

"A flap about what?" He tried mentally to scroll quickly through the profile, but nothing jumped out, unless it was …

"There was a question … I have it somewhere. Yeah, it says 'Reflect on your experience of working with people society describes as different,' and you wrote, 'I have been a member of GLADN—the Gay, Lesbian, and Affirming Disciples Network—since the General Assembly in 1987 and am committed to the full participation of gay and lesbian persons in the life of the church. All persons are created in God's image and are of infinite worth in God's eyes.'"

Matthew felt his stomach tighten. "Well, I have been. Margaret joined too. So, I thought I should say it. But wait a minute. How did … what's his name?"

"Judkins, Harold Judkins."

"How did Mr. Judkins get hold of the profile? I don't understand how this came up."

There was a pause on the other end of the line before Duane said, "We were sending a letter to all of the congregations announcing your nomination, so I said we should include the profile, the one you filled out in March, to let them know who you are. May have been a mistake. May have been. Probably was. I just thought people would have questions since you're pretty young and not serving a congregation or being a regional minister. Anyway, for better or worse, that's what we did."

Would he have edited his answers if he had known they would be sent throughout the church and not just to the General Board?

The question crossed Matthew's mind, followed by the thought that this was God's way of removing such temptation. That's not what he taught about how God works, but he suddenly had the feeling that something beyond himself was making him accountable for his commitments. "Well, what is he saying? What kind of flap are you talking about? He can't be saying very much because I haven't ever said anything about it, except what you just read."

"It's not just this Judkins character by himself. He got the elders at Farmington to issue what they are calling the 'Farmington Declaration,' which they have just sent to the elders in every congregation in the Yearbook—all 4,187 of them, it looks like. Some have already arrived. Harold owns some kind of small company— trucking, I think—and says he paid for this mailing out of his own pocket." Duane paused. "I doubt it will amount to much, the churches don't pay much attention to things I send them, but this so-called 'declaration' says that your refusal to call homosexual activity a sin shows—how do they put it?—your 'disregard for the primacy of the Bible as a Christian's guide to values and living standards.'"

More tightness in the stomach. He straightened his blotter and pad of paper until they were even with the edge of his desk. "Are you getting feedback, Duane?"

"Rachel, who's answering the phones, tells me it's been pretty heavy. Well, very heavy. I stopped taking calls a little while ago. But mainly they just want information— 'How seriously should we take this?' 'Who is this guy Judkins?'— that kind of thing. Somebody this morning reminded me that Farmington was Leo's first church out of seminary."

Matthew pictured in his mind the denomination's most famous preacher and storyteller, Leonard Fletcher—Leo, as he was simply known throughout the Disciples. Leo, now retired in Virginia, had never held an official position in the church, but his influence was pervasive.

"So they've heard good preaching," Duane said. "Apparently, it just didn't stay with them, did it?" There was a catch in Duane's voice as he said, "I'm really sorry this has come up, Matthew, and I really don't want it to lessen your excitement for the position—or your joy. There's too little joy in the church! I want you to be *joyful* about taking over this office. I'm guessing all this other won't amount to much."

Matthew told Duane how much he appreciated his support, which was true, and how it wasn't his fault that this had happened. It was right to send the profile throughout the church, although he wasn't so sure that was true. Then he asked, "What are others saying?"

"We haven't met yet as staff to talk about it. I know that Marvin thinks it could get pretty rough, but that's what the deputies are paid for, to balance me out." He laughed softly. "I'll keep in touch. For now, just concentrate on commencement at my alma mater."

The letters began to arrive the following week. Matthew had occasionally wondered if some of the more contentious letters to the editor in the local newspaper were real or the product of the paper's imaginative staff, and now here they were in his own mailbox—opened, as all his mail was, by Lucinda. He had been getting congratulatory notes since the nomination was first announced, but now these were mixed with statements of opposition, not an avalanche but two, three, or four a day.

Most of the themes were predictable: "The church needs leaders who are Bible-believing Christians." "Don't we have enough troubles as a church without stirring up this hornet's nest?" But there were also ones that felt like personal attacks, and they, naturally, were the ones that stuck to his mind like Velcro: "Whatever made you think that you should be President of our church?" "Stick to teaching if you don't know enough to keep your mouth shut about these kinds of things." One letter that actually made him laugh listed five reasons he should withdraw from being the nominee. "Reason number 3: You said you weren't the best person for this job and at least on this you were right."

Several letters expressed support for him precisely because of his support for persons who are gay, which made him slightly uncomfortable—no, very uncomfortable—for reasons he hadn't yet pinned down. And a couple were from gay members of the church: "Your support is a blessing. Lots of people want us to fake being heterosexual and live a lie. That isn't Christian!" "I urge other Disciples to get to know me as a person before making negative and hurtful comments."

Matthew tried to respond to the most thoughtful letters, whether pro or con. In each one, he had Lucinda include a paragraph reminding the writer of the admonition in Ephesians to lead a life worthy of our calling: "bearing with one another in love, making every effort to maintain the unity of the Spirit in the bond of peace." But even though the volume of negative mail tapered off considerably, this still proved to be overwhelming, particularly as the end of the semester drew closer.

April had already ended before Matthew found time for lunch at The Sizzling Griddle. He managed to get his favorite stool, feeling relieved enough to be off campus that he even loosened his tie. Edgar smiled when he saw it. "Rough day?"

"Rough month."

"That's what Heather and what's-her-name told me?"

Did students come here too? Matthew looked around, feeling slightly less relieved. Edgar smiled again and walked away to fill a coffee mug. When he returned, he said simply, "Man, if I was you, I'd enjoy the people you see and not worry too much about the ones you don't."

"Yeah," said Matthew, "but that's easier said than done. I guess they told you people are saying pretty negative stuff about me, and it's hard to get out of my mind once it gets in."

"Who do you like being around most, apart from that family of yours?" Edgar asked.

"Students."

"Then concentrate on them."

Matthew could still hear Edgar's words when he met the next day with students in his course, "The Unity of the Church: Theological Perspectives." The effort to achieve greater unity among churches was his specialty. He would follow Edgar's advice and concentrate on the students who were studying it with him.

On this particular day, he was planning to discuss differences regarding baptism and how the churches—well, some of them— were overcoming these historic divisions. He intended to start with an especially bad example from Disciples history: a nineteenth-century Disciples leader named Moses Lard who declared that because Martin Luther wasn't baptized by immersion, the practice of the Disciples, he wasn't really a Christian! He was going to ask the students, "Should the amount of water we use be a church-dividing issue? What really is at stake?" and let the discussion unfold from there.

On this day, however, the students were clearly more interested in talking about the current controversy than about one that now seemed quaintly irrelevant. A third-year student, one of his favorites, gave away her own position by how she framed her question. "Do you, our future GMP, think persons should be barred from being ordained just because they happen to be gay?"

"That's not for me, for whomever is GMP, to decide," Matthew told her. "We've said that the church, speaking through its regional assemblies, makes those decisions."

"What if the church continues to say that homosexuality is a sin and gay people can't be ministers?" asked an older student. "Would you still want to be part of this church, let alone be its General Minister and President?"

Matthew could feel his ears turning red. "I don't think that's where things are headed in the long run."

"But what if they are?" she persisted. "What if this country gets more conservative instead of more liberal, and the church just goes along with it?"

"Or what if you're right?" asked another of his favorites. "Should the conservatives stay in the church if they think it's going against what the Bible teaches?"

As he drove home that evening through Lexington traffic, there were now more words echoing in his head.

CHAPTER THREE

As graduation day loomed, Matthew tried to push the nomination to the back of his mind and, following Edgar's advice, allow himself to feel a growing sense of excitement for the students he could see. Duane had wished him joy. Well, he found real joy in the procession of soon-to-be-graduates in their rented gowns, each one a seed of new possibility. It made him not only joyful but genuinely hopeful for the church. And, by God, he would *not* let a few letter writers he couldn't see spoil it!

Since commencement was on a Saturday, Margaret, Abigail, and Zachary were free to go with him to the seminary—early, of course. One thing he would surely miss was going unannounced into the second-floor classroom, where the graduates were putting on their academic gowns, and giving each one a hug, or at least a handshake. This time Abigail went with him, her index finger through one of his belt loops, as it often was when they were in a crowd.

No sooner had they started around the room, however, than a student asked him what he thought of their uninvited guest. "Who is that?" he asked, and they took him to the window that looked out over the great lawn. There, marching back and forth, was a middle-aged man with a large, hand-lettered sign: "Say yes to God, no to homosexuality," on one side, "Say yes to Jesus, no to McAvoy," on the other. Abigail stood on tip toe so she could see out the window, trying hard to read the uneven lettering aloud.

"I'm sorry," he told the students standing with him. "I didn't mean for anything to cloud your day."

"*He* is clouding it," said one of the older women graduates, pointing out the window, "not you."

"I'm proud," said another, "that you are giving me my diploma." Several others agreed, and suddenly Matthew felt slightly phony. They thought he was some kind of crusader for justice, when he knew that all he had done was join an organization; and he had only joined it because friends had invited him to attend a late-night session at a General Assembly. Well, that wasn't quite true, he told himself. He *had* wanted to be supportive. But would he have taken the initiative to become a member of GLADN on his own? He tried to express some of this to the students but, not surprisingly, it came out in a jumble and led to more slightly embarrassing affirmations.

It was Abigail who rescued him. One of the students had brought her ten-year-old daughter, and Abigail now asked if the two of them could run around on the expansive lawn. "You should leave, too, Dad. You've already said congratulations to all of 'em."

As he sat on the chancel of the seminary's chapel—suffering, like everyone else, through the commencement address—Matthew looked closely at each graduating student, and then beyond at the other seminarians who were present to support their friends. Heather and Lisa had suggested he didn't know the other students who were gay or lesbian but, actually, he had a pretty good idea from what he had seen and overheard. And now, even though he told himself it wasn't appropriate, he counted: three ... maybe four ... in addition to Heather and Lisa. One of them had recently received the seminary's top award "for academic achievement and contributions to the community." Of course, these four—and others?—hadn't felt the need to make their sexuality public the way Heather and Lisa had, and that made things easier for him. That would have to change—wouldn't it?—but maybe not right away.

The graduation, in Matthew's estimation, was a fine event if you didn't count the speaker. The forecast had a chance of rain but, in fact, the morning was warm and sunny. More importantly, he had not botched any of the names when announcing students who were about to receive their diplomas.

The reception, however, was more problematic. Spouses, parents, and grandparents usually wanted a picture of their graduate with the dean, but this year several of the older relatives seemed to avoid him. Or was that just a touch of paranoia? After waving goodbye to Margaret and the kids, Matthew moved quickly around the fellowship hall with its art museum posters. He ate a piece of cake, smiled through a few photos, and then, uncharacteristically, left the reception well before it was over, returning to his office to put away his academic robe with its three chevrons on the sleeves. On his way, he glanced out the window toward Limestone, but, as far as he could tell, the picketer was gone. Probably stayed just long enough for all of the trustees to see him, he thought ruefully.

Next to the closet where he hung his robe (and an extra suit and tie, just in case) was what Matthew jokingly referred to as his icon: a nineteenth-century, lithograph portrait of Alexander Campbell he had rescued from a storeroom in the basement of the seminary library. It had been relegated there, he supposed, because the extravagant gold frame was badly chipped and there were ugly splotches on Campbell's head and shoulders.

He now stared at length at this early Disciples leader: his self-assured posture, his high collar and white bow tie, his gaze that indicated such authority. Campbell was the great advocate of Christian unity at a time when fragmentation was the order of the day. So, what would he have to say, Matthew mused, about the current state of the church? What would he counsel Matthew to do in the face of the controversy? Although, to be honest, who really cared what Campbell thought? He was the key figure in the denomination's first generation, his public debates about the meaning and practice of Christian faith were big news on the frontier. But who now, outside of a few Disciples, even knew his name or cared about the issues and disputes that preoccupied him? Looking at the Campbell portrait made him smile. Somehow it seemed endearing that his icon was chipped and splotchy.

Matthew turned toward his desk feeling a bit more at peace. Commencement was over. There was no stack of papers to grade, not a single memo in the inbox. Perhaps he could have a day or two just to catch up on things around the house, go out to dinner with Margaret. Maybe spend some time in the library researching homosexuality, so he would know more about what people thought he was talking about. That's when he saw, at the edge of his blotter, an over-stuffed mailing envelope with a note on it in Lucinda's handwriting.

Matthew,

I have taken the liberty of holding back some of the mail from recent weeks. I didn't read it all carefully, just enough to know that you didn't need all of this while getting ready for graduation. A few I probably should have thrown straight in the trash, but I was sure you wouldn't like that approach! There is one man who has written three weeks in a row that I wouldn't worry about if I were you. He is from the class of 1933! So here they are. For what it's worth.

Lucinda

Although even picking up the envelope made him slightly queasy, as if he were picking up a snake, he thumbed through the sheaf of letters—typed ones on letterhead, note cards with handwritten messages, whole pages with snippets of scripture—until he found three letters paper-clipped together. The handwriting, he saw with some satisfaction, was shaky, like that of a person from the class of 1933. He set the letters on the desk, side by side. Each one was exactly one page long and each ended with the same sentence: "News of your resignation or death will be welcome."

Early the next week, Matthew received the first issue of the denomination's national magazine, *Disciples Forum*, since the start of the controversy caused by the Farmington Declaration. There was a half-page editorial calling the Declaration "divisive" and urging people to check out the nominee for themselves, but Matthew had to admit he was disappointed it wasn't a more forceful endorsement. He reminded himself that this was a magazine that needed to speak to the whole church, not a mouthpiece of the denominational office. Beyond that, all of this was very recent. He had only been the nominee for a month and a half, for God's sake! Still, these editors, people he knew fairly well, might have said *something* more. He was tempted to look up old issues of *Disciples Forum* to see what they had said editorially about previous nominees.

From the editorial page, he turned to the letters to the editor, where he discovered that only seven dealt with him and the nomination. Relief? More disappointment? Two were clearly against having him as General Minister and President, but they were not nearly as vituperative as some he had received. Was the magazine staff screening out the worst ones the way Lucinda had? Two sounded suspiciously like the editorial in calling the church to a period of careful study, prayer, and civil dialogue. Well, he was in favor of that, but why didn't somebody point *that* out? Why, he railed silently, wasn't someone saying that he, Matthew, had been committed throughout his ministry to just this sort of dialogue? One woman from New York, someone he didn't know, lauded him as a man who obviously wasn't afraid to stand up for justice, which made his jaw tighten. One said that Matthew's suits and fun ties would be a welcome change from polo shirts and khakis, although it would be nice someday to have a GMP who wore a dress. Why, he wondered, had they bothered to print something as trivial as that? And then there was a brief letter he read three times.

> *The early reaction to Matthew McAvoy's nomination as our General Minister and President is an indication of the fearfulness that has gripped this culture. In years past, it was the Soviet menace; now it's Saddam Hussein. In the past, it was Jews and Italians; now it's Mexican immigrants and new arrivals from Asia. In the past, it was feminists; now it's gays and lesbians. Middle Americans seem scared to death that some group is out to undermine their way of life. It is time for the church to stop acting like the culture and stand up to such fear.*

Matthew wished he knew the author of this letter so he could call him. The man seemed to have a better grasp of what was going on than he did. This unexpected uproar—did it deserve that description?—left him with a gnawing desire to talk to someone, to share what he was feeling with a friend. He was getting lots of attention—even the *Lexington Herald-Leader* ran a story with the headline, "Controversy Swirls Around Local Educator"—but Matthew felt strangely on his own.

Of course, he was certainly not alone at home, but he couldn't really talk with Margaret about what he was feeling. For one thing, he didn't want to worry her when her own school year was wrapping up, or at least that's what he usually told himself. The real reason was deeper. Margaret had always had reservations about the GMP position and what all the travel and pressure might mean for the family. But now she was worried, to the point of sleeplessness, about what this extra tension might mean *for Matthew*. You can sometimes get overwhelmed, get too anxious, she reminded him—not angrily, but firmly—when the controversy first broke. Maybe you should get back in therapy. No, he told her, also firmly, he could handle a few negative letters.

This whole exchange left him reluctant to complain about any part of the nomination experience. When he did, following the issue of *Disciples Forum*, she said that if he thought there was too much heat it was probably a good sign he should get out of the kitchen … and then seemed to regret she'd said it, or that she said it in such a churlish tone. And if all this weren't enough to discourage conversations with Margaret, whenever they quarreled Abigail seemed to overhear it; and nine-year-olds, he told himself, have better things to worry about.

The person he knew he should turn to, at least in theory, was the minister of his congregation, but he didn't trust this fresh-out-of-seminary pastor to give him helpful feedback. Was this, he wondered, a commentary on seminary education or just an honest acknowledgment that it's tough for a new minister to counsel the person responsible for teaching ministers? It would be like a junior employee being asked to give advice to the boss.

He considered calling Sonny, the regional minister of the Disciples in Kentucky, whose office wasn't far from campus. See if they might have lunch together. After all, wasn't pastoral care for other ministers in the job description of a regional minister? But he had no idea where Sonny stood on this issue. Would he have to worry about that with everyone from now on?

Matthew might have spoken confidentially with Carter, even though they weren't close friends, but Carter was on an extended fundraising trip that would take him and his wife to Florida, where they would slide into vacation. It would be awkward confiding in members of the faculty since he was the person to whom they were most accountable—although he had once spent a productive hour with Loren, the professor who taught leadership. Matthew had just told two popular students that, even though they were passing their courses, they just weren't ready to be in seminary … and there was grumbling in the hallways.

"Those students needed to be ushered out," said Loren. "Your problem is that you wanted them to like you while you were doing it. Nothing wrong with wanting to be a nice guy, but some people just won't like what you've done. For that matter, some people won't like you no matter what you've done or haven't done."

Loren, however, like most members of the faculty, was away from the campus in these precious weeks between commencement and summer school.

Of course, there was Edgar, but theirs wasn't really a friendship. And Matthew didn't like the mental image of pouring out his troubles on a stool in The Sizzling Griddle, like some lonely patron in a local bar. Although, in fact, that's what he had done more than once.

Finally, he decided to call his friend Roberta, who was the Minister of Christian Education at First Baptist Church in Lexington and an occasional adjunct teacher at the seminary. Yes, Roberta was the right person. She was a Southern Baptist who had fought with her church for years, especially about its racist legacy, but still stuck it out. She invited him to stop by that very afternoon.

Roberta's office was unadorned, which was in keeping, Matthew knew, with her modest lifestyle. She had never married, so there were no pictures of husband and children, just one photograph of her home church in Alabama and one of a favorite niece. There was, however, an electric tea kettle. The water was already hot when he arrived, and she made them both a cup.

Once they were seated in comfortable chairs by a window, Roberta began the conversation by saying, "Quite an article in the paper."

"The stuff I'm getting from the church is a little less affirming. Some of it, anyway."

"I can imagine," she said. "I don't play for your team, but my Baptists also hit a foul ball now and then."

They both laughed, and then Roberta listened—intently, as she always did, in his experience—while Matthew told her of the mail he was receiving. "What I need," he concluded, "is to put all of this in some perspective." But even as he said it, he knew what he really wanted was reassurance from a friend that he was doing a good thing, that he was on the right side of the issue.

He didn't get it.

"It sounds tough," she said when he finished, "but I'm not sure why it's bothering you so much. You've faced conflicts before, lots of them, I expect. I remember the semester I was teaching at DTS and there was some incident of sexual harassment. I tried to stay clear of all of it, but I know you had to be right in the middle. And someone told me just the other day that you have a few unhappy trustees over a recent student announcement. Why does this feel so much different to you?"

Yes, why was it? He had been caught off guard by this flap over his joining one group, but being caught off guard was true of nearly every conflict that landed on his desk. As Margaret occasionally reminded him, there is no school to prepare you for being a dean ... or a GMP.

When Matthew didn't quickly respond, Roberta continued, almost as if she had read his mind. "Speaking more personally, I can't say I'm surprised by what you told me. Or I guess what surprises me is that you are so surprised. After all, you're challenging two-thousand years of church teaching and, to be honest with you, that troubles me too."

Matthew's face obviously betrayed his shock because Roberta smiled. "I guess that also isn't what you were expecting."

Matthew took a sip of his tea and nodded. "No, not quite."

Roberta leaned forward in her chair, forearm resting on her knee. "You are a wonderful teacher, Matthew. I have seen you in action. And you can lead by teaching. But what are you going to teach, as a leader of the church, if it's not what the Bible teaches?"

"Unless what the Bible teaches is just a prejudice from another era."

"Yes," said Roberta, "some parts of the Bible can be hazardous to our spiritual health. But surely it's the church, not you, that determines what parts those are."

"I don't get it," he said after a pause. "You grew up in the South and told me yourself how you almost hated your church for its racial bigotry. Didn't you say that? This is the same thing, just a different group to be prejudiced against."

Roberta's response was immediate and forceful, which also surprised him.

"That's how *you* see it, but that's not the picture for most church people, at least not most Baptists. Matthew, I've heard you talk about being pastoral even though you aren't serving a congregation. So, think like a pastor as well as a teacher. This isn't only a challenge to what the church has taught, it's a major challenge to values and assumptions people have held all their lives." She accentuated the last three words. "Good people. And they hear you tossing that aside—at least it seems that way to them—as if there is no other perspective but yours. Is that what a pastor would do?"

"Maybe," said Matthew without much conviction, "the church needs leaders who are prophetic as well as pastoral."

"Really?" She was now on the edge of her chair. "The church honors prophets, after it shoots them! Or after they've suffered enough to be credible. But do you honestly believe church people want prophets in their headquarters? By definition, prophets are not found in church headquarters. They want their leaders to be there when they need them, moving the ship forward without making waves."

Matthew finished his tea, and they sat in silence until he said, almost to himself, "What's funny about this conversation is that in lots of ways I agree with you. I don't feel like a prophet. And I certainly don't want to provoke some kind of war in the church. That's not me at all." He sat up straighter in the chair. "But I just don't understand why people are so up in arms about *this*. Why isn't it better for Christians to affirm people as long as those people aren't hurting anybody, and let God sort it out? And, yes, I guess I am surprised that you don't agree with that."

Roberta smiled. "Oh, I may come out where you are, but I'm a Baptist, for goodness sake, and first of all we wrestle with the Bible. Well, we don't always, but we should. Everywhere I look I see Christians sort of fitting the Bible into their lives, but only when it doesn't contradict some political bias they have."

Now Matthew smiled. "Should I be offended?"

"Maybe," she said leaning forward to grip his arm. "But if so, you have plenty of company, including me much of the time. And if I were a Disciple, of course I would vote for you."

The religion reporter for the *Lexington Herald-Leader*, a woman who went by the initials C. J., also wrote human interest stories for the Lifestyle section of the paper. After her article on Matthew's nomination generated several letters to the editor, she was asked to do a follow up, to put on her human interest hat and dig down on this guy whose views were causing such a stir. So C. J. came up with what she decided was an inspired idea: She would interview Margaret. It would be a way of featuring a woman's voice while learning more about this nominee.

Margaret's immediate response was, "No way!" Matthew encouraged her to reconsider. It would be a chance for people to get to know him as a person, not just as the champion for some cause.

"Then they should interview you," Margaret told him. "Why drag me into it?"

He didn't say aloud *because it would show readers I'm not gay*, but she finally agreed after C. J. said she would be happy to conduct the interview on a Saturday—May 25, the day after Matthew spoke with his friend Roberta—at the McAvoy's home.

As the hour for the interview drew near, Matthew took the kids to the local park so they would be out of the way; but when the three of them returned, he was anxious to find out how it had gone. The first thing Margaret told him was "C. J. thinks you're good looking."

"And I suppose you felt compelled to disagree with her."

They were sitting on the deck in the late afternoon, and even though Margaret's face was in shadows, he could see her smiling as she said, "I just told her what you always say about yourself, that you have big ears and are painfully thin. I think I said 'skinny.'"

Matthew rolled his eyes. "How else did you slander me?"

"She had you pegged as some kind of activist, but I popped that bubble. I assured her that you are much more at home in a library than at a protest rally. Shot down her whole image of a handsome agitator" ... and they both laughed.

"Did you tell her that you're the one who is more likely to be the agitator?"

"Only when people I care about are threatened." Margaret was still holding a glass of iced tea, poured during the interview, which she now finished and set beside her chair. "Actually, I did tell her you are much more likely to look for common ground than I am." She smiled. "Then our friend C. J. wanted to know other ways we are different, so I told her how, when we were first dating, I had to learn to be ready at six forty-five, or even earlier, if you said you'd pick me up at seven." She reached out and took Matthew's hand. "But don't worry, I didn't tell her why you're that way."

Zachary appeared by her chair, complaining first that he had nothing to do and then that he was hungry. "We'll fix dinner soon," she assured him, "so let Daddy and me talk a little longer." Once he wandered off, she said, "There were questions I wasn't sure how to answer. Like, she wanted to know if you had always been deeply religious. That's how she put it: 'deeply religious.'"

"What'd you say?"

"I told her that in college I went to Mass while you slept in on Sunday mornings."

"You didn't really!"

That smile in the shadows. "You are the one who wanted me to do this interview." She leaned forward. "I said that church is in your bones. But I did tell her how you took the LSAT, and how I imagined you, down the road, teaching law, maybe doing something in politics. And how I was surprised when you first said you were thinking about seminary. That's fair, isn't it?"

Matthew nodded and they were silent for a minute, watching Zachary chase bugs, one of his favorite things. "I remember," he said, turning to look at Margaret, "sitting in a corner booth in that Pizza Hut in downtown Champaign, talking about how people kept pushing me that direction when politics is the last thing I want to do. How working in the church is a better fit for who I am."

"And me telling you that I wasn't sure a good Catholic girl like me would fit in as the wife of a Protestant minister. Although, even then I thought you'd end up as a professor."

Zachary yelled that he almost caught one, and Margaret waved to him before turning back to Matthew. "Another thing C. J. asked is what role I played in your career decisions. I told her you may have made church unity a big theme of your teaching and your writing because you married someone who grew up going to Mass and saying the rosary."

They both smiled, and Margaret announced she was going to start on dinner. Matthew said he would help once he rounded up Zachary, but since their son was now playing contentedly in the sandbox, he followed Margaret into the kitchen. "I have a feeling," he said, "there were other interesting questions you haven't told me about."

"Nothing bad. For some reason I mentioned Frank, so she wanted to know if you took after your father."

"I want to hear this!"

"Well, I said you both love baseball. I also let her know that he owns a hardware store while you are useless with tools, and that you're a scholar in religion while he barely goes to church or reads anything other than sports magazines."

"He goes to church," said Matthew, "just not every week. And he reads the paper and a novel … now and then." They both smiled. "So, then I suppose she asked about my mother."

Margaret nodded. "I told her that Betsy died when you were nine. What else should I have said?"

Why, Matthew wondered, was he always embarrassed at how his mother had faded from his memory, as if it were a betrayal? Why over the years hadn't he asked his father more questions about her? "I couldn't answer if someone asked how I'm like her, so there isn't much else you could have said."

They were now facing each other, leaning against counters on either side of the kitchen. "Another question on her list is whether I always knew you would be a leader. I told her the truth, that when we were first married, *I* was the one with aspirations for leadership. I told her about my degree in educational administration and how we talked about me being a principal, even a superintendent … until you got accepted in the Ph.D. program at Yale, and I had to use my teaching credential to keep us financially afloat. I also told her the truth about something else, that I think people are attracted to you as a leader partly because you don't covet the role."

After their years in New Haven, time seemed to speed up, Matthew reflected as he took out the plates and silverware. Abigail was born right as he was offered a faculty position at DTS, Margaret began teaching at a good school, Zachary was born. Then, at age thirty-six, he was appointed dean of the seminary, and two years later a number of people, he'd been told, had submitted his name to the committee searching for the person to succeed Duane. He and Margaret had agreed that he was surely too young to become the nominee for this top position. They agreed that such a position was not a great fit for a family with a nine-year-old and a three-year-old. But he had wanted to let the process play out—it would be valuable experience in case something like this came up again—and Margaret had agreed.

As her husband started for the door, ready to corral their son, Margaret said, "She also wanted to know my reaction to the controversy."

Matthew turned to face her. "What did you say about that?"

"I wanted to say that it makes me anxious ... and furious." She shook her head. "But I won't say that to a reporter. What I said is that the number of idiots making noise is tiny compared to the support you're getting. That's true, isn't it?" Matthew nodded and made a mental note to let his wife—his partner, after all—see more of the good mail he was receiving.

Margaret had turned toward the sink, but now she turned back and seemed to be deciding whether or not to speak. Finally, she said, "I hope you don't take this the wrong way. I'm sure you will be confirmed, but, just in case, I think the kids and I should plan to stay in Lexington through the fall."

On the first day of June, while reading at home, Matthew got a phone call from a minister named Barbara who, he learned, was serving the congregation in Farmington, Indiana, where Harold Judkins was a member. It might be possible, she told Matthew, to arrange a meeting between him and Harold. Is that something he would welcome?

"What's Mr. Judkins like?" he asked. "Is he likely to listen to what I have to say, or would he see this as a time to harangue the heretic?"

"I don't know him well," she said. "I've only been at the church a few months. But he actually seems pretty reasonable. I'm not sure why this issue pushed his buttons, because he doesn't act like a right-wing nutcase."

So Matthew agreed and the next day Barbara called back with an invitation to dinner at her home the following week. She gave him directions and told him to look for a white, two-story house, with tall oak trees and a large porch, down the street from the church. "I like the idea of breaking bread together," she told Matthew, although he still had his doubts about this strategy.

The first half hour seemed to confirm them. Harold, who Matthew guessed was about sixty, arrived in a coat and tie, which he took off at Barbara's urging—perhaps because she and her husband, Phil, were in jeans—but then looked uncomfortable. Matthew was glad he had followed Margaret's advice and, for once, kept his suits in the closet. Barbara offered them all a glass of wine, which Harold refused, but then he said he would take a beer, which they didn't have. They all settled for sparkling grape juice. After Harold said for the third time that he wasn't an intellectual, Phil, who taught history at a nearby university, offered to leave. "One less Ph.D. in the room." But that might have made things even less comfortable since Harold, inexplicably, had been directing nearly all of his comments to Phil. It was Barbara who finally got the real conversation started.

"You know, Harold, Matthew isn't saying anything about the Bible that isn't taught in all of our seminaries, in the seminaries of all mainline churches for that matter." She began to elaborate but stopped when it was clear Harold wanted to speak.

"So you don't teach that it's the Word of God?" He hadn't raised his voice, but his cheeks were turning red. "Maybe that's the problem in all these churches. Maybe that's why the pews are so empty. I've traveled around. I've seen what the story is." Harold shifted to lean more on the arm of the sofa, but still looked uncomfortable.

"They teach, at least in my experience, that the Bible witnesses to God's presence in human life," said Barbara, "but it's a witness written by humans. So it has Good News, but there are also errors and human customs. It reflects the knowledge people had when it was written."

"But your question is a good one," said Matthew, looking directly at Harold. "It may seem sometimes like seminaries are emphasizing the errors more than the Good News."

For the first time—or at least it felt that way to Matthew—Harold looked at him. "I'm not saying you, personally, are out in left field. This may be what everybody teaches, but that doesn't mean it's helping the churches. We don't need a history lesson on Sunday morning. We don't need people in Indianapolis who say that everybody who disagrees with them is uneducated. We need a minister who can read the Bible and say what's right and wrong. And the Bible says homosexuality is just plain wrong. I don't get why this is even a question. It's there for anybody to read."

Phil, who had been busy in the kitchen, invited them to the old, wooden dining room table, where Matthew resisted the temptation to rearrange his silverware and move his water glass to the right side of his plate. He had been anxious about the evening, but his anxiety wasn't out of control. He further relaxed when the dinner conversation stayed on a more personal level. Matthew learned that Harold had two sons in their thirties: one who was married, with two children of his own, and one who seemed like he would always be a bachelor. Harold loved being a grandfather! They even got him to share pictures from his wallet.

After Phil and Barbara told Harold about their children, who were with their grandparents for the evening, Matthew knew he needed to reciprocate, so he talked about Abigail and the biography she put together as her year-end project for fourth grade. Even Harold smiled as Matthew told how he had expected her to choose someone like Helen Keller or Jackie Kennedy. But, instead of pictures and a paragraph or two about someone famous, she had written three pages about a nineteenth-century abolitionist and equal rights campaigner named Abby Kelley Foster.

"How in the world did she even discover this person?" asked Barbara.

"I have no idea," said Matthew, "unless Margaret suggested her." Part of the appeal, he knew, was the name. Abigail occasionally announced that she wanted to be called Abby, and it was her father who insisted on calling her Abigail, probably because he so disliked being called Matt. But there was no doubt, he told the dinner party, that she was also attracted by the thought of one-upping her dad. "Do you know who Abby Kelley Foster was?" Abigail had asked him. When Matthew acknowledged that he didn't, she shouted "Good!" and proceeded to tell him at considerable length about this woman whose motto was, "Go where you are least wanted for there you are most needed."

"You should read about her, Dad," Abigail concluded. "She was a real leader!"

Matthew started to tell them he had looked up Foster, whose other famous saying had something to do with harmony and truth, but decided against sharing this part of the story. It seemed to him that he'd already talked on too long about his daughter. Harold, however, didn't seem to mind. In fact, his tone was friendly, almost tender, when he said, "You seem very proud of her," which made Matthew like him more than he had expected.

Barbara got them back to the topic of the evening. "You must have spent a lot of money sending this declaration to every congregation," she said to Harold.

"Nearly eight thousand dollars out of my own pocket, once you add it all up. More if you count the poster we're going to send." He obviously couldn't resist telling this, but then looked sorry he had.

Matthew was surprised by how aggressively Barbara pounced. "Harold, the church could have done a whole lot of good with eight thousand dollars! There is mission that needs funding from Farmington to New Delhi."

"It *did* do good," said Harold, his cheeks again getting red. "We send money off to Indianapolis and who knows what it's used for. We're told it helps people in Africa or wherever, but we don't see any real accounting of how the money's spent. At least I don't. For all I know, it just keeps the machinery oiled at the headquarters."

"All of the church's units," said Phil, "present audited reports at the General Assembly."

"Harold, have you been to an assembly?" Barbara asked him.

"Not yet. But you can bet the farm on it that I'm going to go this year!"

"How long," asked Matthew, "have you been a Disciple?"

"Two years, almost. I was a Presbyterian, but they seemed more interested in politics than in preaching the gospel, so I started going to the Disciples church, and look where that's got me. But I don't know what difference it makes how long I've been there. I don't make a deal out of whether you're old enough to do this job."

The other three were silent, so after a pause Harold continued. "I want to come back to this business of doing good with my money. I think our declaration was a really good thing. If nothing else, it started a conversation in the church."

This was a moment Matthew had been expecting. "I appreciate that, Harold. I also believe in the importance of honest dialogue. In fact, that's what I teach and try to practice. You need to know, however, that the way you went about it has unleashed forces beyond your control, and not all of them are working for good. I suppose they could even get dangerous." He told them about his mail, including the regular letters (he now had five) from the graduate of 1933.

"You can't blame that on me or our declaration," said Harold. "There are people mean as snakes all over the place—including liberals, I might point out—who are just looking for an excuse to ..."

Matthew cut in. "That's the point. You provided one. But it seems to me we can turn this around, make it a positive."

Harold didn't respond, but he also didn't object, so Matthew continued. "What if we, you and I, write an open letter to the Disciples?"

Harold looked around the room, his lips tight together. "Saying what?"

"Saying we still disagree with each other about important matters; however, now that we've met each other, we respect what the other is trying to say and hope the church can engage in a healthy conversation about the place of gay people in it."

"Did you all cook up this idea beforehand?"

"First I heard of it," said Barbara, "but it's a good one. This church conversation could also be about the authority of scripture."

Matthew nodded. "And the authority of scripture. I'm talking about a conversation that includes anybody who wants to take part, not just those with seminary degrees. We could produce study materials with different points of view."

"I don't know," said Harold. "I have a bunch of people that are counting on me to lead this fight."

"Does anyone," asked Barbara, "really win a fight in the church?"

And so, for the next hour they hammered out a letter, Matthew and Harold talking, Phil writing, Barbara asking questions and clarifying answers. They spent another few minutes tweaking the beginning and the end, but the core remained pretty much as Phil had drafted it:

I, Matthew McAvoy, am convinced that a healthy church welcomes, even encourages, a wide variety of voices as it attempts to follow God's will. Seen in this light, the Farmington Declaration was not intended to be divisive but to be a vehicle for expressing genuine concerns and stimulating constructive debate.

I, Harold Judkins, trust Dr. McAvoy when he says that, if elected to be the church's General Minister and President, he will teach what he believes to be the truth about God and Jesus, but will not attempt to force the church to adopt ideas that people in the pews can't accept.

Both of us realize that this letter will likely come as a surprise to many Disciples. It may even disappoint some who see one or the other of us as the standard bearer for a particular wing of our fellowship. We are convinced, however, that the church must be a community that speaks the truth in love, a community that is able to disagree without weakening its basic bonds.

Harold wanted to add something about agreeing that the Bible is the Word of God until Barbara and Phil convinced him that how we understand scripture should be part of the future debate, and that

Matthew would encourage it. When they had finished, Barbara said, "I think Leo will feel very good about what we've done this evening."

"Who," asked Harold, "is Leo?"

Matthew would not say they parted as good friends, but the departure was cordial, which is why he was somewhat surprised and very disappointed when Harold left a message on the after-hours answering machine at the seminary saying he had changed his mind. He appreciated what Matthew was trying to do, but, after lots of prayer and talking with other people, he had decided that he could not sign his name to the letter.

CHAPTER FOUR

I n early June, not long after the dinner with Harold, Matthew attended a worship service at the Cane Ridge meeting house, which sits in the middle of wooded hills and horse farms just north of Lexington. If Disciples had shrines, Matthew was fond of saying, Cane Ridge might be the most important. It was the site of a great revival meeting, a gathering in 1801 of thousands of church folks for days of preaching and praise that was one of the roots of the Disciples movement. The wooden meeting house, actually a church, had been built in the late eighteenth century. Sometime in the 1950s, the deteriorating building had been enclosed in a protective limestone structure, complete with a series of stained-glass windows depicting significant moments in Disciples history.

Two years ago, Matthew had been the featured preacher at the annual Cane Ridge communion service, but this year he was simply invited to bring a greeting as "the nominee." The service was on a Sunday afternoon, and Margaret declared she had already had enough church for one day, thank you. Abigail, however, agreed to go with him as long as they stopped at the Dairy Queen on the way home. Matthew urged her to stay dressed for church, but Margaret said, "For heaven's sake, she's a kid on a Sunday afternoon!" So, while Matthew wore a suit and tie, Abigail wore an old T-shirt, tennis shoes, and her Cubs cap. He did manage to talk her out of the T-shirt that read "Stop the War."

On the short ride to Cane Ridge, Abigail announced, "Mom says you wear suits to try to look like you're older, since the people you meet with are older. Except the students, they're not older."

"Some of them are," said Matthew, as if this mattered. "And maybe I like wearing suits and ties." This thought was apparently so unimaginable that Abigail didn't respond but spent the rest of the drive staring out the window at thoroughbreds and white board fences.

The service was scheduled to start at two o'clock, plenty of time for people in Lexington to eat lunch after church and drive to the meeting house. But Matthew, true to his usual pattern, got there closer to one thirty. "You're so early I spend half my life waiting for things to begin," Abigail complained as they walked up the path from the gravel parking lot.

"That's a bit of an exaggeration, don't you think?"

"Are you afraid people won't know you're here? You don't need to worry about that, Dad. Everybody knows who you are. Well, not normal people, but everybody at church things. It can get embarrassing!"

As if on cue, two couples stopped to greet Matthew and offer congratulations. As he spoke to them, Matthew could feel Abigail's finger hooked in one of his belt loops. "Okay," he said to her once the couples were gone, "let's go look at the windows. If we pretend that we're looking very intently, maybe no one will bother us."

The first window they stood in front of—Abigail doing her best to stare intently—showed Barton Stone, a preacher at the 1801 revival and a prominent leader among the early Disciples. Stone was signing a document in which, according to the plaque under the boldly colored stained glass, he and others expressed their desire "to sink into the body of Christ at large."

"What does that mean?" asked Abigail.

"It means that he just wanted to be a Christian, not to be part of a particular church, like Presbyterian or Methodist or Catholic. This," Matthew added, "is very important for us, for our history."

"But we're a particular church, the Disciples of Christ." Abigail said the name, pointing with her finger as if reading from a church signboard. "Mom said she used to be a Catholic, but now she's a Disciples of Christ, so it's the same."

"Yes, that's true." This, he thought, was getting complicated. "But we are committed to working for the unity of all Christians. That's a big part of our mission, of who we are ..." He paused and then added, "of what I do. Well, some of what I do."

"So, has it worked? Who are we doing unity with?"

Matthew suggested they move on to another window, one that portrayed a handshake between Barton Stone and a messenger from Alexander Campbell. He reminded Abigail of Campbell's portrait that hung in his office, with no glimmer of recognition. According to the plaque under this window, the messenger's name was "Raccoon" John Smith, and the handshake took place on New Year's Day, 1832.

"This happened right here in Lexington," Matthew told her. "It's an example of two groups uniting, and they became our church."

"Why did they call him Raccoon? Did he have circles under his eyes?"

"I don't know." He smiled. "It seems when I'm around you there are lots of things I don't know."

"Like who is Abby Kelley Foster!"

People looked as if they might interrupt, so Matthew and Abigail stared intently at two quotations from Raccoon John carved under the window, Abigail tracing the letters with one of her index fingers, the other still in Matthew's belt loop.

Let us then, my brethren, be no longer Campbellites or Stoneites, but let us come to the Bible, and to the Bible alone, as the only book in the world that can give us all the light we need.

While there is but one faith, there may be ten thousand opinions; and, hence, if Christians are ever to be one, they must be one in faith and not in opinion.

Matthew had always been drawn to this early figure in his church's history, perhaps because Raccoon John, even though he had almost no schooling, was anything but narrow-minded. It undercut one of Matthew's prejudices. And yet, he reflected, education *does* help you see complexities. He reread the quotations, becoming less satisfied with the sentiments. While it sounds good, it's finally not enough to say "return to the Bible" when people read the Bible so differently. And it's not enough to say "be agreed in faith while allowing diversity of opinion" when so many people regard their opinions as immutable faith and other people's faith as mere opinion.

"So what happened after the handshake?" More questions from Abigail. "Did they just start being one church, or what?"

No, Matthew had to admit. It took three years before even the two congregations in Lexington began worshiping together, not to mention the task of selling their agreement to others who hadn't been there. This struck Matthew as par for the course, but Abigail was clearly unimpressed.

"It takes time," he said, sounding to his own ears a bit defensive. "You need preachers who tell the people that they need to get along, that they belong to each other because they all belong to Jesus."

"Well, *I* could tell 'em *that!*"

Okay, he thought, that was too simplistic. But before he could complicate the meaning of ecumenism, a bell rang, signaling time for worship. As they entered the old meeting house, Abigail asked if they could sit in the balcony. "I need to be down here so I can give a greeting," Matthew told her. "And they don't use the balcony anymore. It isn't very sturdy."

"*Somebody* used to sit there."

"Yes, it was the place where slaves sat when they came to church."

"Did somebody make 'em sit there?" Abigail asked loudly. "Why'd they do that?! I thought you said we're supposed to get people doing unity. That doesn't sound very unity if ..."

The service started, to Matthew's relief. He could see people around them smiling at the overheard conversation. It was impossible not to like Abigail, but, as Margaret often said, she wore you out.

As it turned out, the sermon text from Paul's letter to the Romans was tailor made for their conversation: "Welcome one another, just as Christ has welcomed you, for the glory of God." Yes! This, he told himself, was the perfect passage to use when speaking—well, maybe not to nine-year-olds, but to the church as a whole. God isn't glorified by our wrangling but by the Christ-like welcome we give to one another. He nudged Abigail to see if she was following the words, but she was busy drawing pictures of people falling out of what he decided must be a balcony.

The preacher, a friend of Matthew's, reminded the congregation that the issue facing the first-century church was whether Gentiles needed to become Jews—be circumcised, keep kosher—in order to become Christians. "If this dispute sounds archaic to our ears, imagine how our current disputes may sound to people who come after us."

Matthew made a mental note to use that line. He would have written it on his bulletin, but Abigail was busy decorating it with elaborate question marks.

The preacher, leaning—dangerously, Matthew thought—over the old wooden pulpit, reinforced his point by lifting up another verse from Romans: "Who are you to pass judgment on the servants of another? It is before their own Lord that they stand or fall."

Isn't this what he was trying to say to those who would judge their gay neighbors? Of course, Paul's message cut both ways. Harold was not to judge, but neither was he to judge Harold. He felt instructed and, at the same time, reinforced in his convictions, a feeling that grew as the community took communion together. All except those, such as Abigail, who weren't old enough, according to Disciples practice, to be baptized. Matthew knew he would face a slew of questions about that on the way to the Dairy Queen.

As they were leaving, Matthew stopped to pose for a picture with members of a congregation in Cincinnati. "We drove sixty-five miles to be here," one of them told him, "and this is icing on the cake." When, finally, he got free from all the schmoozing (not his cup of tea), he saw Abigail on the other side of the large fellowship room, talking to a man he didn't recognize. As Matthew approached, the man squeezed Abigail's shoulder and walked out the nearby exit.

"Who was that?" he asked her.

"How should I know? You're the one who knows everybody. He said he knew you. Said he even knows where we live."

It had been a grand celebration. So why did he leave Cane Ridge feeling slightly uneasy?

Matthew had no doubt that Margaret supported him. But he also knew she hated conflict—as did he, if he was honest with himself—and all the turmoil was making her unhappier by the day, despite his efforts to minimize it at home. The elders of their congregation, New Circle Christian Church, had, of course, received the Farmington

Declaration, and while they rejected it as "divisive," it was still the talk of the coffee hour. Margaret told Matthew she thought she overheard Carol, one of the elders, saying, "Where there's smoke there's bound to be fire," but she couldn't be sure. And she wasn't sure what Carol might have meant by that even if she said it.

Then came the June issue of *Disciples Forum*, with its page after page of dueling letters to the editor. One of them read, "It is my conviction that God, in response to prayer, has indeed lifted up for us a great leader suited to our times and needs." This was from a member of the Executive Committee. But there were others, which Margaret also read (Matthew could tell by her expression), that were far less complimentary. One declared, "It is a blasphemous mockery of the cross to even consider someone who would advocate the ordination of lesbians and homosexuals into the ministry or affirm that this sinful lifestyle is compatible with the gospel of Jesus Christ."

"I have never talked about ordination," Matthew fumed. "Apparently I need to remind people that the GMP has no say in who is ordained. That's up to the congregations and regions."

"But you do support it," said Margaret. "They know how to read between the lines. You say you won't have much power, but they know you'll have lots of influence. And, besides, as soon as you say something like that, the GLADN people will say you're waffling."

Another letter writer declared that liberals should consider how they would feel if a KKK supporter were the nominee. That, according to the writer, is how conservatives felt about the choice of a nominee who supports the "gay agenda." Matthew railed about the absurdity of comparing someone who affirms persons different from himself to those who condemn nearly everyone who is different from themselves.

"I'm going to write a response," he told Margaret. "These people, these … idiots, can't just say outrageous things and get away with it!" But when he cooled off, she told him what he already knew: If he wrote a response, all that people in the church would remember was his defensiveness. He would lose either way.

He also realized that venting his irritation only served to increase Margaret's agitation … and her concern. "Are you really sure you want to do this?" she asked him. "I'm not saying you should withdraw your name, but there's no law that says you have to go ahead with it if you don't want to. It's not just me. It's not good for you to get too anxious. That's when you start getting compulsive about things."

Abigail's complaint was of another sort. "It isn't fair!" she told her father one evening as he sat in his study. "Kids get dragged wherever parents want to move them. What if I don't want to move to Indianapolis? What about what I want? Or Zachary? Well, Zachary's too little to have any say in it, but ..."

"Maybe," Matthew interrupted, "you're also still too young to have the final say."

"I knew you'd say that! But that just shows you don't know how grown up I am. I even know what a homosexual is." She paused, apparently to see what effect this would have on him. When Matthew said nothing, she continued. "It's when a boy likes a boy instead of a girl. Like Keith and Alvin at church, even though they don't hold hands because nobody is supposed to know, I guess. It's all pretty silly, if you ask me. Jennifer likes Ryan even though he's a dork and in the fifth grade. People just like who they like."

Matthew started to ask why she'd brought this up, but Abigail was on to another subject. "When you're the GMP," tracing the letters in the air, "will you have to go to Australia like your friend who brought me the stuff?"

"Probably not. That was a special meeting, a one-time thing. But I might ... I will have to do a lot of traveling."

"Why is Mom so upset?"

How much of this should he tell her? Surely a going-into-fifth-grader, as she called herself, didn't need to be worried about such things. On the other hand, she obviously could feel the tension in the house. "People," he said, looking at her across his desk, "have been writing things about me, letters in the church magazine that aren't very nice. Well, lots of them, most of them, are nice, but some aren't."

"Have I met 'em?"

"No, most of them aren't even people I've met."

"Then what are they so mad about if they haven't even met you?"

Despite the seriousness of the topic, Matthew nearly laughed out loud. When, he wondered, do people stop being so refreshingly blunt and start beating around the bush. He made a mental note never to discourage Abigail's in-your-face honesty, even when it got on his nerves. Then, before he could respond, she added, "Must have to do with homosexual people. Why are they so against *them*?"

"Some of them, some Christians, think that the Bible doesn't approve of people who ... act in a homosexual way." He immediately regretted putting it like this, but she didn't ask him what he meant by acting "in a homosexual way" because her mind was on a different track.

"Does it?"

"Does what?"

"Does the Bible say that?"

How could he explain the problems of biblical interpretation to a nine-year-old? Would she understand about the Bible being written in times very different from our own? Would she understand that some biblical themes, like loving neighbors and honoring the image of God in everyone, are more important than others?

Abigail took him off the hook. "That's okay, Dad. We can talk about it some other time." She picked up the book she had set on the corner of his desk, but before leaving she added, "If they don't really know you, you can just ignore 'em, like you told me to do with Chelsea in third grade."

Of course, Margaret and Abigail were not the only ones who heard about the controversy. Matthew had given his father a subscription to *Disciples Forum* (a gift he now regretted), so if Frank didn't hear about it at church, he might well read about it at home. After finding two days' worth of reasons to put off the call, Matthew finally telephoned his father ... at the hardware store, when there likely would be little time for conversation.

Matthew started by talking about baseball, which he thought of as their shared passion, but that simply opened the door for Frank, a lifelong White Sox fan, to ridicule his son for following the Cubs. "You suppose they'll ever have a winning record again in your lifetime?" he said derisively.

"Come on, Dad. I didn't call to fight about the Cubs. And, besides, they aren't that bad: Dawson, Sandberg, Grace ..."

"Are you kidding me! I wouldn't trade Frank Thomas for your whole team. Your shortstop throws harder than any of your pitchers. I'd have Maddox on my team, but other than that, you can keep 'em all."

"I don't see that the White Sox are in first place," said Matthew, although he immediately regretted prolonging the topic.

Frank ignored him. "And how many managers are your Cubs gonna to go through this year? I wouldn't want to manage that group, I'll tell you that." But he added, "We would win it all this year if it wasn't for those damn Twins."

Matthew took that as an opening. "I just called, Dad, to see if you'd heard anything about the ruckus over my nomination. It's been ..."

"Oh, yeah. The reverend said something about it. I guess somebody was raising questions, some kind of fuss. Beverly, I suppose. Sounds like Beverly. Of course, this isn't something we talk much about around here. Better that way. No need to stir things up if you don't need to."

"I hope you know," said Matthew, "that *I* didn't stir this up."

"She never has had anything good to say about Jeffrey, never has."

"Dad, who are you talking about?"

"Beverly! And don't tell me you don't remember Jeffrey. Worked for me for a few years. Nice fellow, just different. I knew him in high school. Never liked girls. Never did."

Matthew started to say that, yes, he remembered Jeffrey, vaguely. But before he could complete a sentence, Frank was back to the earlier topic. "So I suppose you know what Sandberg is hitting?"

"His average," said Matthew, more calmly than he felt, "is around .310." He could picture his father's office: a short, dusty bookcase with hardware catalogues; a hook on the wall for his winter coat; a brick Matthew had given him from old Comiskey Park, which had recently been torn down; the Frank Thomas bobblehead.

"You always were the one for statistics," said Frank. "You were better at that than you were as a player ... always were." He apparently had second thoughts about that remark. "I'm not saying you were a bad player. You know you weren't a bad player. Let's just say I'm not surprised you're a professor. That's what your mother said one time: 'That boy's gonna to be a professor.'"

Now Matthew wanted the call to go longer. His father seldom spoke about his mother, and he wanted to ask him, *What made her say that?* But, sure enough, Frank was summoned to deal with a customer, and Matthew was left with questions: What did his mother see in him? Was she a closet academic? Is that where his interests had come from? Should he stick to being the professor she thought he would be? It was a great occupation, even a vocation. But he was more than that, wasn't he? Wasn't that why he had been asked to serve as dean at a young age, because he was also a leader?

Such questions were still in the back of his mind when, later in the day, sitting in his seminary office with its portrait of Campbell, he received a call from Carter. "I talked to all the faculty," he told Matthew in his southern drawl. "All but Wallace, and you know where he is, sifting through dirt on that archeological dig in Israel. He likes playing in the dirt." He paused for a brief chuckle before adding, "They voted unanimously to put you on sabbatical for the fall."

Matthew was stunned. "Don't you want to start the search for a new dean? I assumed you would want me to turn in my resignation so you could start that process ... if, that is, the General Board confirms the nomination."

"Oh, we have no doubt that the General Board will confirm you," said Carter. "But the General Assembly, with people from all those rural congregations, that could be another story. So, this way you have a job to come back to if you need it. And we get the benefit of having you introduced as dean of DTS during this whole nomination. As they say, any publicity is good publicity." He laughed at his little joke before saying, "I thought you'd be pretty happy with this."

Matthew acknowledged that it was a very gracious gesture by the president and faculty. Yes, he was happy for the news, but, although he didn't say this to Carter, it also troubled him. People really thought it was possible he wouldn't be elected! First Margaret and now the faculty hedging their bets. Every previous GMP had been affirmed at the assembly overwhelmingly, practically by acclamation. Even Duane, who, from what he could tell, was few people's first choice. Was he, Matthew the reconciler, really so toxic that the church would vote against him? Was his membership in GLADN—no, say it like it is, he told himself—was his *support* for gays and lesbians really such a big deal to that many people?

The day after Matthew spoke with his father, the family drove the three hundred miles from Lexington to Effingham, Illinois, to visit Margaret's parents. As her mother occasionally observed, three hundred miles isn't that far; it seems like their daughter and her family could manage to visit a little more often. It was just far enough, however, to rule out weekends, so they squeezed times with this set of grandparents into breaks in the schedule. Like now, before the seminary's summer classes and whatever else was in store for Matthew.

Matthew was very fond of Gretchen—his gentle, deeply religious mother-in-law—but the relationship with his father-in-law, Walt, had never been easy. Walt later insisted he'd been teasing when he'd wondered aloud how his daughter could have married someone who was both a Democrat and a Protestant, but Matthew wasn't at all sure that was true. They were on opposite ends of almost any spectrum. Walt looked like the football lineman he had been in college, Matthew more like someone who might play baseball, a sport Walt claimed to detest. Walt, a mechanic, was amazingly handy around the house, whereas Matthew was thankful that the seminary's maintenance man often gave him a hand when something needed fixing. "How," Walt wanted to know, "can you be the son of a fellow who owns a hardware store?" Walt took pride in "telling it like it is," Matthew in being tactful … although he didn't feel like being tactful when, from time to time, Walt called him Matt.

The plan was to stay three days, and the first went smoothly. Walt had filled a small, plastic pool near Gretchen's vegetable garden in the backyard of their modest, ranch-style home, and, since it was hot, Abigail deigned to play in it with Zachary. Matthew happily supervised because it kept him out of the house.

In the middle of the afternoon, when Zachary had crashed and Abigail was reading some book that her grandfather declared was too old for her, Matthew told Margaret he would like to visit the church where they were married. "Take your time," said Gretchen. "I'm always glad for time with the kids."

The interior of St. Anthony of Padua Church, a brick building from the 1870s, was pleasantly cool. Matthew took Margaret's hand and they stood silently, their eyes adjusting to the dimness, until he said, "This must feel like home."

"Catechism, first communion, a thousand dinners, Christmas pageants, our wedding." He could see her smile in the sunshine that filtered through the stained-glass windows, dust particles hanging in the shafts of light. "I don't think I ever told you my greatest worry on that day: that my side of the church would be filled and your dad and sister would be all alone on your side. Your grandmother had just died, and you told me your aunt in Dallas wouldn't come. But then all those friends showed up from the seminary, and *so* many people from the church you were serving as a student. ... I can't tell you how relieved I was."

They walked slowly down the center aisle, Margaret genuflecting as they neared the chancel steps. Matthew, who had walked on, now turned to face her, which meant he was looking down the aisle toward the back of the church. "I'll tell you my secret from that day, and it's related to yours. I stood right here, on this very spot, waiting for you to walk down the aisle."

"With my father."

"Yes, with your father. I can't forget Walt," and they both smiled. "Anyway, standing here gave me a chance to actually see all those people you were talking about on my side of the church, and it was amazing! A bunch of future ministers, but not just them. Conservative, old farmers like the Jorgensens. Remember them? Housewives like Gwen and Patricia, Gary was a mechanic who never got through high school, Lois worked at Schnucks as a cashier. There were three or four teachers. I remember thinking, "This really *is* my family. Well, you were now my family, but these others too."

Margaret's look was tender. "Why didn't you tell me about that before now?"

"There was lots going on. Besides, it's not always clear that a moment is pivotal until you think about it later. In college, I would have said that my deepest source of community was with peace advocates or other students. We liked the same things, thought the same way about things. When I look back on it, this, right here, was when I knew all that had changed, and my community was now the church." He stepped toward her. "Of course, you were at the center of it." She started to kiss him, but several people entered the sanctuary and they settled for a short hug.

The smooth visit got decidedly bumpy at lunch on the second day. They were squeezed around the table in what Gretchen called the "breakfast nook"—the adults eating sandwiches, the kids, macaroni and cheese—when his mother-in-law asked Matthew how things were going at the seminary. It was Margaret who jumped in to explain, as briefly as she could, about the nomination. "There's not really a position like it in the Catholic Church," she concluded, speaking quickly, "but I guess you could say he'll be like the archbishop of our denomination." Matthew grimaced and raised his eyebrows, but held his tongue.

"Most of the bishops I've had anything to do with," said Walt, "arch or otherwise, aren't worth a damn. You could put 'em all in a boat and send it out to sea without a paddle, far as I'm concerned. Especially these newer ones."

Gretchen was looking distressed. "Now Walt, what do you know about it? You haven't been to Mass since Easter." Turning now to Margaret, "You remember how we used to go all the time as a family when you were growing up? Now he says weekends are his free time away from the garage, and he'd rather watch football or golf or whatever." Walt started to speak, but his wife cut him off, eyes still on Margaret. "Why didn't you tell us about this big news before now?"

"I guess, Mom, because it's not a done deal. The board of the church still has to vote on his nomination, and then the whole church assembly votes on it in October. But if he's elected ..." She looked at Matthew. "*When* he's elected ... he doesn't like to call it an election. When he's *confirmed*, we'll be moving to Indianapolis, and that's quite a bit closer to Effingham. So that's good."

Gretchen clearly wanted to hear more about the position, which, she said, sounded very important and exciting. Abigail, however, set the conversation in a different direction. "The students at the seminary aren't sure Dad's gonna be elected. They think he should be, but they say there's a lot of trouble about it in their churches."

Now it was Margaret's turn to grimace. Her father opened his mouth, but Matthew spoke first. "How do you know all this, Miss Gossip?"

"Beth tells me things. Well, she doesn't tell me exactly, but I hear her talking to her friends, and then when I ask her about it she has to tell me what they're talking about."

Margaret clearly wanted to speak, but Abigail, now looking at her father, was on a roll. "The other day, when you and Mom went somewhere—I forget where—and Beth stayed with me and Zachary, we went to her apartment at the seminary, and that's when she talked to Heather and Lisa. They said you were supposed to go with them to a parade in Chicago, but then you didn't." She giggled. "They said you 'finked out.'"

"What's she talking about?" asked Margaret, now also looking at Matthew.

"Some of the students wanted me to go to a parade they're going to in Chicago, but I told them I didn't have time for it. Because we wanted to come here," he said, looking at Gretchen and trying to smile.

"What kind of parade?" asked Walt, not smiling.

Matthew and Margaret looked at each other before he began to explain, tactfully, that he—he started to say "we" but stopped in time—had been part of a group of gay persons in the church. Well, not all persons in the group were gay or lesbian. (He could see his mother-in-law looking anxiously at Abigail.) Many were simply supporters, like he and ... like he was. This had led to some controversy around his nomination. And some of the gay students at the seminary wanted him ...

"So," said Walt abruptly, "you need a new job because you got fired from the seminary."

"Dad! Why would you say such a thing? Matthew didn't get fired!"

"If I was associated with that school and heard the head of it was part of a group like that, I wouldn't give any more money to it. And I bet I'm not the only one who feels that way."

Gretchen tried to smooth things over, even scolding her husband for causing such a fuss when he didn't know anything about it. That, however, led him to launch into a diatribe about what happens when you mix religion and politics the way some of these new bishops were doing. Even families got split up by this nonsense.

Zachary, who had been silently eating macaroni and cheese in his booster chair, began to fidget, finally spilling his juice. Three of the adults jumped at the chance to clean it up.

Margaret spent time with her mother the next morning, and then, after conferring with Matthew, announced to her parents that she and her family would be driving home that afternoon. "Matthew has to get ready for the General Board, and Abigail has to get ready for church camp," she told them, even though the board didn't meet until the middle of July and camp wasn't until the middle of August.

CHAPTER FIVE

Despite the continuing trickle of negative mail (the most recent issue of *Disciples Forum* seemed to stir it back up), the first telephoned threat came as a shock. The call came on the home phone at about nine in the evening. Matthew was in his study, listening to an album of string quartets, making notes for his presentation to the General Board, when he picked up the receiver.

"Is this the big man, the big shot, the queer lover?"

It felt to Matthew as if the blood was draining from his body. "Who is this?"

"Getting your picture in the paper, sitting there with all your books—yeah, all your pretty books—pretending you're somebody, while you ruin the church."

Matthew thought of hanging up, but something inside compelled him to hear more. He started to say, "Who is this?" again, but stopped himself. What was the point?

"My friends and I want to know if you're queer, too. That pretty family just a front? Your wife do it with someone else so you can pass in respectable company? There are plenty like me who can't stand phony big shots. I'd be extra careful, if I was you, big shot. I wouldn't mind at all hearing that you've quit ... or died."

Matthew sat at his desk, his heart racing, for five minutes, ten minutes, thinking of all the things he wished he had said—"It takes a coward to threaten someone anonymously by phone rather than confronting him face to face." "Who else are you afraid of besides gay people?"—even as he knew it was better he hadn't said them. That would just have played into the caller's hand. He was also trying to decide if he should tell Margaret, but even then he knew he would. This was not the kind of thing you should keep secret. And, to be honest, he didn't want to. Was this, he wondered, a sign of ego? Some perverted notion that only important people get threatened?

Once the initial shock wore off, Matthew wasn't sure it was worth the time to file a complaint, but Margaret insisted ("Why is this even a question?"), and so he called the police. To his surprise, instead of telling him to come to the station, the dispatcher said a patrol car was in his neighborhood and would be at his house shortly.

The officers who arrived took the threat seriously … sort of. "So," said the one taking notes as they stood on the landing inside the front door, "a male voice. Any distinguishing characteristics? Old? Young?"

"I don't know. Middle aged, maybe. No real accent. Probably not a Kentucky native, now that I think of it. Probably not a Ph.D."

"Why do you say that?" asked the second policeman.

"I just mean he didn't sound highly educated. But he may have ties to the seminary, mentioning my quitting, although he may have been talking about my quitting as the nominee for a church position."

That led to an awkward discussion of his nomination. The first officer took notes, looking up occasionally. Matthew also mentioned how the phone call somewhat echoed a series of letters he had been receiving, although the voice on the phone didn't sound to him like that of a man who'd graduated from seminary in 1933.

"It did sound as if he has seen our house. He talked about me sitting in my study with lots of books." But that, he acknowledged, could also be a reference to his office at the seminary, where he had most of his rather large library. "He might have been drunk, kept repeating some words, maybe slurred a little."

"Was there any background noise?" asked the second officer. "Anything that might indicate where he was calling from?" Matthew thought for a moment, then shook his head.

"There's no doubt this is threatening," said the first officer, "but it isn't quite a threat, if you see what I mean. He didn't directly threaten you." He flipped through his notes before adding, "We could turn this over to the detectives, but I'd bet money they'd say this doesn't strike them as the kind that gets violent. If you get one of those, you'll know it. We'll keep this on file, of course, and if you hear from him again, of course let us know."

The whole episode was further unsettling for Margaret, who had been listening to her husband's conversation with the police.

"I should never have done that ridiculous interview," she said to Matthew once the police were gone. "That just called more attention to us, to our family, and made all of this seem ... 'normal,' like something that belongs in the Lifestyle section." She obviously had more to say, and Matthew didn't interrupt. "There are other people, you know, who could be nominated for General Minister and President, people who may not have as much baggage."

Although the kids had slept through the police visit, they were still trying to keep their voices down, so she exaggerated each word, which made them sound more strident than she might have intended.

"What baggage?!" Margaret signaled for him to lower his voice, which only ramped up his irritation with her, with the whole thing. He had just had a threat, for God's sake! This was a moment when he needed her to be supportive and keep all the worries for another time.

"Tell me, what's this baggage I'm supposed to be carrying? That you and I joined one organization? Margaret, the Executive Committee chose me, at least I think they chose me, because I can bring different parts of the church together. That's what I do."

"It doesn't look like it to me," Margaret said sharply. "Matthew, these aren't students you can reason with, give assignments to. They are uneducated, prejudiced people who now are resorting to threats. In our home! Think about that ... *in our home!*"

"We don't know that this guy had anything to do with the Disciples. It could just be some right-winger who read about it in the paper." Seeing Margaret grimace, he quickly added, "Not your interview, I don't mean that ... I just mean it could be some fool from another church or no church who hates gays, somebody who heard a rumor and decided ..."

They sat for a minute in grim silence before he continued. "Besides, that's not fair. You can't lump them all in a basket marked 'uneducated.' Some of the people who oppose me, like Harold, are trying to be faithful to what they think the Bible says. That's completely different from this name-calling creep on the phone."

Margaret looked away and shook her head. "You are always so understanding with everyone else, aren't you? Everyone but me. They say all kinds of crazy stuff and you find ways to justify it. But I tell you how I'm feeling, how I hate what this could do to our family ..." Her voice trailed off and she turned back to face him. "Last week you told me about some guy who practically called you the Antichrist in a letter and you treated it almost as a joke. Matthew! We read all the time about crazies who hear voices telling them someone famous is Satan or who knows what."

"You talk about Carter blowing things out of proportion," he said. "Aren't you exaggerating just a bit?"

"See! I try to say something that's serious to me and you respond with some condescending bullshit you might say to Abigail."

Matthew's mind felt blank, his stomach in a knot, as they sat for a while in silence. He would not let anxiety get the best of him, he told himself. He would not! Concentrate on the good things, not on this one call. Concentrate on how much he loved his wife, not on this one area of argument.

Perhaps Margaret had similar thoughts because when she next spoke her tone had softened. "I didn't mean to suggest ... You *do* know how to get people to talk with one another, assuming they'll give you a chance. And *of course* I'm with you; that's not the issue. But, honey, you don't *have* to save the church, especially when it seems that parts of it don't want to give you a chance. All I'm saying is that they could nominate someone who isn't a member of GLADN and doesn't have small children."

Later that week, Matthew received a scheduled visit from two leaders of Disciples for Biblical Witness. Much to the surprise of some of his seminary colleagues, he occasionally assigned materials produced by DBW, the evangelical caucus within the Disciples. It was a group perpetually upset by decisions of the denomination, which they saw as going the way of "the heretical United Church of Christ." Disciples for Biblical Witness had criticized Matthew, in their eponymous journal, for various ecumenical activities. But the criticism wasn't harsh ... perhaps because he had never been publicly critical of DBW.

He recalled one journal editorial that attacked the Disciples dialogue with Roman Catholics, naming him specifically as a member of the dialogue team. Catholics, according to the editors, give authority to an earthly Pope when all authority belongs to Jesus. Catholics also act as if the Lord's Supper is some kind of magic ritual, so special that others must be kept away. Why were the Disciples involved in dialogue with them instead of with other Protestants, such as the Baptists or the Nazarenes? However, there are two issues, the editorial noted, where Evangelicals and Catholics are on the same page: abortion and homosexuality. "Unity in animus," Matthew called it. Unity on the basis of shared disparagement.

Duane and other leaders in Indianapolis counseled against an interview with the group, but, as Margaret noted, that wasn't Matthew's style. He tried to put himself inside the perspective of conservative members of the church. Yes, as he saw it they had swallowed the culture's prejudice against gays and lesbians, and that was harmful. But *they* also felt harmed ... threatened by an attack on values that shaped their very sense of identity. That, too, should matter to him. "Who are you to pass judgment on the servants of another?" He was going to be the leader of the whole church, he reminded himself, not just the parts of it with which he was most comfortable.

Beyond that, he told Duane, they at least asked him for an interview. Why hadn't *Disciples Forum* done the same? Duane reported that he had inquired about this and been told that the magazine had already devoted enough inches to Matthew by printing parts of his information profile. Now they needed to let other voices be heard. It was clear Duane did not agree with this decision.

Matthew had previously been introduced to the two interviewers, an older man named Chuck and a younger one named Jeremy, but he didn't know them well. They met for the interview around the wooden table in his office at the seminary, the portrait of Campbell looming in the background. Lucinda offered to get everyone coffee, which Chuck and Jeremy first declined, then accepted, before Jeremy changed his mind and asked if she had a Coke. Matthew saw Lucinda roll her eyes as she left the room, and that, at least, made him smile.

The first question, one Matthew half expected, came from Chuck. "Dr. McAvoy, we have heard from several Disciples seminary students, students that identify themselves as evangelicals, who tell us how difficult life is for them in a liberal environment. There are students at DTS who felt that way after the event, I think you call it a convocation, that celebrated your nomination. Could you comment on that?"

"I'm sorry students felt that way," said Matthew. "Every seminary, I imagine, needs to work at being more open to theological diversity. But I'm not sure why anyone would have felt excluded by that convocation. No one was pushing any agenda, except congratulating me."

"That's not how they felt," said Jeremy quickly. There was an aggressive edge to his voice. "They said the whole thing was a glorification of liberal ideas. Maybe you should talk to them occasionally."

"If they have a complaint," said Matthew, "*they* should talk to *me*. I imagine, by the way, that gay students have also found seminary life pretty difficult over the years."

Jeremy was ready to respond, but Matthew didn't let him in. "Okay, we'll work on it. I may not be here after October, but I'll urge my colleagues to pay attention to this."

He shifted in his chair. "I have to add, however, that seminary education is designed to make *all* students feel uncomfortable. You get here and meet people who have different ideas, have had different experiences. We had a visiting student from India this past year who tried to convince his American friends of the merits of arranged marriages. You can imagine how that went over!"

He smiled, but the interviewers' expressions didn't change. "Conversations like that make you reconsider things you once took for granted. I recommend it for everyone," he added, again smiling.

Both interviewers ignored the insinuation, or didn't catch it. "Would you agree," asked Chuck, "that conservatives are also seeking to promote the good of the church, even the unity of the church?"

"Sure." Matthew considered adding *some of them at least,* but decided not to. He didn't think he was feeling overly anxious, but it still bugged him that Jeremy's Coke bottle was leaving yet another ring on his well-worn table. He grabbed a magazine from his desk and slid it across for Jeremy to use as a coaster. When it ended up at an angle, he reached quickly across the table and straightened it before sitting back in his chair and saying, "As I see it, the gap, tension—whatever you want to call it—between liberals and conservatives may be the most pressing church unity issue of our era. Our congregations need both perspectives. One thing I appreciate about DBW—this may get me in trouble with my liberal friends—is that you have tried insistently to call us back to our biblical foundation, as have I." Matthew paused, but he clearly intended to continue and they didn't interrupt. "I would like to know, in this same regard, if you acknowledge that I'm a faithful Christian who takes the Bible seriously."

Jeremy started to respond, but Chuck cut him off. "We don't attack you personally," he said.

"You're as slippery," said Matthew, "as my father."

"Your father doesn't agree ... ?"

"Yes, he does! I'm sorry I mentioned him. Please don't write about my father, except that he's a faithful member of a Disciples congregation in Iowa."

They talked about an eclectic list of other matters—his commitment (or lack of it, in Jeremy's estimation) to evangelism, whether the World Council of Churches has supported left-wing terrorists, what the seminary teaches about the resurrection—before getting around to the elephant in the room. "Please explain," said Chuck, "your support for homosexual practice in light of your stated commitment to the authority of scripture."

Matthew spoke about the priority of love in the Bible, about scripture's frequent denunciations of judgmentalism, about the danger of applying ancient ethical codes to contemporary situations—aware that none of this was convincing to his questioners. Aware, as well, that questions could be raised about each of his points.

"My real concern here," he told them, "is that we not become distracted by focusing too much energy and attention on matters that aren't central to the gospel. How many times did Jesus talk about homosexuality? Zero that we know of. I am pleading with you: Don't divide us further over this issue. For now, let's agree to disagree. We can continue to talk about it, that's fine. In fact, when I'm General

Minister, I will try to promote a church-wide conversation on this. But let's not polarize prematurely. My plea is for a moratorium on our internal squabbling, a moratorium for the sake of our common mission."

Chuck and Jeremy pointed to their notes, as if deciding what question should come next, and so Matthew added, "You know, I would be the best friend DBW ever had in that office. For my whole ministry, I have been committed to dialogue that includes diverse voices, even yours" … the last words said with a smile. This is what he had intended to tell them, the main point he wanted to get across in this interview. Why, then, did it feel slightly off target once he said it?

That evening Matthew talked about the interview, perhaps exaggerating how dumb he thought some of the questions were, while Margaret ate quickly, said, "Better you than me," and left for a meeting of their congregation's education committee. When her mother was gone, and she and her father had cleaned up the dishes, Abigail said, "Let's go to the park. Zachary's been a pain. He keeps saying he's almost four and can do everything himself, which just makes a mess. Mom says going to the park wears him out." Zachary thought it was a grand idea, and the three of them set forth, Abigail wearing her Cubs cap and carrying a Wiffle ball and bat.

They walked the four blocks at a pretty good clip, considering the length of Zachary's legs. Past modest, split-level, two-color homes that looked a lot like theirs, across a narrow stream on a wooden footbridge, and into the neighborhood park. For several minutes, Matthew pitched the Wiffle ball, which Zachary happily chased whenever Abigail happened to hit it. But eventually Zachary tired of this and wandered off to the playground, with its slides and swings and teeter totter. Matthew followed to help him go down the slide, but the slide was fairly short and Zachary announced that he could go down it by himself. He had done it lots of time when Mom brought him to the park. So father and daughter headed for a bench near both the playground and a large oak tree, evening shadows lengthening around them.

As soon they were seated, Abigail asked, "Did you tell them to buzz off?"

It took several seconds before Matthew realized she was referring to his dinner conversation with Margaret. "What makes you ask that?"

"Mom says you need to tell a bunch of people to buzzzzzz off." She spread her arms, pretending to be a bee. She also looked to see if Zachary, her usual audience, was watching, but he was crouched on the other side of the playground equipment, apparently looking at another kind of bug.

"She does, huh?" He started to ask what else her mother had to say on the subject, but then decided against it. She told him anyway.

"She says you want everybody to like you, even though you told me in second grade that not everyone will like me when I told you about Sarah being mean. Mom calls them 'knuckleheads.'" She giggled. "Maybe those men you talked to today are just knuckleheads, whatever that is."

Was that true? he wondered. Had he wanted Chuck and Jeremy to like him? Margaret was not the first person to say that about him, to suggest that he tolerated too much in an effort to be liked or at least to get along. On the other hand, Chuck and Jeremy were members of the church too. Being inclusive meant including those who didn't agree with how he defined inclusive, didn't it? How did leaders make sure the circle was as wide as it needed to be, but no wider?

While pondering these things, Matthew had been staring up at the massive tree that loomed over their bench. Now he turned to Abigail. "Okay, starting today your bedtime is seven thirty."

Her eyes widened. "What for?!"

"You don't like that? Well, you just told me I shouldn't care whether people like me or not."

"Dad! I didn't mean *me*!"

He smiled and gave her a hug. "Speaking of bedtime, it's getting past Zachary's. Let's head back." But when they stood and turned toward the playground, Zachary was nowhere to be seen.

The next ten minutes were among the longest of Matthew's life. "You look for him around here," he told Abigail, trying to keep his voice calm. "You know how he likes to chase bugs. I'll go check by the stream."

Matthew could hear his daughter calling her brother's name, sounding increasingly frantic, as he walked quickly in one direction, then the other, paying particular attention to the tall weeds that lined the stream, the shadows lengthening by the minute and changing shapes as tree leaves blew above him. Zachary couldn't have gone far. Was he hiding behind some bushes or a tree? If so, why didn't he answer them?! Zachary had seen where his father and sister were sitting, hadn't he? He wouldn't have panicked and started for home, would he? Matthew headed quickly toward the entrance to the park, although he saw no one, let alone a little kid, on the path ahead of him. His mind had just begun to play tricks, raising the possibility that someone ... when he heard Abigail say in a loud voice, "Where have you been?!"

As it turned out, Zachary had decided he was big enough to use the park's bathroom by himself, and then got scared when he was able to push the door open from the outside but wasn't strong or tall enough to pull it open from the inside. It wasn't until a man came in that a crying Zachary was able to slip out and hear his sister calling.

Margaret had just arrived home from the church when Matthew and the kids returned from the park. He had hoped to say little about losing Zachary—his wife had enough to worry about as it was—but Abigail, of course, was more than ready to share their adventure, playing up her role in finding her brother after they had looked "absolutely everywhere." Margaret was basically silent during Abigail's narration, comforting Zachary who was tired and fussy. But, to her husband, the tightness around her mouth spoke volumes.

During the first two weeks of July, Matthew not only beat himself up for nearly losing Zachary, he agonized over his speech to the General Board. This was obviously a crucial moment to clarify who he was and why having a GMP who is an educator and a reconciler could be good for the church. But how to focus it? How to show the nuance of his thinking? Originally, he had been told he had thirty minutes to speak. "Don't worry about the time, take what you need," Duane had assured him. But then Marvin had called to say that the controversy over the nomination had been added to the agenda, so shorter was better. Could he keep it to twenty? How, Matthew fumed, was he supposed to give the most important speech of his life in twenty minutes? He had given sermons longer than that, although afterward he usually wished he hadn't.

Once he had a draft, Matthew was anxious to try it out on Margaret. They settled after dinner into their usual living room chairs, but five minutes into the speech Margaret interrupted to check on why Zachary was being so quiet. They moved to the deck, ostensibly to preclude interruptions, but then Margaret stopped him in order to get bug spray, and Matthew gave up on the whole idea. "You can just read it," he said in a slightly irritated tone, "when you don't have anything else to do."

The board meeting happened to be in Louisville, so Matthew could simply drive the seventy miles from Lexington, for which he was thankful. As always, he arrived early but decided to skip the session before his address. He wasn't sure why, but it just felt better not to be hanging around until time to speak.

On the dais, Duane greeted him with a hug, leaving no doubt that he was in Matthew's corner. Raymond, the moderator, was far more measured, cordial but not particularly warm. Matthew sensed the same ambivalence in the room, or was that just him being insecure?

There were various announcements to be made before Matthew was introduced. He used these minutes to arrange the water glasses and note pads set out on the front table and to look around the small ballroom, where perhaps a hundred people were seated at tables strewn—too haphazardly, for his taste—with papers, glasses, and coffee cups. Several friends smiled in his direction. Other members of the church's governing board looked anything but cheerful. A few seemed ready for a post-luncheon nap. And then there were two men he had never seen before, standing with hands folded against the back wall. "Are those security guards?" he whispered to Duane.

Duane followed his gaze and nodded. "There have been a couple of fairly nasty calls to the office," he whispered back. "But nothing to be too alarmed about. We just wanted to be extra safe. You've probably heard that, as it turned out, the man who caused the explosion at the WCC assembly also had a gun."

No, he hadn't heard! Matthew wanted to ask more about this revelation, but he was already being introduced. He used the minute while his credentials were being read to line up his pen and note pad.

"We meet," he began, once the applause had ended, "in the midst of a difficult, but potentially creative, period in the life of the Disciples of Christ denomination. The past three months have brought a number of latent problems to the surface. If nothing else, we have managed to eliminate much of the apathy that often accompanies transitions in church leadership." The muted laughter told him the Board was definitely in a serious mood. Suddenly, he wondered if the threatening caller could actually slip into a ballroom like this, which made him momentarily lose his place.

"It is not particularly pleasant to be told I'm out of touch with the church, or I don't take the Bible seriously, because of my conviction that gay and lesbian persons should be fully included in Christian community. But I have been equally troubled by some—no means all, but some—of the many supportive letters I have received. To say 'I am pleased with your nomination because we agree on a, b, and c' is not fundamentally different from saying 'I urge the church to reject your nomination because we disagree on x, y, and z.' Both responses point toward what may be the critical issue before us: namely, the growing politicization of our life as a church family."

Had this been a mistake? It was hardly the way to solidify his base, as a politician might put it. But wasn't it true? He was bound to be a disappointment to those who saw him as their spokesperson for whatever cause.

"In a politicized environment, the perspective of one's wing or group is often confused with *the* position of the church or *the* position of scripture, which leads to the conclusion that 'our agenda' must prevail, 'my side' must be victorious. And in a politicized environment, leadership is selected on the basis of whether the candidate," he smiled at his own misstep, "the nominee, agrees with us on certain key issues."

His text moved on to cite the work of a well-known theologian and his own experience with other churches, but already the speech was feeling far too heavy. He skipped the next two paragraphs, taking a drink of water to mask his search for the right place to reenter the manuscript.

"You are familiar, I am sure, with other symptoms of this disease, symptoms," he added, "that are closer to home: the tendency to evaluate ministers by the extent to which they say things that are agreeable to powerful members of the congregation; an approach to general assemblies that seems more intent on political victories than on celebration, communal decision making, or education; a tendency to caricature or ridicule one's opponents in the church, explaining away their theological concerns on sociological or psychological grounds. We are all too familiar with this kind of rhetoric: 'Disciples for Biblical Witness is just a power play, mostly involving people who aren't very well educated.' 'Liberals aren't serious about their faith; they just use the language of the gospel for social purposes.'

"As General Minister and President, I will oppose this kind of thinking and speaking, no matter where it comes from. As GMP, I will insist that whoever preaches half the gospel is no less or more a heretic than the person who preaches the other half."

Still not much laughter. The first draft of his speech had said he learned about reconciliation from growing up with a father who, for reasons known only to God, was a White Sox fan. But he had dropped it because being personal made him uncomfortable. He now realized, however, that a little more humor would have been good. Nothing to do at this point but forge ahead. "As GMP, I will urge us to recover our commitment and capacity to seek God's guidance together, not as a collection of special interests but as a community of faith."

There was more—*much* more, he realized, as he cut additional paragraphs, feeling rivulets of perspiration under his suit coat. And then, mercifully, he was on the last page.

"The church, of course, is a human institution. When serious arguments flare up within human institutions, members can resign or form political caucuses aimed at winning the next election. But the church is also more than a human institution. Christians recognize that we belong together not because we think alike or look alike, but because we have all said 'yes' to the One who has graciously welcomed us. At times, it may seem that this is all we have in common, but it is a commonality far greater than the differences on which we concentrate with such energy.

"Friends, we have had too much us–them, win–lose thinking. Too much fighting. And as a new friend recently said to me, 'No one really wins a fight in the church.'"

The ovation was strong, even prolonged, but for the second time in recent weeks, Matthew felt dissatisfied in a way he couldn't put into words. He had said important things, he told himself, but he couldn't escape the feeling that what he had said needed to be, in some way, qualified.

Later that afternoon, Harold was given five minutes to talk about the Farmington Declaration. Duane had been against giving him any time at all, but Matthew, the message of Cane Ridge still in his head, urged Duane and Raymond to let Harold speak. "Okay," said Duane, "but that troublemaker had better not see this as some sort of rebuttal to what you have to say."

In fact, he didn't. "Matthew McAvoy," said Harold toward the end of his brief remarks, "is no doubt one of the most gifted persons in our Brotherhood." Matthew could imagine board members wincing at the use of this anachronistic term for their denomination. "He is exemplary in his compassion for the forgotten souls of humanity. Nobody should question his honesty and integrity. However, his biblical interpretations are seen by lots of people, from all I hear, as being far out of step with the mainstream of folks in the pews."

Matthew smiled at these words. While certainly not an endorsement, they were a real improvement on the Farmington Declaration.

"I believe," Harold concluded, "that if a person who has such far-out views is presented to the General Assembly the majority will not accept him as their leader."

There was applause but scattered and half-hearted. Matthew later heard people say that he had started what applause there was. While he never denied this rumor, he actually couldn't vouch for it, either.

The meeting ended the next day at four o'clock, the board having affirmed Matthew's nomination: 78 percent in favor, 19 percent opposed, with two persons apparently abstaining. Why in the world, he wondered, would anyone abstain? He would have liked an even more favorable vote, but this was well over the two-thirds needed to send his nomination to the General Assembly in October, where he would again need two-thirds.

The whole experience left Matthew exhausted but not sleepy, so he eagerly agreed to go with Duane to a Louisville Cardinals game that evening. Unless it went extra innings, he could still get back to Lexington before midnight.

"They're the AAA franchise for the Cardinals," Duane told him, as if Matthew didn't know.

Duane reveled in their seats, second row behind the third base dugout where, of course, Duane ran into people he knew. "I loved playing ball," he told Matthew once he returned from greeting them. "And I was pretty good, if I do say so myself. Pretty good. It just seemed to come naturally. How about you? You play high school ball?"

The recent conversation with his father flashed through Matthew's mind. "No," he said. "I played Babe Ruth league but not an all-star or anything like that. What I really like," he admitted, "is the strategy of it and the statistics. I would have made a good manager."

He wanted to ask, "How do you think they liked my speech?" but that felt too self-serving. And, in any case, Duane kept the conversation on baseball for the first two innings. In the middle of the third, the older man left to relieve himself, returning with more beer, and Matthew saw it as an opportunity to change the subject.

"That young minister on the board from Virginia told me she had spoken with Leo—or, I guess, she had spoken with someone who had spoken with Leo—and he said Leo isn't in favor of my nomination. Is that true? Have you talked to him?"

"Oh, I've heard that rumor," said Duane, his eyes on the game. "But as far as I know, Leo's working on a book and isn't in touch with anybody. Not even preaching these days. Won't commit to speaking at the assembly. So I doubt he's said anything one way or the other."

Nothing to do but take the bull by the horns. "Duane, how do you think things went this week—the meeting, my speech ... ?"

Duane turned to face him, wearing his perpetual smile. "Fine. Yeah, it went fine, don't you think? They liked what you said, most of 'em. Of course, now people out in the church need to hear you. We've been thinking ..."

"Who is 'we'?"

"Raymond and I, Marvin, Isabel, a few of the other colleagues. We've been thinking that you should do a kind of 'Meet the Nominee' tour. Speak to people, let them hear you defend your positions."

"Duane, it's not up to me to defend the nomination. That's for the Executive Committee to do, and now the board. They nominated me, for God's sake."

"Yes, yes. I agree." Still smiling. "Raymond sometimes talks about you defending the nomination, but I think we're all pretty much on the same page. We'll send out an invitation to invite you, so to speak, and then my office will coordinate your schedule so you can go where it will have the most impact. The biggest impact. I know most of the regional ministers are on board. They'll help set up the meetings."

"You're sure this is necessary."

"I wouldn't say it's absolutely necessary, but I think it's a good idea, don't you? Think of this as Dr. McAvoy making house calls on the church."

They watched the game for a minute before Matthew said, "I can see the point of visiting different places, but please don't supervise it too much. If Backwater, Arkansas, invites me, I think I ought to go there. That itself will say something about how I see the church."

"Good. That's good. But let's at least put a priority on regional gatherings or large congregations, so you can reach as many people as possible. I imagine they'll want to ask about your pastoral experience. That may be an issue."

"See, that's what I mean about the committee defending their decision. My background is what it is. I didn't choose me! The Executive Committee must have thought I have other qualifications. Or maybe they didn't want a safe nominee, business as usual."

Matthew wished he could take that back. "I didn't mean, Duane, that your leadership is business as usual. I just meant that they may have wanted someone who would help the church think about what it believes."

"That may be," said Duane, "although some people on the committee have told me that in March they didn't really get a full picture of what *you* believe."

He looked as if he wanted to take *that* back. "Matthew, you did fine yesterday, just fine. They heard the voice of a reconciler. I think that's just what the church needs. Now I guess we'll find out if that's what it wants."

CHAPTER SIX

The invitation to come to Switzerland for a long-range planning meeting of the World Council of Churches took Matthew by surprise. It seemed that now he was the nominee to be leader of his own church, other groups also got more interested in his leadership potential.

Margaret suggested—perhaps more than suggested—that he not accept the invitation. Abigail would be on her way to church camp not long after he returned, and then he would be on the road going God knows where to speak about the nomination. Abigail would only be nine once, she reminded him (as if he had somehow overlooked this fact), and he needed to think about spending time with her ... not to mention Zachary, who would soon turn four, and the rest of the family.

But this, he tried to point out calmly, was his first real opportunity to have an influence on the global church. Surely, she could see that this was important, not only for him but for the Disciples. It would also be a welcome break from the nomination uproar, although he didn't say that to Margaret. So he went, but somewhat under a cloud.

The World Council's headquarters is a two-story, rectangular building with three taller wings, set amid gardens in a section of Geneva filled with international organizations. The meeting was scheduled to begin at nine in the morning, but Matthew, having arrived at his hotel the night before, was at the headquarters by eight thirty. Friends had raved about the chapel, and he wanted to be there early, both to see it and to spend time in prayer.

The chapel was empty when he got there, and he entered slowly—walking across the floor mosaics, designed to look like water in a baptismal pool; wandering past the wooden, lattice-work walls and modern stained-glass windows—before taking a seat on a side aisle. His intention was to not think about the nomination, which, of course, made thinking about it inevitable. Okay, he would pray that God be in the process.

Before long, however, he found he was also fretting about Abigail. Last night, he had eagerly looked for the usual note in his suitcase and was slightly disappointed when all he found was a six-word sentence, "I am glad you like cheese!" and a smiley face, scribbled on a sheet of paper torn from a notebook. Was Margaret right? Was he paying less attention to his daughter because of this nomination? And was she, therefore, paying less attention to him? Should a dad even think such things?

Once the meeting started, however, he had little time for such stewing. All twenty members of the working group agreed that it was tough to plan for the future when the world was changing so rapidly around them. They reviewed developments in Iraq, although the war (despite the still-burning oil fields in Kuwait) almost seemed like distant history. There was lots of discussion about the disintegration of the Warsaw Pact just the previous month, and even as the group met, two republics pulled out of the Soviet Union, which seemed to be in its last days.

Patterns of relationship that the church leaders had taken for granted were falling apart before their eyes. The question was how they were to interpret such events. Some wanted to speak of God's hand in these historical developments. If scripture is the lens through which we look, they argued, then the God we worship is One who intervenes in history. Our task is to discern where God is acting and become co-actors with God. Others were wary of this kind of thinking. Humans, as they saw it, have far too often claimed to see God's hand in ways that served their own interests, justified their own beliefs. There was also little clarity about the role of the church in this period of upheaval. The WCC took pride in being a sign of unity in diversity, but didn't the events of the era show that some forms of unity—human alliances created by humans—*ought* to fall apart?

Everywhere Matthew looked there was ambiguity. The meeting included two observers from the Vatican, one of whom carried on at length about the part Pope John Paul II had played in bringing an end to the Communist bloc. Matthew knew, however, that the Pope had also written letters to Bush and Hussein in an effort to avert the U.S. attack on Iraq, and you could see how effective that was. If the leader of the world's one billion Catholics, a man with rock star status, had little diplomatic clout, how much less would other church leaders have.

Still, Matthew couldn't help but picture himself, General Minister of an admittedly small American denomination, playing some role on the international stage. Before becoming dean, he regularly taught a course on Jewish–Christian dialogue with a local rabbi, so maybe he had something to contribute to the church's peacemaking efforts in the Middle East ... although the Disciples' partners in the region, he knew from his reading, were Palestinian churches, and their priority was justice. Could you be a true champion for justice and also be a peacemaker?

There was discussion, of course, of the WCC's recent assembly in Australia, and this led Matthew to think about the Disciples General Assembly, now less than three months away, where representatives from various global partner churches would be present. The church's biggest mission field had been in Zaire, so the head of that Disciples community would be in Tulsa, wouldn't he? What was his name? Matthew resolved to find out, to welcome the man warmly at the assembly, and to discuss a time when he could visit central Africa. Perhaps he would speak with Duane about drawing up some kind of certificate that he, Matthew, could present to all of the visiting church leaders in October—although as soon as the idea was in his head his gut told him that such gestures, as his father would say, didn't amount to a hill of beans.

The meeting ended with lunch, but since the afternoon flights would get Matthew into Lexington very late, he had booked his return for the next morning, giving him the afternoon to explore Geneva. After saying his good-byes, he headed downtown, his first time to walk along the lakefront, see the famous *Jet d'Eau*, admire the bridge with its colorful flags, stroll by the clock made of flowers at the base of the old city that is crowned by the Saint Pierre Cathedral. He picked up an array of colorful postcards for Abigail, and was looking for something to take to Margaret and Zachary, when he ran into another member of the committee, the president of the United Church of Zambia, who was also window shopping. They quickly agreed that the shopping could wait and found an outdoor table near the clock tower on the Place du Molard.

Most people at the meeting had seemed completely unaware of what Matthew was going through back home—or, if they were aware, showed little interest. This struck him as appropriate. How trivial the Disciples brouhaha seemed when set alongside the problems facing the Methodist Church in Sri Lanka or the Congregational Church in South Africa or the Orthodox Church in what was left of Yugoslavia. He had made a note to use that line when speaking to Disciples gatherings.

So it was a surprise when, after they had ordered coffee, his Zambian friend said to him in Oxford-inflected English, "I hear you are going through a rough patch in your church."

Matthew explained briefly about the nomination, uncertain how much he should say about the actual issue behind the controversy, while the other man sipped his coffee, nodding slowly.

"It seems to me," he said once Matthew had finished, "this is a sign of the decadence of American society."

"Look," said Matthew, "I understand that African culture has a real problem with homosexuality, but for many people in the United States this is a justice issue. Maybe we can agree …"

His new Zambian friend cut him off. "My dear Matthew, I'm not one of *those*. All Africans, you know, are not the same. I'm talking about the decadence of a society that gets so worked up over a person's sexual preference when half of all Africans live on a dollar a day. In my country, it's actually worse than that."

He took a long drink of his coffee and shook his head. "And now we have a disease that threatens to wipe us all from the face of the earth. Our own president's son died of AIDS, which we know full well is not just a disease of homosexuals. My friend, what I'm saying is that I'm afraid you live in a country whose priorities are all askew."

Matthew made a mental note to talk about this conversation at every opportunity. He started to agree, to say thank you for upsetting his stereotypes, but before he could respond the man again surprised him.

"What," he asked, "makes you most anxious about this ruckus?"

What, indeed? Matthew asked himself. Was it all the opposition? That wasn't fun, but it also wasn't what kept him awake at night. Was it the threats, if you could call them that? No, those would pass, wouldn't they? Was it that he wasn't up to the job?

"I think," he said, after a long pause, "it's that I can't see around the corner. The churches are changing, have *got* to change. We need new ways of doing Christian education, new models of congregational life, and I can't see clearly what they look like."

This felt true, but for the rest of the day he thought of other things he might have said, like his anxiety that denominational labels meant less and less. As a scholar who talked and wrote about Christian unity, he had often questioned the value of denominations, had advocated the blurring of their boundaries. But now that he was to become the head of one, the picture looked considerably different. Was this nomination simply an ego-boosting way of being co-opted? Was he about to become a physician whose charge was to keep a dying patient alive?

Once he boarded the plane for the flight to Lexington, by way of New York and Cincinnati, instead of taking a book from his briefcase, he simply sat—eyes closed, head against the headrest—replaying conversations from the past four days. All of the talk about the Pope led him to think about other "heroes"—authentic leaders— popping up in this era: Mandela, Suu Kyi, Tutu, Havel. Could he include Gorbachev? Walesa? What configuration of internal traits and external events made them right for such a time as this? Did they have anything in common? And who were America's heroes? Michael Jackson, Sylvester Stallone, Cher? What was the phrase his Zambian friend had used?

This led to reflection on skewed priorities. He could still see the bishop of the tiny Church of Bangladesh as he described villages that had all but disappeared into the sea when a cyclone whirled up the Bay of Bengal at the end of April. The bishop brought pictures, including a color photograph of two bloated bodies, face up, arms extended as if in supplication, which Matthew couldn't get out of his head. What had he been worrying about at the end of April? Had he even prayed for the people of Bangladesh? Had Disciples sent assistance? Would he know what to do when such things happened in the future?

The meeting had been intended to do long-range planning for the world church community. But he now wondered how this was possible when the churches had such different concerns. For the past four days, he had felt genuinely connected to the church in such places as Zambia and Bangladesh, but he knew that back in Indianapolis he would be expected to focus on how to increase the Disciples' market share, on whether to move the headquarters to a new building, on how to keep the church together when so many members were so up in arms over homosexuality.

He took a glass of wine from the flight attendant, careful not to spill any on his suit, and dug around in his briefcase for a book he had decided he should read on church growth. At least it would put him to sleep. As he tried to read, however, the lyrics from an old hymn they had sung during the closing worship in Geneva kept intruding:

O God of earth and altar, bow down and hear our cry;
our earthly rulers falter, our people drift and die;
the walls of gold entomb us, the swords of scorn divide;
take not thy thunder from us, but take away our pride.

Matthew returned to the U.S. to find that the national press had picked up the story of his nomination, or at least the debate swirling around it. The Office of Communications at the Indianapolis headquarters had sent him a packet of articles, along with a note saying, "Any publicity is good publicity," although Matthew wasn't sure that was any more true now than when Carter had said it.

From the *Indianapolis Star*: "Church Board Approves Controversial Candidate." From the *Des Moines Register*: "Gay Stand Clouds Bid to Lead Church." From the *New York Times* (the *New York Times!*): "Choice to Lead Church Faces Challenge." From the *Tulsa World*: "Controversy Expected at Disciples Convention." That headline made sense, Matthew reflected, as Tulsa was the site of the upcoming General Assembly. From the Associated Press: "Theologian Selected for Top Office Opposed by Conservatives." He particularly liked that one, as well as one from the *Louisville Courier-Journal*: "Candidate Refuses to Fight to Lead Disciples of Christ." They had obviously picked up on his statement that defending the nomination was up to those who nominated him. And then there was one, from the *Columbus Dispatch*, that he didn't like in the least: "Theologian Campaigns for Church Post." No! He was not campaigning. Although it felt more like that all the time.

Matthew also discovered that during his absence in Europe the national office had sent out three-fold, two-color brochures to every congregation. They included excerpts from his address to the General Board, a brief biography, slightly embellished (he didn't really speak three languages, at least not well), and pictures of him with Margaret and the kids, even one of them holding the cat. Had Margaret given them the photos? What else was going on that he didn't know about? Matthew read through it a second time, wishing that the brochure included a prayer, maybe one from his book of daily prayers. That, he thought, would have been a good touch, although he then wondered if that would be using prayer for political ends. No, he told himself. This was a time of discernment for the church, and it was important for the whole church to be in prayer. But it sure felt political.

The third time through, he studied the pictures more closely. Abigail, he saw, had an almost defiant look on her face. She was such an interesting mix of completely vulnerable little girl and I'll-do-it-my-own-way budding teenager. Are kids, he wondered, really getting older that much faster? Was he missing some of her growing up? He resolved to take Abigail to a baseball game before she left for camp.

As it happened, the Reds were at home in Cincinnati that very week; so, the next afternoon, father and daughter were on the road headed for Riverfront Stadium. Abigail liked baseball, sort of, but she also covered all the bases by taking along a book that was all the rage, *Jurassic Park*, "in case the game is boring." He wanted to ask *Isn't that pretty scary for a going-into-fifth-grader?* but, knowing how that would go, he simply asked, "Do you like that book?" As if she knew his real question, she answered, "I like scary things when they can't be real."

Since they left before five, he expected her to let him know they would be early, even with the hour drive from Lexington, or to give him mock grief because he wasn't wearing a suit, but the conversation in the car went another direction.

"I want you," Abigail announced, "to call me Abby. That's what the kids call me ... teachers too."

"The teachers call you Abby?"

"I asked them to. Mom knows that because she went to the fourth-grade open house. Really, Dad, only you and Mom call me Abigail. And Grandpa, but that's because you do."

"We named you Abigail," said Matthew, "because it's a name from the Bible, like Matthew and Zachary." After a quick pause, he added, "Abigail is described as a beautiful, intelligent woman in the Bible, a wise person who even stopped people from fighting. And besides that, it means 'father's joy,' which you ... "

"Mom's name isn't from the Bible, is it?"

"No, but ... "

"I bet Abigail was your idea. Mom wouldn't care so much about it being a Bible name."

"What do you mean? Your mother goes to two churches. Sometimes, you know, she goes to Saint Peter's Catholic Church, plus she's one of the leaders in our congregation. She's very active."

"Yeah," said Abigail, "but it's really your thing, like baseball's your thing. We all know that, Dad. It's okay ... but I want to be called Abby."

"Well, I guess when you grow up you can choose to be called whatever you want."

"And drive my own car!" She straightened up in the seat and rotated her arms, as if driving. "Mom says I should never have you go with me to buy a car."

"Why not? Why did she say that?"—trying hard not to sound defensive.

"She says you're too honest for your own good, so I'm just thinking that means you're no good at buying cars."

Matthew chuckled softly. "What else does she say to you about me?"

"Well, she says you're not very good at fixing things, I guess things at home that are broke. She says I should marry a man who is 'handy.' She's glad she married you anyway, but face it Dad, you're not handy."

Matthew started to protest, although he wasn't sure why since it was basically true, but Abigail wasn't finished. "I guess it doesn't have to be a man. If you're gay, does that mean you marry a girl if you're a girl? Are Heather and Lisa gonna get married?"

How, he wondered, did she hear these things?

Once they got to the game, Abigail holding on to his belt loop as they made their way through the crowd, his daughter was back to being her interrogative self. Why are there two stripes down the first base line but only one everywhere else? Why do some players have short pants legs that show their socks and others don't? Why do people get to keep the ball if it's hit into the stands? They didn't pay for it, so shouldn't they give it back? What is the manager good for? The players do all the work. They know they're supposed to hit the ball when the pitcher throws it at them and catch it when somebody hits it at them, so why have a manager? Are any of the players gay?

Since there were people sitting on both sides of them, Matthew tried to change the subject by pointing out some of the nuances of the game. Watch the shortstop when there's a runner on first base, he told Abigail. When he holds his glove up to his face, he is giving a sign. She interrupted him to ask for cotton candy, even though she had earlier announced she was going off sugar, like her friend Kayla, who had diabetes. Is diabetes something you can catch? Can you play baseball if you have diabetes?

After a relatively long period without questions, perhaps because she was eating the spun sugar, Abigail asked, "Why do you and Grandpa fight about the Cubs and the White Sox? They're both in Chicago, aren't they?"

"That's part of the fun. People choose teams to cheer for."

"You and Grandpa don't seem to be having much fun about it. If they're in the same city, why can't you cheer for 'em both?"

Before Matthew could answer (although he wasn't sure what he would answer), Abigail asked, "Why do you like baseball so much anyway, Dad? You don't play it."

"I was actually not a bad player once upon a time," he said defensively, thinking of Frank. "I usually was an infielder, which is why I was telling you to watch the shortstop."

"Then why don't you play now?"

"Because at some point you have to stop being a player and just be a fan, or a coach. That's the way life is. You do something for a while and then move on to other challenges."

"What's the challenge in being a fan?" asked Abigail. "I mean, all you have to do is sit here and yell."

"Well, I didn't mean being a fan is a big challenge. I was just talking about life in general. As you get older, you have to be prepared to give up some things and take on others. When Major League baseball players get to be my age, they retire and do something else."

One of the Reds hit a home run, and Matthew stood to cheer. When he was seated, Abigail said, "It's pretty funny, isn't it?"

"What's funny?"

"In baseball, you're too old, but everybody at church thinks you're too young."

"Too young for what? Who says I'm too young?"

"Too young to be the GMP." She said the letters slowly, one at a time, tracing them with her finger in her typical way. "That's what I heard Reverend Tim say other people were saying. I told him," she said, giggling, "that I think you're pretty old."

Matthew felt a swell of emotion as he said, "I'm really glad I'm the right age to be your dad," but Abigail was already on to other topics.

"Are you sure, Dad, this is the right job for you?"

Again he was caught off guard. "Why do you ask that? I know you don't want to move ..."

"Because you don't try to get all the attention, like people on TV do. You told me crowds make you tired, and I bet the GMP"—tracing the letters—"has to be in lots of crowds. Face it, Dad, you like to be alone in your study. You don't even like it when Mom or somebody, like me, calls it an office, and now you're probably going to have a super-huge office with people coming in and out all the time."

Matthew had been trying to keep one eye on the game, and Abigail paused as he cheered. As soon as the cheering died down, she was back on topic. "When you came to career day, you told my class you were a teacher—at least you didn't say you're a theologian!—and now you won't be a teacher. You'll be general ministering, whatever that is. What is a 'general minister,' anyway?"

On the ride home, Abigail more awake than he had expected, Matthew tried to steer the conversation in other directions. After asking if she was looking forward to fifth grade, he asked, "Are you a leader at school?" As soon as he said the words aloud, Matthew wondered if that was a fair thing to ask, but Abigail took the question in stride.

"The other kids think I'm too bossy to be the leader."

He savored the irony of this before saying, "But you have lots of friends."

"Yeah, sometimes, unless they think I'm acting too smart. Unless they need help with homework or something. Then they're happy I'm smart."

There were so many things, he realized, that he didn't know about her life. "Do you do things with other girls, like at recess?"

"We don't call it recess, Dad! I do free time things with Andrea, we call her Andy like they call me Abby, and Maria—some kids call her Mary, but she doesn't like it—and Stephanie. But sometimes I just go off on my own so nobody knows where I am."

"What about camp?" he asked her. "You have good friends there, don't you?"

"I don't want to go to that stupid camp!"

So much he didn't know. "Why not? I thought you liked it. We have—how many?—five kids from our church who are going."

"They're not fair at camp."

"Who? What isn't fair?"

She took a big breath before speaking rapid-fire.

"Last year, that stupid Dave said Laura's cabin made a big mess around the fire circle, only they didn't do it. So I told the counselor, Scott, they didn't do it. But then Dave said I was with them, so we all got blamed, like I was part of their cabin because I stood up for them, and I had to help clean it up and then stand up with them while we got some stupid lecture about 'keeping things clean for everybody'"—the last words said in a sarcastic sing-song. "I don't want to go to that camp!"

"That *doesn't* sound very fair," Matthew admitted. They drove in silence for a minute before he added, "When you are in a situation like that, try to think about the good things, the blessings in your life. Sometimes that can help."

This time it was Abigail who broke the silence. "Then why don't you do that?"

"Do what?"

"Think about the good things. All you and Mom talk about is the bad stuff you're hearing from people that don't even know you. Why don't you talk about all the good things," she giggled, "like me and Zachary?"

When Abigail fell asleep, Matthew spent the rest of the ride counting blessings and wondering why he was so prone to seeing a half-empty glass.

Friday, August 16, turned out to be a day of memorable phone calls—three of them. It started with a call to his father. Matthew intended to tell him about going to the game with Abigail, but Frank was eager to talk about the nomination brochure that was now on display in the church narthex. In fact, Reverend Wainwright had apparently ordered a bunch of them for members of the congregation to take and read.

"Quite a spread," said Frank. "Good pictures of Margaret and the kids."

"Did you read the speech?" Matthew asked him. "I hope people will actually read what I say and not just listen to what others say about me."

"You know," said his father, "your mother was a protester. What do the papers call it? A 'dissident.'"

This whole comment took Matthew by surprise. Finally, he said, "I am hardly a dissident, if that's what you're getting at. I've heard that some people say they oppose me because I'm too much of an insider, though I'm hardly that either."

"I'm not saying your mother marched in the streets or anything like that. She—how would you say it?—she just didn't care very much whether other people agreed with her. Spoke her mind and let the chips fall. Well, *I* know some things people said bothered her—got her pretty depressed, to be honest about it—but she stuck to her guns anyway. Always did."

Matthew realized this was a side of his mother, dead now for twenty-eight years, that no one had ever shared, or at least he didn't remember it if they had. He could feel a tingle, almost like a rush of adrenaline, as he asked, "What did she protest?"

"Oh, nothing big, I guess. Big to her, though. I remember one time when this student got dismissed from school. I don't remember what he did, but, whatever it was, your mother didn't think it was fair. She told the principal—his name's on the tip of my tongue—that if he didn't take it back she was going to resign as a teacher and let people know why she did it. Said she'd work at Woolworth's, if she had to, but she wouldn't be party to treating anybody that way. I said, 'Are you crazy?!' but she wouldn't back down. That's who she was." ... these last words said with an obvious tinge of pride.

"What happened?" asked Matthew. "Did the student get reinstated?"

"Oh, there was a big hubbub. Went on for a while, but then it blew over. These things come and go, and nobody remembers 'em. But your mother, she was a fighter. She'd go for a time, trying to help people get along, and then something would hit her the wrong way, and she wouldn't back down. She would fret about it, that's for sure. I could tell because she would start to clean the house like crazy, straighten up stuff in the drawers, line up all the glasses in the cupboard, but she wouldn't back down."

"Do you have some of Mom's things around the house, you know, in boxes in the basement or somewhere? Things I haven't seen?"

There was a pause before Frank said, "I kept a couple of her books, but ... it's been a lot of years. Your aunt took some of her stuff, including a collection of some sort. Ask her about it."

Matthew had called his father from home, but after hanging up he told Margaret he had to go to the seminary, in large part so he could eat lunch at The Sizzling Griddle. He waited until after one o'clock, when it was more likely Edgar would have time to talk.

After taking a bite of his cheeseburger, Matthew asked the older man, "Is your father still alive?"

"Nope. Dead ten years."

"Edgar, can I ask, did you have a good relationship with him? Could you talk to him about important things," he paused, "and get a straight answer?"

"Neither of us," said Edgar, "was ever much for talking." He filled a coffee mug, took an order, and when he returned said, "Sounds like you're having trouble with your old man."

"Not trouble exactly. It's just that he says a lot about trivial things, but not enough about what I wish he'd talk about."

Edgar wiped his hands, then wiped the counter, before saying, "I guess that's who he is. You can't want him to be you." Matthew hadn't yet asked for pie, but Edgar set a piece of key lime in front of him anyway. "You told me once your ma died when you were young. That right?"

"I was nine."

"And now you wish you knew more about her."

Matthew put down his forkful of pie and stared at his friend. "How'd you know that, Edgar? Did your mother die when you were young?"

"Nope, still alive. Almost ninety. But you never learn all the things you want to know from parents. Take a look at who you are and you'll get a pretty good idea of who she was, even if your old man doesn't tell you."

Later that afternoon, Matthew was back on the phone in his office, joining a conference call of church leaders convened by the National Council of Churches. Although Matthew was not yet the head of his church, Duane had asked him to represent the Disciples—"in anticipation," as he put it—on a call to discuss a possible collective response to the nomination of Clarence Thomas as a Supreme Court justice.

Before dialing, Matthew sat for five minutes, staring at the portrait of Campbell, with its splotches and nicks. He arranged the papers on his desk until they were perfectly lined up, putting his pens in a neat row, and was still the first one on the line. While others were calling in, someone (Matthew couldn't yet recognize all the voices) asked him how he was "holding up." Even as he answered, Matthew felt a surge of resentment that not one of these future colleagues—with the exception of his friend Gerald, at the United Church of Christ—had bothered to send a note of support. "I've been surprised by the tone of some of the opposition," he said honestly, "but at least we are having a conversation about the acceptance of gays and lesbians. I'll know more in a week when I begin a series of local meetings in different regions."

"I wish," said the man who had asked the question, "that *we* could have an honest dialogue about homosexuality."

"I don't," said another, to general laughter. Matthew wished he could see their faces.

Gerald then spoke up, talking about how beautifully Matthew was handling the controversy they'd all heard about, which Matthew appreciated, but then he wondered: How would he know how I'm handling it? Probably from talking to Duane, who was hardly an unbiased source.

"Well, we will be praying for you," said the first voice—which Matthew also appreciated, but then wondered: Is it true? Would this church leader actually say his name in a prayer to God? Or was this simply something one said at such moments? Should a church leader wonder such a thing about a colleague?

The moderator of the telephone meeting, a member of the council's staff, asked for people to introduce themselves, and Matthew heard the names of the fourteen voices on the call, in addition to himself. All were men and all, it was quickly apparent, were united in their opposition to Thomas. The most strident voice was that of the Stated Clerk of the Presbyterian Church, a man he knew but not well.

"Say more about your concerns," the moderator said to the Presbyterian leader. "What worries you the most?"

"Where to begin?" He said this with mock resignation, and others laughed. "Clarence Thomas opposes affirmative action, which could set civil rights back decades if, God forbid, he were to end up in the majority on the court."

"How could the President appoint *him* to replace Thurgood Marshall?" Matthew knew this was the presiding bishop of one of the Black Methodist churches, but he wasn't sure which one. "He's so far out of step with us," said the bishop, "that I find it hard to believe he's African American."

The Presbyterian leader, who hadn't finished, cut back in. "His stand on guns is also way out of sync with what our church teaches ... all of our churches, if I'm not mistaken." Others agreed with this point and added further objections to the list.

"So," said the moderator, "it sounds like we agree in saying no to this nominee."

"No question there," said the Presbyterian.

"So, the only thing now is to decide how to proceed. We can certainly issue a statement. I think we will want to do that for sure. But what else?"

Matthew could feel the knot in his stomach tighten as he tried to sort through the thoughts colliding in his head. What was the point of speaking up? Their opinion was clear, and it would hardly endear him to these future colleagues if his first words were ones of opposition. But it really wasn't opposition, he told himself, just another perspective. Maybe they would respect him for speaking his mind. Beyond that, why did he care what they thought? He found himself thinking of what Frank had said about his mother. "Actually, I'm not very comfortable with the direction of this conversation ... so far." Silence. "This is Matthew, by the way. From the Disciples of Christ."

"What," asked the moderator slowly, "is your concern?"

"I'm not a fan of Judge Thomas. Obviously. Well, I hope that's obvious. I suspect he's not qualified to be on the Supreme Court. But I'm not comfortable opposing him because he disagrees with us on certain issues. We should be examining whether he knows the law and how he thinks judicially, not just whether he passes our issue litmus test."

Again silence, so he continued. "That's what's happening in our churches. Ministers get chosen because they say things that echo the opinions of powerful members of the congregation, when the church should be trying to evaluate whether they know the Bible or have a good track record of pastoral care or are willing to listen to those who disagree with them. At least as I see it. I mean, this is what's happening to me. 'Do you agree with my view of homosexuality?' That's how people are evaluating me—not, do I have the knowledge and faithfulness to be a leader in the church."

"I'm glad you spoke up," said a voice he couldn't place.

"Thanks. I just don't like politicized behavior in the church."

"But isn't that a little naïve?" It was the Presbyterian. "This is a political process. What this man Thomas thinks, not just *how* he thinks but *what* he thinks, will make a hell of a difference to a lot of lives and for a long time to come."

"I appreciate your point, Matthew," said a voice he recognized as that of the presiding bishop of the Episcopal Church, "but I think we all need to realize that we are in a struggle for the soul of this great nation. And churches other than the right-wingers need to be heard. I'm afraid we can't afford the luxury of your more academic perspective."

Now Matthew felt his anxiety turning to anger. *There was nothing academic about the church acting like the church! Modeling a different way of making decisions and choosing leaders was the churches' best possible witness to the God who stood in judgment of all political processes. Show the world that you—that we—aren't just another political caucus!* At least that's what he later decided he should have told them, if only he'd been ready and willing to say it. In the actual moment, however, he sat staring at the Campbell portrait in his office and was silent. When the common statement, apparently written by one of them in advance, was read, he added his name to it on behalf of the Disciples.

That evening, he got the third call. Matthew was becoming less troubled by the critical mail. After all, as Abigail had reminded him, they didn't really know him. And while it had been disconcerting when a caller last week had told him that "the statute of limitations has run out on you" (whatever that might mean), he hadn't even bothered to call the police. They would simply take the information and tell him there was little they could do. "It's threatening but not quite a threat, if you see what I mean." Why waste the time?

This call, however, was different. He could sense it immediately in the tone: cool, slightly ironic.

"Hello Dr. McAvoy ... Matthew." He drew the first name out slowly. "Are you having a good summer?" Matthew started to ask *Who is this?* but his mouth went dry. The caller continued, still drawing out his words. "I bet you're having a fine summer, imagining all the ways you can do the work of Satan from the heart of the church. Unless—or, maybe I should say, *until*—someone stops you."

"Is that a threat?" Matthew realized that his own voice sounded hoarse. Absurdly, the thought came to him that the telephone can be a bad way to communicate.

"A threat? I merely asked if you were having a good summer. Oh, and I wonder if your daughter, your precious Abigail, is having a good summer, too, at Camp Rise and Shine. Let's see, that's just south of Danville, isn't it? Out in all those woods. I know it well. Yes, I know it well."

This time the police listened more intently. It could be someone using the controversy to make a splash, a detective told him, someone who gets his kicks out of spreading fear. Well, if so, it had worked, thought Matthew. He tried calling the camp, but since it was quite late, no one answered in the office. He then called Duane who, once he was awake, promised to notify every local host of the upcoming church visits so they could arrange for adequate security. What, Matthew wondered, did he mean by "adequate"? And how did that help protect his family?

Not surprisingly, Margaret wanted to leave immediately for the camp. Matthew convinced her to wait until morning, but, when neither of them could sleep, they changed their minds. They started to take Zachary to a neighbor's house but finally decided just to buckle him in his car seat in his pajamas.

Both of the adults were quiet for most of the fifty-five-minute drive, whether from lack of sleep or anxiety Matthew couldn't tell. At one point, Margaret, while staring at the road, said, "This has to end." Matthew was about to say, *It hasn't really started*, but, realizing this was hardly a comforting thought, he kept silent. She also told him— tersely—that the position of assistant principal had just opened up at her school. She did not have to add that this was a position she would enjoy, one that would further her own ambitions, and one she could likely have without controversy ... in Lexington.

Their plan, although they didn't discuss it in so many words, was to pick up Abigail when she arrived at the dining hall for breakfast. When they got there, however, dawn just breaking, they discovered that her cabin and its counselor had spent the night in the forest and were not due back until afternoon.

Margaret was near the end of her rope. "Fourth graders out in the woods?!"

"Fifth graders," the head counselor corrected. Matthew quickly jumped in to explain the situation, and he and the counselor set off down a well-marked trail, leaving Margaret to be agitated alone.

Abigail, despite her stated aversion to camp, was having a good time in the woods and not happy to be found. Her displeasure was no doubt compounded by the tension she could sense in the car, but her parents were unwilling to discuss. And so she bounced and grumbled in the backseat until she made Zachary whine and Matthew told her to knock it off. At one point, Margaret, looking out the window, said in a low voice, "You of all people know what it would be like to lose a parent," and Matthew was tempted to tell *her* to knock it off. All of this made the trip back to Lexington one he preferred to forget.

CHAPTER SEVEN

A week later, August 26, it began: a gauntlet of thirty-eight meetings in the sixty days leading up to the General Assembly in Tulsa. The scheduling was too much for Lucinda to handle, given everything she had to do at the seminary, so it was done out of Indianapolis. And before Matthew realized he had to block out certain days if he didn't want them on the itinerary, he found he had meetings on Zachary's fourth birthday and the beginning of Abigail's school year.

Since the invitations often came from areas where opposition was most vociferous, Matthew also discovered he was scheduled for gatherings in places he had never been, never imagined being: Washington, Pennsylvania, where a man asked how many small-town ministers needed to pay the price to satisfy his ego; McAllen, Texas, where an Hispanic man told Matthew, without a trace of irony, that his support for homosexuals showed he was insensitive to minorities; Lynchburg, Virginia, where a woman announced that "around here we like down-home preachers like Leo, and I hear he's not even for you"; Pine Bluff, Arkansas, where a man, waiting at the entrance to the church, announced, "I'm going to pin your ears back." What in the world did that mean? Should he be worried? Did this count as a threat?

Following the very first meeting, a woman who professed to be a fan told him that throughout the evening he looked "inscrutable." "I couldn't tell," she said to him, "if you were happy or sad." Is that true? Matthew wondered. He often worried that his face gave too much away. Was he really so out of touch with how he appeared to others? And was she actually telling him that he seemed distant, unapproachable?

The next evening, he tried smiling more and nodding whenever someone spoke, although this just made him more self-conscious about what his face was conveying. Afterward, he asked the regional minister, a pretty good friend who had been at both sessions, if he could see a difference in the way Matthew presented himself. "No," his friend told him, "you seemed about the same."

The meetings generally followed a pattern. People—for the most part Disciples, but also a few curious folks from other denominations—would gather in the fellowship hall or sanctuary of a local Disciples church, usually after supper, where there would be homemade desserts to go with coffee and soft drinks. The numbers varied from forty to several hundred, but the crowds overall were bigger than Matthew had expected. Naturally, he remembered the vocal opponents most vividly, replayed their comments like a tape in his head. But it was gratifying to realize that—with two or three exceptions, maybe four—supporters seemed to outnumber antagonists, with most people apparently there because this was their church and they cared about it.

After the local pastor, or someone official, said why they were there and Matthew was introduced, he began with a presentation. No more than fifteen minutes, he told himself, although sometimes it would be twenty, and once even twenty-five. We, Disciples, he would tell them, are a people who celebrate both unity and freedom. This is not an easy way to be church! But it rests on an important conviction: that unity is not synonymous with agreement. We are free to disagree. What we shouldn't feel free to do is split from one another because we disagree.

One of his favorite stories, told repeatedly during the first weeks, was of Aylett Raines, a man who wanted to join one of the early Disciples congregations despite being a "universalist," a person who believes that everyone will ultimately be saved through the work of Christ. The congregation in Western Pennsylvania wasn't at all sure about Mr. Raines's worthiness because they believed in the eternal punishment of sinners, and this was no small disagreement in the early nineteenth century. But then Thomas Campbell, Alexander's father, spoke, saying that he and Mr. Raines had "freely unbosomed" themselves to one another in recent months. Because of these conversations, he knew Mr. Raines to be a man of God. And so, said Campbell, their deep theological differences notwithstanding, "I would put my right hand into the fire and have it burnt off before I would hold up my hands against him."

Matthew found this story deeply affecting and instructive, although he had to acknowledge that it didn't have the same impact on all his listeners. Some people apparently had a tough time seeing the monumental disputes of another era as instructive for their own. Others just got hung up on the word "unbosomed."

Following his presentation, the floor would be opened for questions and comments. The host pastor would say something like, "Please don't give speeches. We're here to listen more than talk," which always drew a chuckle. Matthew saw early on that the same questions were repeated from meeting to meeting—"Do you believe in the bodily resurrection of our savior, Jesus Christ?" "Do you believe in the divine authority of Holy Scripture?" "Do you believe that the blood of Christ can cleanse us of our sins?—questions having nothing directly to do with the topic that, he was sure, had drawn people to the gathering. They were delivered as if to the accused in a courtroom, evidently intended to reveal that he was, in all things, a dreaded liberal.

His suspicions were confirmed when a somewhat-sympathetic minister in Enid, Oklahoma, showed him a letter, sent to members of Disciples for Biblical Witness, listing "Questions for the Nominee." "You know," said Rev. Owens, "this gay thing isn't the only reason people are against you. For some of them, you just aren't one of the good ol' boys. You're one of those east coast intellectuals who are stealing the church from people out here."

"I'm from Iowa," said Matthew. "Rural Iowa."

"Doesn't matter. You're one of 'them.' The Judkins letter, it just put blood in the water, and now everybody with a gripe against church leaders in Indy or their latest seminary-trained minister or whatever feels free to nibble away."

It's true, Matthew realized. One recent letter that stuck in his craw took him to task for being a poor steward because he and Margaret didn't give ten percent of their salary *before* taxes to the church. Why, he wondered for the hundredth time, did they have to send that damn profile to every corner of the denomination? And why

had he felt compelled to be so nitpickingly honest when filling it out?!
He could talk about all of the other causes to which they contributed
until he was hoarse and it wouldn't matter to this person, who had
decided not to support him ... not to *like* him.

He was prepared for challenges to his stand against the war
in the Gulf, would have welcomed a chance to talk about it; but
surprisingly, at least to him, this was almost never mentioned in the
letters or church meetings. When he was criticized, it was often in
personal terms, and when he was lauded, it was usually for taking a
stand on an issue that, if it hadn't been for Heather and Lisa, would
barely have been on his radar before April.

As he got further into the gauntlet, following a merciful break
for Labor Day, he found that challenges also came from less expected
quarters. Several people, clearly wanting to be supportive, asked
about Disciples for Biblical Witness. What should we do with groups
like this that seem intent on stirring up trouble? Yes, he would say
to them, DBW can be a problem since their literature contains false
generalizations that inflame more than inform. He was glad they
were part of the church, however, because they called attention to
issues, like the importance of a personal relationship with Jesus,
that more liberal types often minimized. "Instead of focusing on
DBW," he would say, let's ask ourselves, 'What is the deficiency in
the theological diet of our church that leads to the existence of such
a group?'" He liked that line a lot.

At least until the evening in Nashville when, after what he
thought was a pretty good meeting, he was stopped in the parking
lot by the Tennessee regional minister.

"I appreciate what you are trying to do," she said, "but are you
aware that Disciples for Biblical Witness has been working overtime
to pull eight of our congregations out of the region? Telling them
to stop giving to the Disciples mission fund? And that's just in the
past two or three years. I agree with you, we need conservatives
as well as liberals in the church, although I hate these labels. But
these people aren't some benign conservative think tank. They say
their purpose is to reform the Disciples, but look at the literature of
their funders, like the Institute for Religion and Democracy. What
they want is to destroy mainline Christianity because it gets in the
way of their right-wing political agenda. You really need to read this

material, Matthew, before you defend them. There has to be a limit to our openness. At least I hope to God there is!"

Then there was the GLADN supporter who confronted him, not in the parking lot but in the midst of an actual meeting. Matthew had just finished his presentation with its story about Aylett Raines, and she was the first to speak.

"Okay, we get it, Dr. McAvoy. The unity of the church is important. When you are GMP, you will be Reconciler-in-Chief. But maybe there are times when the church needs to be divided. Maybe too much reconciliation language just allows bullshit to continue instead of naming it for what it is."

There was a buzz in the audience, probably, he thought, because of her choice of words as much as her ideas.

"Sorry," she said, looking at the crowd. "Some things, however, are just wrong. Just plain wrong." She turned back to Matthew. "I know … we all know your heart is in the right place. And I'm glad that you can rattle off the history of our church. But not all of that history is good, Dr. McAvoy. You know this stuff better than anyone. Alexander Campbell, if I remember correctly from my seminary history class, didn't think slavery was a big enough deal to split the church over. Really? Really?! Is that what *you* think?"

This remark haunted him, and his unease grew two nights later at a small church in Cleveland, Ohio. In this case, he had expected a bigger turnout and found it hard to get the juices flowing. The second or third person to speak—an ordained Disciples minister, he was later told—started out rather blandly. Clearly a comment, not a question. Matthew was listening with half an ear, vaguely anticipating where the man's remarks might go, when he heard him say, "After all, these homosexuals are just scum."

Back in the hotel room, which now seemed much smaller than when he was getting dressed, he replayed this scene in his mind over and over. "After all, these homosexuals are just scum." *Scum.* Was that really the word the man—a minister in the church of Jesus Christ!—had used? Yeah, no doubt of that. Scum. Then why, why, why, *why* had he not denounced it? Okay, he was caught off guard. And he did speak forcefully, once the man was finished, about how everyone is a valued child of God. But why *at that instant* had he not told him to sit down and be quiet? Why had he not said—no, *shouted!*—that anyone who calls another human being "scum" has forfeited his right to be heard in a gathering of the church? Wasn't there something fundamentally impoverished about an understanding of reconciliation that left him unprepared for such a moment?

Matthew had never been very good at praying by himself. As an introvert, he liked time alone, just not alone with God. He had urged students at the seminary to organize a morning prayer group because *he* needed this daily discipline to keep him at it (if only he could get there more often). He had written his book of daily prayer, *And Praise Your Name Forever*, because it was a way of helping himself do what he told others they should be doing.

Now that he tried to pray in sterile hotel rooms, his efforts seemed particularly futile ... or desperate, as was the case that evening in Cleveland. "Give me the strength to speak the gospel. And give me the wisdom to know what it is."

Back at the seminary, he was always telling students to pray for the people of Yugoslavia in their time of turmoil, or for those who'd lost loved ones in the earthquake in Costa Rica. But now, when he tried to turn to God, when he *needed* God, his prayers couldn't escape the gravitational force of his own self. He walked down the four flights of stairs to the lobby, then once around the parking lot in front of the hotel, trying to clear his mind. He thought of going for a run, but he had done that early in the morning and now his whole body—legs, arms, back, head, and mind—felt drained of energy. Back in the room, he found himself simply praying, "Give me the strength to pray."

On Thursday, September 12, Matthew took a break from the local gatherings to meet in Dallas with the men, and one woman, who pastored the largest flocks in the denomination. Theirs, he knew, were mockingly referred to as Big Steeple churches, especially by ministers with little steeples. Matthew wasn't particularly thrilled with this invitation (a few of these pastors struck him as glad-handers), but he looked forward to the trip because Dallas was the home of his aunt—his mother's sister, Frances—and, for the first time he could remember, he wanted to speak with her.

The discussion with the ministers was scheduled to begin at ten in the morning and run through lunch, but Matthew, who arrived early, was still waiting to be invited in—to be summoned, he thought sourly—at ten thirty. It turned out that two of the younger big steeple ministers, both self-styled conservatives, had held things up with questions and comments that many of the others found superfluous. Matthew learned later that one of them had even objected to him on the grounds that he was married to a Catholic—"That's as far from Disciples as you can get!"—until it was clear that this argument had no traction. According to one of the seasoned ministers, "The whole delay was a deliberate attempt to insult you." So, when the doors were finally opened, most of the room was disposed to be on his side.

But with muted enthusiasm. Matthew knew several of these colleagues fairly well, had been warmly welcomed to speak in their churches, and so he pressed them: Why the reticence? Why doesn't this group use its influence and issue a statement of support for my nomination? Finally, as lunch was being served, one of them put the matter bluntly: "Your stands are causing the pot to boil over, and we're the ones who have to clean up the biggest mess." "Our churches," said another, "have some of the Disciples' wealthiest members, and they like their church run like a business. They think you might be bad for business."

After the meeting, Matthew walked to the parking lot with Harrison Honeycutt, one of the two living former GMPs. Harrison was nearly eighty, but as he put it, "They invite me as a courtesy. Makes them feel gracious." As they reached Harrison's car, the older man turned to face Matthew directly. "You probably know—you're a perceptive man—that you only got half the story. These people like you. As far as I can tell, most people like you, once they get to know you. I heard from somebody on the General Board that even Harold what's-his-name likes you. But if the members of this group don't seem supportive enough, it's because they think you haven't paid your dues. They think one of them should have been the nominee."

Matthew nodded. "Yes, I get that."

"Good," said Harrison. "Put yourself in their shoes. They may have big churches and lots of resources, but as far as they're concerned, they've been marginalized for a decade or two while the church looks for young, disabled, black women, or whatever, to put on its boards and take its overseas trips."

"Or young seminary professors."

"You're just a final straw. No matter how impressive your academic credentials, you won't be what some of them are looking for. This homosexual business just gives them cover to say they think someone else—that is, one of them—could do a better job. I know a couple of them would like to have seen Ralph Wilkins be nominated, told him not to agree to be chairman of the search committee so they could put his name in. But he decided not to do it. Anyway ... as a seminary dean, you have their full support, but they think running the church is their bailiwick."

Matthew held the door while Harrison climbed slowly in. He fiddled with his keys, and then, through the open window, said, "Of course, they aren't the only ones having second thoughts about your nomination."

"What do you mean? You're not ..."

"No. No. I'm in your camp. But surely you're hearing rumblings from some of our friends in Indianapolis."

When Matthew said nothing, Harrison added, "I am sorry if they don't have the backbone to tell you directly."

Later that afternoon, Matthew rang the doorbell at the home of his Aunt Frances. All of the houses on the street were brick, but, as she had promised, hers was one of two sporting an American flag. He had hoped to meet her right after his session with the big steeple pastors, so he could catch an early evening flight, but Frances informed him that Wednesday was her day to play bridge and have lunch with the "girls," so she couldn't possibly see him until after her nap, around four o'clock. Fair enough, Matthew told himself. In previous years, he wouldn't have bothered to contact Frances during a short trip to Dallas. The truth was they had had decreasing contact in the years after his mother's death. Some of his friends talked about aunts and uncles who were warm and fun to be around. This would never have been his description of Aunt Frances. But now Matthew wanted to know: Was her sister, his mother, the person his father described?

The answer from his aunt was emphatic: "Heavens no! Betsy was no 'dissident.' Where'd you get that idea? From Frank?" Matthew knew better than to nod, but Frances continued as if he had. "He never did understand her one whit."

"Maybe I used the wrong word," Matthew said a bit sheepishly. "What my dad has said, hinted at, is that she stood up for what was right, that she ... " he paused looking for the correct word, "protested when people weren't treated fairly." He took a big drink of the heavily sweetened iced tea, which nearly made him gag.

"A 'protester,'" said Frances, shaking her head. "Betsy loved this country as much as I do. Volunteered with the USO during the war doing something, I forget what."

"I wasn't suggesting ... "

"She *was* stubborn though. If he said that, that part's right. Though so is he." She nodded while sipping her tea. "I will say this, too, she didn't like to see anybody left out. In games at school, she would just grab their arm and pull 'em in, even if they didn't want to. Just keep pulling. She was stubborn. That part's right."

She settled back in her chair, with its lace doily and flowered upholstery. "I remember I asked her once, 'Why do you do that?' And she said, 'What if it was me standing there?' Never would have happened. People were always attracted to Betsy. Well, either really liked her or really didn't like her. She just didn't always know it, either way."

She paused and looked at her nephew. "She's been dead seems like forever. If you wanted to know more about her, why didn't you ask me before now?"

The question played in Matthew's mind while his aunt went to the kitchen for more iced tea. No one had seemed eager to talk about his mother's death at the time, and then he got busy in high school, went away to college, started a career and a family, began teaching, became a dean. His aunt returned with a pitcher, frowned when she saw he still had a nearly full glass, and spent considerable time arranging the pitcher and coasters until everything was apparently to her liking.

"I guess," said Matthew, once she was seated, "I'm at a point in my life, maybe because of this nomination I told you about, when I want to know more about myself, where I come from. And I'm realizing that Mom is still something of a mystery to me."

Frances sighed and shook her head. "Why she ended up with Frank, that's the mystery for the ages. When we were kids, Betsy had such big plans. Although she was always too anxious for her own good. She'd seem like she was having fun, doing fine, and then before I knew it she was worried sick about this or that, second-guessing herself. Maybe Frank made her feel ... I don't know. ... Well, to each his own."

Matthew wanted to ask about his mother's big plans. Had she wanted to be a professor? Did her plans have anything to do with politics? What about his mother and the church? How did his father make her feel? How did she act when she got anxious? His aunt, however, was clearly ready to change the subject, telling him about her own back surgery, which is why she needed the afternoon naps, even though it meant they had to put a strict time limit on the bridge club, which didn't make her popular with a couple of the members, as if she cared a whit one way or the other. ... So when she got up to relieve herself of tea, he took it as an opportunity to say he needed to be on his way.

Before going, however, he had one more question: "My father said Mom had a collection of some kind, and he thinks you might have it. Do you know what he's talking about?"

His aunt looked briefly puzzled and then smiled, slightly. "Oh, he must mean that box of old campaign buttons."

"Political campaigns?"

"I have no idea why she wanted to save that sort of thing or where she got most of them. She had a bunch, but I threw that box out years ago. That and some old scrapbooks. Couldn't imagine why anyone would want any of that."

Matthew looked in vain for pictures of his mother as he left. But he later decided that anger may have clouded his vision.

He had wanted to get an evening flight because, with no church meetings for the next three days, he was headed back to Lexington. His flight the next morning, with a change of planes in Cincinnati, still got him there in time to spend a couple of hours at the seminary before Margaret would be home. He picked up his mail and messages from Lucinda, who assured him that she was no longer withholding anything except a few items that struck her as generic propaganda. He started to say he wanted to see all of it, but then decided that wasn't true. Instead, he simply said, "Thanks for taking care of things. This whole nomination has probably given you a lot of extra work."

"Are you kidding! With you not here writing a dozen memos a day, I'm practically on vacation." They both smiled, and she added, "But you will want to speak with Carter about something that happened earlier this week. And Heather and Lisa said they just need ten minutes." She rolled her eyes. "Have they ever kept it to ten minutes?"

The seminary's president had apparently overheard part of the conversation, because he appeared at the door to his office and beckoned Matthew in. Once they were seated, Carter asked the obligatory questions about how the meetings were going and how Margaret was holding up. After Matthew gave his general response, Carter said, "We're getting a taste of it here," and handed him a piece of notebook paper with scotch tape hanging on its corners. "This was taped to the front door of the library when Nate got here on Monday."

Matthew read: "IF HE STAYS REST OF YOU WILL HAVE TO GO TO," written with a black magic marker in large printed letters. "I don't think it's someone who knows much about DTS or else they would've put it on the door to this building, not the library."

Matthew nodded. "I'm really sorry, Carter, that this has spilled over ... " But the older man went on as if Matthew hadn't spoken.

"Once Nate gave this to me, he and I tried to figure it out. 'He' obviously means you. If you stay, the rest of us have to go where? Then we decided the fool meant 'too,' not 'to.' That still doesn't make much sense, but at that point we took it as a threat."

"I hope you called the police right away."

"That afternoon, after we determined it was a threat ... of a sort. Told them all about your nomination, which they seemed aware of. They wanted to know if we wanted some kind of protection."

"What did you tell them?"

"We talked it over here for a while and decided that that would be an overreaction. No need to create unnecessary anxiety with school just starting back up."

Not long after Matthew left Carter's office, the students arrived at his ... all seven of them. Matthew's face must have registered his surprise because Lisa, smiling, said, "You probably weren't expecting so many of us."

"No, I wasn't." It was hard to keep the irritation out of his voice because this felt like an intrusion, even a bit of an ambush. He was eager to get home, and the arrival of a group promised to delay his departure, just as Heather and Lisa had complicated ... He stopped the thought and stood up. "Well, we won't all fit in this office." Since classes weren't scheduled for Friday afternoons, the classrooms were empty. They migrated in silence to one down the hall, taking seats around a rectangular conference table.

As soon as they were seated, Robert, one of the older students, said, "My seventy-year-old mother was at one of your church meetings, and she told me she wasn't happy with some of the questions you got."

Matthew smiled. "Was she happy with my answers?"

"I suppose so," Robert said with a shrug. "She mainly talked about what she called the 'troublemakers.' She's not a fan of conflict, especially in the church."

"Neither am I," said Matthew. He looked around the table. "If your family—or your home ministers, for that matter—are at these gatherings, tell them to come up and introduce themselves. Really, I mean it. Tell them I would like to meet them."

Lisa, who had apparently been chosen to be the spokesperson, nodded. "Good suggestion." Others nodded as well. "My minister," she added, "was at the meeting in Kansas City, but he said there was a big crowd, so maybe that's why he didn't say something to you. He also said you were very articulate, which wasn't a shock to any of us." More nodding and smiling. "But the other thing he told me is that you talked about queer people like we're one big group ... "

"I don't think that's fair ..."

Lisa was not to be interrupted. " ... so we," she gestured around the room, "thought it would be good for you to see individual faces from your own student body."

"Some of our faces are better than others," said Heather, and everyone laughed.

Lisa jumped back in. "Everyone's story is different. My parents are fantastic. They have always supported me in being who I am, they march in gay rights parades, the whole thing. For some reason, they even get along fine with Heather," who punched her playfully in the arm. "But Larry's parents ... Well, you tell him."

"They act like I'm dead." No more laughter. "They told me I'm a blasphemer for going to seminary when I won't renounce my sinfulness."

It didn't surprise Matthew that Larry was gay, but he had never before noticed the nervous twitch around the student's mouth, or the way this quiet man looked down after speaking. How had he missed these things? "I'm very sorry," he said softly. "Where do you go at holidays?"

"I planned on going to my sister's, but she got pressure from my parents, so usually I just stay here." He looked down. "I guess you don't remember asking me that same thing my first Christmas in Lexington. But this past Christmas, I went home with Patrick"—a student not in the room.

It was Robert who broke the ensuing silence. "My situation is a little different. I'm graduating, at least I hope I am"—more smiling—"it should be next spring, and I would like for my partner—Greg, you met him once—to be with me publicly, to celebrate with me openly. Wear the robe, take pictures, eat cake together, the whole thing."

"Why not?" asked Matthew. "People are free to bring whomever they want to Commencement. For all anyone knows, he could be your brother."

"That's missing the point," said Robert sharply. "How would you feel ... "

Matthew could feel his ears burning. "Okay, I get it. I wouldn't want to tiptoe around, having to act like my wife is my sister."

He looked around the table, pausing long enough to register each face, and they waited for him to finish. "I also get it that things aren't changing as fast as you—or I—would like. But you've got to admit they are changing, aren't they?" No one nodded. "Come on, friends! This isn't 1950, when you wouldn't have dared speak to the dean about being gay. I want to hear what you're saying, but cut me a little slack. This also isn't 2020, when openness may be taken for granted. I'm trying my best to nudge the church in that direction."

For the next few minutes, others talked about their experiences: of enduring taunts in high school, of being grateful for the support of a sibling, of having an uncle disrupt a family meal to express his disgust, of trying to hide tears while a beloved minister denounced homosexuality from the pulpit. When they were through speaking, silence settled in the room, and Matthew found that his irritation was gone. It was important to see through the eyes of these students. If they pushed him, they had good reason, didn't they?

"I think," he said at last, "that we should pray."

He was about to start when he heard Lisa say simply, "God, bless our dean with wisdom and courage to face whatever comes his way."

Matthew originally wanted to tell Margaret about the note on the library door, but as they settled into their usual living room chairs after dinner, he changed his mind. She didn't need more aggravation, and *he* didn't need her being aggravated. He did tell her about his meetings with Aunt Frances and the students, she told him about a parent who complained about something, he remembered to ask what book she was now teaching to her ninth-graders, she reminded him that she wasn't teaching ninth-graders this semester, and eventually they drifted to different parts of the house. Which is why Matthew was in his study, listening to opera, needing something to lift his spirits, when Abigail bounced into the reading chair on the other side of his desk. "So, Dad," she asked without introduction, "why do you like opera when you don't even like to sing?"

"I like to sing. I sing in church all the time."

"But Mom says you sing so quiet no one can hear you."

"That doesn't mean I don't like to sing. Besides, people can like things they don't do very well themselves."

Matthew was ready to elaborate on this life lesson, but Abigail was already on another topic. "So, Dad, why do you still listen to records instead of CDs, like everybody else in the world?"

"Look at all these records I have." He pointed to two long shelves of the bookcase behind where Abigail was sitting. "Why not enjoy them rather than buy CDs of music I already have? Just because other people ..."

"You could listen to some new music. These operas you listen to are *old*, and you listen to the same ones over and over." Matthew started to protest that he actually listened to lots of different operas (although he knew that was beside the point), but Abigail had bigger things on her mind. "Dad, you're very ... it's a word that starts with the letter t."

"Terrific? Tremendous? *The* best dad?"

"Dad! It means stuck in the past. Well, not exactly stuck in the past, but you like things from the past, the way they are."

"Traditional."

"That's it! You're a traditional." Matthew was relishing the irony of this, wondering how he could work it into one of his presentations, when his daughter asked, "Who's this singing?"

"Do you mean the name of the singer, or ... "

"I know it's an opera singer, but who's she supposed to be?"

Matthew smiled. "It's an opera singer playing the part of an opera singer."

"That's weird. Who's this?"

"That's Mario, her ... boyfriend."

"So, does he die?" asked Abigail, looking at her feet. "You said one time that all the best characters in operas die."

Matthew watched her for a few seconds before he said, "Yes, he gets shot. He isn't supposed to, but ... it's a complicated story." When she didn't say anything, he added, "But not all operas are tragedies. Some are comedies, although bad things can happen in comedies, and there are a lot of great love stories in tragedies."

Was she following this? he wondered. And why, in any case, was he explaining opera plots to a nine-year-old? "That's the way life is: not all happy, not all sad."

"It's pretty sad for his girlfriend if he gets shot when he isn't supposed to. Did he do something so he deserved to get shot?"

"Sweetie, it's just a story. One that's told with lots of beautiful music." He tried to change the subject by asking about her violin lessons. "I don't hear much practicing."

"That's because you haven't been here to hear it."

Okay, fair enough. He decided to change the subject again by asking what was the most interesting thing she was doing in school. Instead of answering, she said, "I'm not reading books like *Jurassic Park* anymore."

"Why not?"

She twisted in the chair until she was sitting on her knees. Finally, as Matthew was about to ask again, Abigail said, "I don't need to read about scary things in books." She hopped out of the chair. "But I still think you should give up records. I know, get a boombox!" And she was gone, leaving Matthew trying to remember what he had been doing when she arrived. And what to make of what she had said.

CHAPTER EIGHT

The brief break in Lexington made the string of church meetings, five in the next five days, feel even more like a slog. He wanted to hear what people in the church were saying, Matthew kept telling himself and others, but, while this sounded good in theory, the practice was often not enjoyable and seldom very enlightening. At most meetings, he tried to push his idea for a church-wide dialogue about difficult issues, including homosexuality, but he could tell that it was not particularly well received. People, he told Margaret, are more than willing to speak, far less willing to listen. "We need to be an action church," was the way one man put it, "not a church that talks and talks and talks some more." There were times when, following his advice to Abigail, he resorted to thinking of the crowd as so many heads of cabbage.

To be fair, some of the meetings were quite positive, like the time he was introduced by a young woman who thanked him for his "courageous witness on behalf of the gay and lesbian community." This was certainly gratifying, but later in the motel he knew it not only wasn't true, he didn't want it to be true. He was not the nominee "on behalf" of any group in the church. If they thought that now, he would inevitably disappoint them later. He tried to express some of his thinking about all this at the gathering the following evening, but he could tell it sounded forced ... convoluted. In the seminary, he felt confident in sharing his mental gymnastics. They were a sign of nuanced reflection. But here, out in the church, he wasn't sure. It was like playing a game when he didn't know all the rules.

Beyond that, some things he had taken for granted, had devoted his professional life to, now seemed less certain. He still believed what he taught about the unity of the church as a central tenet of the gospel, but increasingly he found himself saying, "It cannot be unity at any cost." His hero, Alexander Campbell, was an ardent pacifist, declaring that "the precepts of Christianity positively inhibit war." He wrote scathingly of those who pray for military victory—through which are created the orphans and widows on whom they can exercise their Christian charity. But during the Mexican-American War of 1846, Campbell was silent, lest his words divide the emerging community of Disciples. Back in March, when he was nominated by the Executive Committee, Matthew would likely have applauded Campbell's silence. But now? Aren't there times, he asked himself, when the church needs to risk even its unity for the sake of gospel-based justice? Aren't there false unities, shallow harmonies, that implicitly bolster unjust policies and practices? Such questions streamed through his head during his early morning jogs.

Matthew found that he approached each gathering with a curious combination of emotions. Before a meeting began, he would inevitably be anxious, sweat glands in high gear, stomach churning, obsessively arranging and rearranging the pens and water glasses (which he hoped people didn't notice). But once it was under way, time would often drag, and he would have to resist the temptation to glance at his watch or keep an eye on the clock, if there was one, on the wall of the sanctuary or fellowship hall. And while he tried to keep a calm demeanor, there were times when he could hardly resist saying aloud just how utterly ignorant he found some comment or question. *Do you really think your homosexual neighbor is a bigger sinner than you, you judgmental old biddy?!* But, in his better moments, such thoughts only made *him* feel judgmental.

It bothered him that some of the attendees—many of them, to be honest—were obviously there to have their preconceptions, whether positive or negative, confirmed, not to learn about him, to sense his leadership ability, to hear what he thought about Christian faith. It was, however, the often-personal nature of the attacks that he couldn't get used to or understand. Like the man in Huntsville who, after asking how old he was, said, "I bet you never fought in Vietnam, did you?"

Matthew had realized earlier in the week that he had started clenching his jaw. The more he tried not to do it, the more he did it. And he was really clenching it as he asked, "What does that have to do with the price of tea in China?"

"What?" The man raised his hands and turned to face the audience, mouth open, as if to ask, "Where did that come from?"

"Why is whether I fought in Vietnam relevant to our discussion here this evening about the future of the church?"

"It has everything to do with it. It tells people what kind of person they're being stampeded to vote for. Someone who's not willing to stand up for the Bible or fight for his country, seems to me."

Was it because he was tired? Was it because he was in Huntsville instead of in Lexington for Zachary's birthday? For the only time during the nomination, Matthew set the microphone down. He turned to the local minister, who was sitting to his right. "I don't need to put up with this," he said in a low voice, not knowing what he would do next.

The minister, a stranger to him before that evening, came to his rescue. As the crowd began to whisper, he stood and said in a voice that needed no amplification, "There is no call for attacks on this man's character. You may disagree with some of what he thinks, but he has proved himself as a leader of one of our seminaries. I know the pastor of the church where he grew up, went to seminary with him, and he says Dr. McAvoy is a church-going man of God, and he deserves to be treated like one. So let's take a ten-minute break, and then come back to talk about the church." It was a gracious word that left Matthew feeling both grateful and embarrassed.

That night, back in his cookie-cutter motel room, a sense of injustice washed over him. He knew lots of Disciples ministers, including Duane, who favored the full inclusion, including ordination, of what some were now calling LGBT Christians. Why had *he* become such a lightning rod? Why did *he* generate this kind of scrutiny and animosity? But once the anger ebbed, he could hear the voices of Heather and Lisa and Larry and Robert as if they were there in the room: *Welcome to our world! What makes you think you're the victim here? You are a white, straight man who has gone to the best schools in the world's richest country, with a wonderful family and a rewarding vocation. It is laughable to think anyone would feel sorry for you!*

He needed to sleep, but the evening had left him too keyed up. He turned on the television, but nothing was of interest. He tried to read, but the room felt claustrophobic. Finally, even though he had jogged that morning, he decided to go for another run. Tire out his body. Clear out his mind.

The hotel was on a major street. Behind it, however, was a residential area, and Matthew, in sweatpants and T-shirt, went in that direction. There was only a sliver of moon and few street lights, and it was late enough that most houses were dark, so he could see little. Since there was almost no traffic, he ran in the street, trying not to think. Just run. Tire out his body. Clear out his mind.

Soon he was far enough from the main drag that the noise from it was only a distant hum. Occasionally, a dog would bark as he passed, but otherwise there was little sound—until he heard someone cough. That was a cough, wasn't it? He turned to look, but the darkness kept its secrets. He resumed his jog, picking up the pace. Was that the sound of another runner behind him? He turned again, and as a car went by tried to see what its headlights revealed. Nothing. He turned right at the next corner, heading now in the direction of the hotel, listening intently. Another cough. Or was his mind just playing tricks. He ran faster, reaching the hotel out of breath and more awake than ever.

The next afternoon, after a flight from Birmingham and a rushed connection in Dallas, Matthew arrived—exhausted—in Amarillo. A layman from the host congregation met him at the airport and dropped him off at a rather run-down Best Western. "I'm not sure why they put you here," said his driver, "except that it's not too far from the church. Of course, the brand-new Marriott's even closer, but I guess I shouldn't tell you that."

After thanking the man and checking in at the motel (where he found that no one had left a credit card to cover his expenses), Matthew rolled his large suitcase, with its extra suit and sport coat, to the room and hoisted it onto the bed—an activity, he reflected, that was becoming all too routine. As was being alone, waiting in a dreary room for someone to drive him to a church, hoping they wouldn't heighten his anxiety by being late.

He decided to call Margaret and found her in an upbeat mood. Zachary had had a fun day playing with the neighbors' kid, and Abigail had discovered a book in the library titled *The Diary of a Major League Shortstop*. "She's already read eighty pages of it," Margaret exclaimed. "I never would have guessed she would check out a book like that," which made Matthew smile. Finally, she asked him about that evening's meeting. "I don't have a very good feeling about it," he told her. "I'm tired before it even begins."

His intuition was confirmed once he arrived at the church, a typical 1950s structure with a newer narthex added onto a long sanctuary filled with blond, wood pews. He tried without enthusiasm to mingle with people who were arriving, but there was no one he knew, and no one paid much attention to this single man in a suit and tie. *Do they know who I am?* he wondered. He saw one girl, about nine, looking at the garish stained glass in the narthex, which reminded him of Abigail at Cane Ridge. But when he walked toward her, her parents moved her along toward the sanctuary. Did *they* know who he was? Then, on a table in the back of the sanctuary, he discovered, not the flyer from Indianapolis with its family pictures, but the newsletter from a congregation in Lubbock, listing six reasons to oppose his nomination. At least twenty copies were stacked neatly under Harold's poster. "Did you say they could put these here?" he asked the minister, his ostensible host, and got a run-around answer.

Unlike most other meetings, hostile speakers at this one got right to the point. "Homosexuality is clearly written in the Bible as being something which the Bible clearly says is wrong," said a red-faced man in his fifties. "Why is this so tough for you to understand? I hear your father doesn't even agree with you on this. If we base our beliefs on the Bible, like we say we do, then we got to follow what it says. You seem to think you can quote parts and ignore the rest."

There was applause, not overwhelming but substantial. Was that what made him feel more aggressive? Was it the reference to his father, a gratuitous smear that likely came from DBW? Was it his fatigue? Was it the persistent memory of the man in Cleveland?

"That," he said, "is exactly what *you* are doing. There are a half dozen passages on homosexuality in the Bible, but hundreds on poverty. Why don't you concentrate on those? Aren't you focusing on the half dozen and ignoring the hundreds?"

"You're just confusing the issue!" said the man, turning even redder. "Do you take the Bible as the literal Word of God or not?"

"Let me ask you," said Matthew, "have you sold everything you have and given to the poor? That's Luke 18:22. If you haven't, then please don't talk to me about taking the Bible literally."

He had envisioned using this line, but immediately regretted using it here. If members of the audience were with him, it would be heard as a clever comeback. If they weren't, it would be heard as an elitist putdown. And this evening, many of them weren't.

Matthew plowed ahead, talking about how teaching the Bible had been a major theme of his at the seminary, and how from the beginning of his nomination he had lifted up the goal of fifty percent of adult Disciples in regular Bible study. He could tell, however, that a lot of the people weren't buying it.

"Your philosophy," said an older, smartly dressed woman, "seems to be, 'If something feels good, it's okay.' Do you have *any* absolutes?"

He could feel his composure slipping away, along with any sense of joy in being called to lead. How far removed this all seemed from the joy he had felt when he first decided to become a minister instead of a lawyer. From the joy he still regularly felt in worship.

"You all are not listening to me!" he said, too stridently. "Please don't say that I don't have a center of faith or that I think anything goes just because you disagree with me, and on one issue at that. I'll give you one of my absolutes, and it is definitely rooted in scripture: All people—that is, *all* people—are loved by God and made in God's image. So, whenever society treats a group of people as somehow lesser, the church needs to step forward and say 'No! These, too, are our brothers and sisters.'"

He was tempted to turn to the red-faced man and ask, *Why is* this *so tough for you to understand?* but mercifully refrained. Instead, he took a step in the direction of the well-dressed woman. "I'll give you another of my absolutes: Avoid if at all possible doing things that harm the neighbor. For the life of me, I cannot see how two people of the same gender loving one another is harming their neighbors. So why do you, a Christian, insist on making life difficult for them?"

Matthew was surprised, pleasantly so, to hear more than a smattering of applause, but he raised his hands to stop it. "We've already had enough polarization for one evening. This isn't an election campaign. It's a time to talk about the church and how we witness more faithfully to Christ. Please, friends! This is a time to talk about things like congregations and how we make them healthier, or our priorities for mission and evangelism."

"From what I read," called out a man near the front, "you are the last person to be talking about evangelism. Your ideas about 'gays' and all will drive people out of the church, sure as I'm standing here." A few people tittered, probably because he was sitting.

"Really?" said Matthew. "I wouldn't be so sure about that if I were you. According to studies I've seen, our golf courses are filled on Sunday mornings with people, good people, who are fed up with an intolerant church"—despite his admonition, this got a louder burst of applause—"with a church that insists that everyone else be 'like us.'"

"You didn't talk one word about evangelism," said the man, now standing. "In all that business about burning your hand off or whatever, in all that there wasn't *one word* about evangelism." More applause.

"*Everything* I said was evangelism! If the church wants to witness to Jesus Christ, if it wants to speak to a new generation, then it needs to stop making social prejudices worse by giving them a veneer of religion." A number of people, he saw, were on their feet, clapping.

If asked to estimate, Matthew would have said there were equal numbers of men and women at these church meetings. The men tended to ask more questions, and make more speeches, during the public discussion. The women were more likely to approach him on the side for a private word about their gay cousin, or their concern for the well-being of their minister who seemed to be "that way." Matthew generally liked these conversations, so he didn't immediately say no when an attractive, thirty-something woman invited him to have a drink at the end of this hellacious, but curiously satisfying, evening. She didn't flatter him as others had tried to do. After introducing herself, she simply said, "I'll bet you could use a glass of wine. You do like wine, don't you? There's a place not too far from here, but far enough."

He had already spent an obligatory five minutes with the local pastor—who, in any case, was an ungracious jerk. The crummy motel, which he was in no hurry to return to, was within walking distance, which meant he wasn't dependent on anyone for transportation. And, once again, he was tired but not sleepy. So, even though he didn't know her, he said, "Why not, especially if they have food. All I had for dinner was an apple."

It wasn't until they were seated in the bar that he realized he had seen her before. At the meeting ... was it in Wichita?

"This is the third time I've heard you," she told him, "because, unlike most churchy types, you have something to say worth listening to."

It wasn't until she began to tell him how glad she was that *he* wasn't gay that he got the picture.

After he had spoken at twenty or so local gatherings, Matthew took a "day off" for a meeting in Indianapolis with Disciples leaders. It would be a time, he was told, to check signals before things got really intense.

Duane, of course, was there—they met in his office around the large, oval table—along with his deputy, Marvin, and Raymond, the assembly moderator. Matthew had been with Raymond at the meetings of the Executive Committee and General Board, knew he was a businessman from Kansas City, but certainly didn't know him well. Hardly at all. So, despite feeling deep-down fatigue, he looked forward to this time together. Surely, he told himself, these weren't the people Harrison had in mind when he spoke of backstabbing in Indianapolis.

The meeting, however, got off to an unexpected start when Duane introduced him to the other person in the room. "Matthew, meet Ross. Ross is a management consultant Raymond hired—with his own money, I should add—to help improve, well, not your presentations but—how shall we say?—the way you are presented."

"And," said Raymond forcefully, "the way you present yourself, at least sometimes."

Now that he looked closely, Matthew realized he had seen the consultant before. "You have been at some of the church meetings," he said while shaking hands.

"Four of them."

Matthew turned to Duane. "Don't you think someone should have told me about this?"

"No," said Raymond, "because then you would have changed what you were doing, played to the camera. I wanted a report on what you do *au naturel*."

"Report?" Matthew was getting testy, which he didn't like in himself and was always sorry for afterward.

Raymond held up a professionally labeled binder that Matthew now saw was at every place around the table. He felt a nearly overpowering need to turn them so they weren't at different angles. "Not all of it is about what you are doing," Raymond told him.

"That's right," said the consultant. "One of the biggest problems I saw is the sheet that was sent, I guess from this office, that people use to introduce you. I heard basically the same introduction in three of the meetings: 'Yale Ph.D., international experience, published books.' This won't fly. Period. That is, if you want to win. It makes you seem distant, like you're putting on airs, and it turns people off before you ever open your mouth. People won't listen to what you're saying if they think they're being condescended to by somebody with fancy credentials."

"Tell him, why don't you, what you're recommending," said Duane.

The consultant quickly grabbed a piece of paper from his place at the table and read: "'Born in Oak Grove, Iowa, son of a Disciples lay leader from whom he gets both his love of the church and his love of the Cubs. Husband of a school teacher, father of two young children. A teacher himself who is committed, not only to raising his children in the faith, but to raising up a new generation of ministers for the church.'"

Now Matthew was really getting testy. He could feel his stomach churning and a need to clench his jaw. "Those things, some of them anyway, come out in a natural way during the meetings. And some are wrong. My father goes to church, but he's certainly not a leader in it. And he's a White Sox fan; he hates the Cubs." He mentally kicked himself for this last, beside-the-point comment. "But I *am* a scholar. I don't want to hide what I am."

"Not hide it," said Duane, "but put the emphasis elsewhere, don't you think?"

"Look," said Matthew, "I think the church wants leaders who know our history, who think carefully about what it means to be a Christian in ..."

"No!" said Raymond sharply. "They want someone they can relate to. A pastor, not just a goddamn academic!"

His vehemence created a momentary silence. It was Duane, his voice going higher, who broke it. "People do value your scholarship," he said, with an anxious smile. "They admire that. They really do." This was said looking at Raymond. "But they need to see the other side of you."

"The side we see," added Marvin.

Raymond continued as if neither of them had spoken. "The report says you were asked about your prayer life, and you responded by talking about a book you wrote. What's it called?"

Matthew took a deep breath. "*And Praise Your Name Forever.*"

"Okay, they know you wrote books, we've all got that, but do you actually pray? This is what they want to know: that you're a man of faith, a family man with children and a wife ..."

"So is that what this is all about? I need to prove that I'm a macho guy who watches football and drinks beer, not some gay or gay-loving intellectual who writes books and listens to opera?! Which, by the way, I do!"

"Don't get so defensive," said Raymond. "This is pretty obvious stuff. People may admire professors, but they love their pastors. You are the nominee to be the head pastor. That's the title of the position: 'General Minister,' not 'General Theologian.'"

"But they have pastors," said Matthew. "What we also need are teachers of what it means to be Christian and how to be church together. That's what I do, what I can help others do."

"Not if they don't elect you."

"It's not an election!"

"You know what I mean. Not if they don't confirm you, which means voting for you." Raymond's tone softened. "Just take a look at what Ross has written. The idea is to be helpful."

"Actually," Ross said, "I think you are all pretty naïve about how leadership works in this country. Church members may have wanted pastors in the past, but the churches that are growing these days don't have pastors, they have celebrities. Think of Schuller. Think of Hybels. Think of this guy Warren. Or the Pope, for that matter. You," he pointed to Matthew, "have some potential for this, if you change a few things."

He picked up the report and looked at it, as if searching for the thing he wanted to say, before putting it back down. "They aren't reacting to *you*," he said finally, "but to an image of you. All this hate mail you talk about getting, they don't know you. They know an image of you that others have painted. We need to paint a different image, one that people in the pew can cheer for. Period. You can be sure you've made it," he added, "when people start commenting on your choice of ties and after shave."

"This report can help you," Raymond said again. "I didn't waste my money ... that is, if you take it to heart. I'll give you another example. When someone asks you straight out if you're gay, you need to answer straight back, 'No.' It's not just in Ross's report. We're hearing from others that you take so long saying 'no' people are getting the impression the real answer is 'yes.'"

"It's an insidious question," said Matthew. Why was it, he wondered, that Raymond was irritating him even more than the consultant? "It implies that you can't like a group of people unless you are one of them."

"It's a fair question!" Raymond slapped the report hard on the table. "They want to know who you are, who they're voting for."

"No, it's not! If I say 'no' without challenging the assumption behind the question, it makes it sound like being gay is something dirty. 'No, of course, *I'm* not a homosexual.'" He said these last words in a mocking tone, and then added, "I can't do that."

"Yes, you can," said the consultant, "just save the footnotes for another time, for some book. While we're at it," he continued, "you need to stop reacting if someone calls you 'Matt.' I was there in Fort Worth when some rancher called you 'Matt,' and, I'll be damned, you corrected him."

"That's not my name," said Matthew. "I haven't been called Matt since grade school, and hardly then. If someone I don't know decides he can be on a first-name basis with me, then he can at least use the right one."

Matthew could see Duane flinch as he said this. Before Ross could respond, Duane said, "Does it really matter? Really, it isn't so important, is it? I always say 'call me what you want, just don't call me late to dinner.'" Duane started to laugh, but no one joined him, and it was Matthew's turn to flinch.

"Maybe you can say things like that, Duane, but I can't. It isn't who I am."

"Let's be clear about this," said Raymond. "You may get to be prickly in your school, where the students don't vote on whether to make you dean, but not in the church, not now. Every time you correct someone, it makes you seem ... well, prickly. It convinces people on the fence that you aren't the good old boy they want for GMP."

"*I'm* not a good old boy," said Duane.

"There are a whole lot of Disciples who don't want a good old boy, who think having a good old boy is precisely what we don't need," said Matthew.

"Okay, bad choice of words. But they sure as hell don't want someone who corrects them if they address him with a common nickname. Many of them are looking for reasons not to vote for you, and you keep serving them up on a platter."

"There's another item in the report that's harder to talk about." Duane's voice was very high and barely audible. "I'm sure it's nothing, can be explained, but ... well, Ross says he saw you leaving one of the meetings with a woman, one who seems to be ... following you."

"Oh, my God! I had a glass of wine and a sandwich. Surely, I get to unwind with a glass of wine and a quiet conversation after these lovefests you've set up for me."

"All it takes," said the consultant, "is for her to start telling people how she comforts you while you are on the road. From what I heard, you don't really know her."

"I know her well enough to know she wouldn't ... "

"Matthew," said Duane, "we think it's likely that Disciples for Biblical Witness put her up to this."

Matthew sagged backward as if punched. "What?! So you all know about my glass of wine ... " He felt himself growing more outraged the more it all sank in. "And now you've concocted some conspiracy theory about evangelicals? I don't know what to say, I really don't. This whole thing feels like Alice in Wonderland. Maybe that's it. I fell down the rabbit hole last March."

"Don't be naïve," said the consultant.

"Stop saying that to me!"

"This kind of thing happens all the time in politics."

"But this is the church, for God's sake. Do you really think the position of General Minister and President of the Disciples of Christ denomination is important enough to warrant dirty tricks?"

"Well," said Marvin, who was the only one sitting, "speaking of dirty tricks, we think that Judkins was probably paid, or at least strongly encouraged, to send that letter by DBW."

Now it was Matthew's turn to slap the report on the table. "Oh, come on! I met with Harold—that's his name, Harold—and he strikes me as a good man who came up with a bad idea all on his own. I've heard that he's actually told people not to put up his posters," although he knew better than the rest of them that there were still plenty of posters out there. "Please don't spread any rumors about Harold and DBW working together."

He straightened his copy of the report so that its edge was even with the edge of the table. "Not unless you have real proof."

Matthew realized with some chagrin that he had been raising his voice, but the consultant—he couldn't think of him as "Ross"—remained unruffled. "Who was it said academic politics is so vicious because the stakes are so small?" Ross thought for a moment. "Doesn't matter. The point is, you could say the same thing about the church. This is the only political arena in which some people get to play. But, who knows? I'm not saying this right-wing group put Harold up to it, or put this woman up to it. But they might have, so you need to be careful who you go home with."

"I didn't 'go home' with anyone!"

"But it looked like you did," said Raymond. "Don't you get it? Perception is what counts. Your days of doing what you please and thinking it doesn't matter ended, well they should have ended when you left the ivory tower, but certainly once this controversy began."

"This is your fifteen minutes," said the consultant, "and some people resent you having it, or else they are going to use you to get a little of the spotlight for themselves."

The rest of the meeting was spent going—laboriously, Matthew thought—through the report. Having said they would leave it for him to read at his leisure, they did anything but. The local gatherings were certainly tiring, but there were usually parts of them that Matthew found somewhat enlivening. This meeting, however, was simply enervating. Was this what he had to look forward to? He found it hard not to tune it out, visually search the bookshelves for autographed baseballs, until, when he thought they were getting ready to leave, Duane brought up the matter of the threatening phone call. Matthew now argued against hiring security to guard him at the church meetings. The further he got from the phone call, the more having someone guard him seemed like an overreaction, although he appreciated the agreement they reached to have extra security at the assembly. The consultant troubled everyone, however, when he told the church leaders that on this point they might be out of their league.

"There are forces in the culture," he said, "that are truly evil, and you appear to have attracted them."

Matthew left Duane's second-floor office quickly in order to avoid walking out with Raymond. As he neared the exit of the building, he realized that, in almost three hours of talking, they never once asked where God was in all of this. He called Duane from the receptionist's desk and suggested they meet in the building's chapel.

As they were going in, they met Raymond coming out. "Marvin told me I should check out the stained glass windows," he said, as if needing to explain why he was there, "especially since we may need to move out of this old building before too long."

"He is a good man," Duane said to Matthew once the moderator was gone.

"I don't doubt that."

"He just thinks like a businessman, which isn't such a bad thing. There are plenty of days when I wish I had more of the businessman in me. That and politics are a big part of the job."

Once more, Matthew found that his prayer had a note of desperation.

CHAPTER NINE

I t was another of those phone calls he wasn't expecting. Matthew was in Omaha, having survived one of the rare afternoon church meetings, when Margaret called him. "I just heard from Karen," she said without the usual words of greeting. "Your father has had a heart attack. They don't think there was major damage, but they've taken him from that little hospital in Oak Grove to Methodist Hospital in Des Moines. I know you've said that's where he should go if he had another something with his heart."

Thank God, thought Matthew, that the schedule didn't have him in Miami or Seattle. He quickly rented a car and was in Des Moines by early evening. He had called his sister, Karen, before he left, telling her when he expected to arrive, and they met in the hospital's reception area.

"So, did he call 911? Does he even know about 911? Did he call you? What exactly happened?"

"You know how he is, ignored the pain as long as he could, then finally called me. Said he first thought it was just bad indigestion. I'm glad I live so close."

"Had he been having more trouble with his heart? He sure didn't tell me about it."

"Well, you've been pretty busy. I don't think he felt like he could call you for the past few weeks. He told me," she said, not looking at her older brother, "that he hasn't heard from you since you first got back from ... was it Switzerland?"

"Like you said, I've been a bit preoccupied." But he felt his ears turning red.

When they entered the room, their father was slightly elevated in his bed, oxygen and IV hooked up, watching baseball on ESPN. Matthew greeted him as they approached the bed, but Frank's first words were, "Can you believe this, baseball on TV during the week. The world is changing. Nearly time for the playoffs, although I guess you won't get to see much of 'em this year."

"But next year, we'll drive up to Chicago for some Sox games. I won't even make you go to Wrigley Field."

They talked for a while about how Frank was feeling, how the hospital had changed since he was there for his last angioplasty, and how the doctors had decided to put what they called a "stent" in his blocked artery. Frank was obviously fascinated by the idea of it. He joked about how medicine was a lot more reliable than prayer. Then he joked about how this disease was part of his inheritance to the two of them, although neither of them laughed, so then he joked about how the patient was in better spirits than the sad sacks coming to visit him. After that, he joked about how it was the Methodists who were taking care of him in Des Moines, while in Oak Grove "that Methodist church isn't worth a damn. Wouldn't even come to a potluck when we invited 'em. Said they had an event of their own. Too busy to be ecumenical." He looked pleased for having used the word.

"I told Dad," Karen said to Matthew, "that he needs to relax more." Then, turning to Frank, "You get too worked up about things. The way you carry on! Some things just aren't worth worrying about the way you do."

Frank smiled. "I guess there's just too much excitement in my life."

"Is there a problem with the business?" Matthew asked.

"I was talking about you," said Frank, but then added, "just kidding," although Matthew got the clear impression he wasn't.

They talked about Matthew's travels through the church, with Matthew downplaying the level of opposition. He did list some of the places where he had spoken to Disciples groups—Fort Worth, Austin, Wichita, Enid, Pine Bluff, Memphis, Knoxville, Dayton, Bethany, Raleigh, Lynchburg, Owensboro—perhaps because it made him feel less guilty for not having called. And they all laughed about the difficulty he had finding postcards for Abigail's collection from Enid or Owensboro.

He had just started to tell them in general terms what he was saying at the various meetings when his father interrupted. "How'd you get to be so religious?" he asked, with a chuckle. "Your mother was a Christian, wanted a Christian burial with all the trimmings, but it wasn't like it was the be all and end all of her life, I can tell you that."

Karen looked as if she was going to say something, but Matthew's expression stopped her and, after a sip of water, Frank continued. "Of course, we always went to church, except maybe in the summer, because that's what I had to do with the business and all. She said a prayer at meals—well, at least at dinner—that's true. And read those books of hers. I still have one she wrote all over: *Bread and Fish* or something like that. Guess it rubbed off, but I never dreamed you'd be a professional religion guy, never did, though I won't say that to Beverly."

They left—following a brief prayer together, during which Frank seemed to be watching the game—with Matthew promising to spend another day in Des Moines, and his father telling him to do something useful instead, like watch baseball. Besides, he didn't want to keep his son from being in such fine places as Lynchburg and Pine Bluff.

As brother and sister were walking out of the hospital, Karen said, "You know how worked up he gets. He has really been on a tear about how the church is treating you."

"How would he know about that? As you've pointed out, I didn't tell him."

"It's come up at church. I don't know what people read, but they're talking about it. Some of them, I guess, said they wouldn't vote for you, and it makes him so mad. I really thought something like this might happen. You could almost see it coming."

"What about you, would you vote for me?" The question felt inappropriate as soon as he asked it, but there was something in her tone that made him want to know.

Karen stopped walking and looked down before saying, "You're my brother."

"And if I weren't your brother?"

Keeping her eyes on the ground, Karen said softly, "Maybe not."

"Just because of one issue?!" his voice loud enough that a couple turned to look. "What about all the other things you know I stand for?"

Now Karen, too, was animated. "If I wasn't your sister," she said, spreading her arms, "I probably wouldn't *know* about them. You've made it so this is all anybody talks about."

"*I* made it? I didn't make this Issue Number One. I never said a thing—publicly, at least—about homosexuality before the nomination."

"You put it somewhere, in some questionnaire, didn't you? You had to know people would latch onto this, especially in places like Oak Grove. Come on, Matthew. You asked me, and I told you. Maybe I should've just kept my mouth shut."

"What about Rev. Wainwright? What's he have to say?"

Karen fiddled with her keys, clearly ready to leave. "He doesn't say much. I heard him tell Bernie that it's not a done deal because the church gets to vote at the General Assembly, but they should all listen to what you have to say. It puts him in a tough spot, like a lot of the ministers, I imagine."

When they first walked out of the hospital, Matthew wanted to ask Karen what she remembered of their mother, but now he had lost his appetite for more conversation. Besides, he told himself, she would only have been four when their mother died, too young to remember much about her. After another minute of small talk, they agreed to see each other at the hospital the next morning. Matthew noticed that neither of them mentioned meeting for breakfast.

The next day was a trial. Frank let everyone know he was not happy being in the hospital, where people didn't let him sleep and stuck him with needles every hour until it was a wonder he had any blood left. "Don't you have somewhere you're supposed to be?" he asked Matthew brusquely. Matthew told him he had canceled the meeting scheduled for that evening in Jefferson City because seeing his father was obviously more important. Frank rolled his eyes.

"If you're so concerned about my health, then why don't you call occasionally instead of showing up when I'm stuck here like an invalid? You ever see such a mess of wires and tubes? You need to go take care of yourself."

He then told a story about a man who lived in Edisonville, near Oak Grove, who went to see his mother for what he thought would be the last time because she was near death. But the man was killed in a crash driving home from the hospital. "So it *was* the last time all right, but he's the one who died." Frank laughed loudly at his own story, which left Matthew somewhat appalled.

"Are you suggesting ... well, what are you suggesting?"

"I'm not suggesting anything, just that you need to be careful too. Especially since you seem to have a knack for getting people riled up."

Having been assured by the cardiologist that his father was out of danger, and having nothing more to say to Karen, Matthew caught a flight that afternoon to Lexington, by way of Cincinnati, for a day at home before his next church gathering. He hadn't always gone back when there was only one free day (he felt funny about spending the church's money when he didn't have to), but something about seeing his father made him want to be close to the kids ... and to Margaret. She had accused him just after the General Board meeting of not thinking of her and what this whole business would mean for her life. "You worry about Abigail changing schools," she had said to him, "but you seem to overlook the fact that I'll have to change schools as well."

He had argued that the decision about letting his resumé be sent to the search committee was one they had made together, but, in his heart of hearts, he had to acknowledge she had a point. He took her support for granted, which in one sense was right. He knew that his wife would stand by him; she was tougher than he was. But, in another sense, it wasn't. He needed to focus more on how all of this was affecting her.

While dinner baked, they sat together in the living room, talking about Frank, which led Matthew to ask if Margaret had heard lately from her mother. Yes, she told him, Gretchen had finally spoken with her priest about "you know what," and he had surprised her by being very supportive of Matthew's position. The church has to change, the priest had told her, although he also said the time wasn't right for him to talk about the matter publicly. She hadn't yet shared any of this with Walt.

Matthew had hoped for a longer conversation after dinner, talk with her about his jumble of emotions and thoughts, but Margaret had a back-to-school open house, mandatory for all teachers, so he spent the evening with Zachary and Abigail. After reading Zachary a story—

from *The Children's Bible*, which he managed to find—and putting him to bed, Matthew followed Abigail to the back deck. Both of them were bundled up against the early fall chill as they sat looking at the evening sky. He usually loved these times with his daughter because there was no telling what her prolific, never predictable imagination would spy in the clouds. Most intriguing to him was how she would often see good images in dark thunderheads and threatening images in clouds he found particularly benign. He was also interested to see if Abigail had heard any seminary student gossip about his travels. Her revelations at his in-laws' made Matthew realize that his daughter was a potential source of inside information.

This evening, however, she had other things on her mind. "Andrea, we call her Andy, her grandma died. She used to have two grandpas and two grandmas, but now she just has three."

"I'm sorry," said Matthew. "Did you talk about it at school?"

"Andy's gone, I guess to the funeral, and Mrs. Hoskins told us." She was quiet for a minute before asking, "How old were you when the grandma I didn't know died?"

Matthew sat forward in his chair, now looking, not at the sky, but at his daughter. "I was nine, Sweetie." He started to say more, but Abigail was off in a different direction.

"I've been thinking about it, Dad. You should quit wearing a suit to these meetings you're always going to." When Matthew raised his eyebrows, Abigail rushed on. "People think you're stuffy or something, which you aren't really, not all the time, but they won't know because they don't know you. Maybe not stuffy, but like you're in business or something. At least don't wear the tie."

"But," he protested, "my ties are fun, from Save the Children ..."

"Dad, a tie's a tie. You either have one on or you don't, and it's better if you don't."

This clearly wasn't the only subject she wanted to discuss, so he waited until she asked, "Dad, are you a hero?"

"I hope I'm your hero, at least sometimes," but there was obviously more to the question. "What makes you ask that?"

"At church, some kids, like Jacob and Beth, said their parents say you're a hero and others said you aren't. Their parents, I guess, said you aren't."

"What did their parents say I am?" It was the second time in recent days when he wondered if he had asked an inappropriate question.

Abigail stared at her feet which were sticking straight out in front of her. "I don't remember."

So Matthew tried, once again, to explain the conflict in terms a precocious nine-year-old could understand. He started to leave out the word homosexual but then remembered she knew what it meant, at least somewhat. He ended by saying that it just isn't possible to stand for what you think is right and still have everybody like you, that it is hard to be everybody's hero all at one time.

"Okay," she said, after his long-winded speech, "but I still don't like those people that think you're just trying to be a big shot."

"God," said Matthew, resolving to keep it short, "loves those people too."

After a couple minutes of silence, he suggested they go inside. "It's time for you to get ready for bed."

Abigail, however, didn't move. Then, not looking at her father, she asked, "Did Mario have kids?"

"Who are you talking ... " Matthew could feel his tears welling up. "You mean Mario in the opera?" When Abigail didn't respond, he added softly, "No, I don't think he did."

That night he found it nearly impossible to sleep. When this happened after one of the church meetings, he often got up and read, but now he didn't want to disturb Margaret. So he tossed and turned, which undoubtedly disturbed her more.

His father was certainly a worry. He made a mental note to call him, perhaps tomorrow from the airport. A bigger worry was Margaret ... and now Abigail. It was normal, he told himself, for his daughter to be uneasy about the move, even about his being gone so much. But what she was expressing now was deeper. How had she picked up on the threats when he and Margaret had tried so hard to keep them from her? The ride back from camp hadn't helped, although even then they hadn't let on that there was any danger, had they? He knew what having a cloud hanging over the family can do to a kid.

From there his thoughts moved to the larger story of his life and how to read it. Seen from one angle, he was unlucky, growing up without a mother, in an out-of-the-way place like Oak Grove, with a father who didn't much value education. And now, nominated for leadership in the church right when membership was declining and churches were torn by society's culture wars. Could there be a worse time to be the nominee?! But from another angle, his life was charmed. So many things had converged to make him the choice for GMP: Duane's decision to retire, not to mention his whole-hearted support; the widely felt desire for a younger leader; his own prominence, itself unexpected, as the seminary's dean. This was an opportunity to test himself that few people got. Wasn't it? So why was he so prone to see a half-empty glass? Why was he feeling weighed down rather than lifted up?

Eventually, his middle-of-the-night thoughts became more concrete, drawn as if by a magnet to the red-faced man in Amarillo, the regional minister in Tennessee, the time he put down the mic in Huntsville, the awful meeting with the smug consultant, and, especially, the Disciples minister—a Disciples minister!—who had referred to other human beings as "scum." And he hadn't denounced him! The sense of his own embarrassing inadequacy made him cringe, until his jaw ached from clenching. He turned over, sat up, lay back down, turned the other direction.

The memory he now couldn't shake was of the time a woman asked, not graciously, how he would feel if his son or daughter were a homosexual. He never answered her because a man had immediately stood to say that his son was gay, and he was damn proud of him. But here, in the middle of the night, Matthew wondered: How *would* he feel? He and Margaret wouldn't love Abigail or Zachary any less. That was a given. He did want grandchildren, but being gay or lesbian didn't preclude that, although it would be harder. Their whole life would likely be harder.

He tried thinking of other things—the baseball game with Abigail, graduation day with the students, the Cubs' batting order—but pictures of the meetings, the worst moments in the worst meetings, kept replaying in his head, along with the GLADN supporter lecturing him on Campbell and Ralph talking about backstabbers in Indianapolis and Rev. Owens warning of blood in the water. And mixed in with it all, yet again, was a sense of grievance he knew was a sign of spiritual immaturity, but couldn't get rid of. Why was all of this focused on *him*? Was there something negative about the way he came across to people? Why was he now so associated with a cause he hadn't thought much about until six months ago? Why was he supposed to be some kind of champion for justice when that wasn't his natural inclination? Where was God in all of this? Why didn't he ask that question more often?

The next morning, more exhausted than the night before, Matthew made up his mind to call Duane, hoping fervently he was not out of town. He could picture the older man—white hair, slightly anxious smile, rumpled khakis—at his desk in the office with the autographed baseballs and large conference table. Matthew realized, while the phone was ringing, how much he liked him.

Duane immediately asked about his father, then about Abigail and Margaret. Matthew started to speak, but Duane hardly took a breath as he began talking about the assembly. "You know we've been having seven thousand or so, but Isabel now tells me we can expect upwards of eleven thousand people, maybe more, in Tulsa! That's pretty exciting, don't you think?"

Instead of responding, Matthew used this as an opportunity to jump in, speaking quickly. "I've been thinking, Duane, that I ought to withdraw my name. This nomination is dividing the church, which is pretty ironic for someone who teaches about bringing Christians together."

Duane's response was immediate and forceful, as if he had been waiting to give it. "Matthew, you just can't do that. Well, you can, but you don't want to. It would be terrible for the church. Absolutely terrible! All those people who have put themselves on the line to support you, how are they going to feel?"

They were both silent for several seconds before Matthew said, "That's one of a whole bunch of things that keeps me awake at night." He paused. "Yeah, that would be hard, but it would also make life easier for a lot of people, like rural pastors who are feeling squeezed."

"Matthew, listen to me. You don't want to be known as the guy who only plays eight innings. And if you withdraw now, what will the litmus test be next time? Abortion? Support for going to war? If it's not this, it'll be something else, always something else." There was a long pause before he added, "I know this has been tough for you and Margaret, and now with your dad ..."

"Yes, but that's not it." Is that true? he wondered. Was this just a way to relieve some of the tension he felt? Was that a bad thing? "You've seen what's happening. I seem to be a provocation for some people. I mean, you're just as liberal as I am, maybe more so, but something about me pushes their buttons." He stopped, but Duane said nothing. "I think I've started a good discussion in the church, been a good nominee. It may be, however, that the election of a GMP is getting in the way ... "

Duane, uncharacteristically, cut in. "Do you really think *you* started this discussion?"

"Sorry," said Matthew. "I know you and others raised these issues before I ever did."

"That's not what I mean." Matthew could hear a sharpness in Duane's voice that he had not heard before. "Don't you think God is present in this process? You've said yourself, I've heard you say it, that gracious welcome for everyone is the gospel, the bottom line for Christians. Then surely God is in this debate, dialogue, discussion, uproar ... whatever you want to call it. You can't just walk away from it. Can't walk away. How many theologians actually get to have a dialogue with the church about the gospel?"

There was another long pause. Finally, Matthew said quietly, "You truly see God in all this?"

"Yes. No question. Every day. Every single day."

For the first time since it all began, he felt as if he might cry. His voice even cracked as he said, "Thanks, Duane. This helps more than I can tell you. In fact, it is practically the answer to a prayer."

After sitting by himself for a few minutes, he found Margaret at the breakfast table and told her about the call, not quite knowing how she would respond. "This has been hard for all of us," she said, her eyes focused on his. "I know you are the one who has to bear the brunt of it, but I'm not sure you can realize what it's like knowing that people have threatened your husband, your family. I could stand it if they threatened me, but ..." She straightened in her chair and cleared her throat. "Some nights, when you're gone, I can hardly get to sleep."

Matthew rose from the table, gently pulled Margaret to him, and they stood embracing for thirty seconds, a minute, before she said softly, "It's not easy for me to say this, but we both know Duane is right. You can't stop now. As much as I hate it when you leave ..." She wiped the corner of her eyes and again cleared her throat. "It would give the wrong signal, like *they* won, and you would regret it. I don't want to live with that."

CHAPTER TEN

That afternoon, Matthew was back on the road, but things felt different. To begin with, a very friendly driver dropped him off at a nice hotel, and when he unzipped his suitcase, spreading it on the bed, there on top was his LP recording of *Tosca*, along with a note from Abigail.

Dear Dad!

Mom said this is the one with Mario the boyfriend. If you can find a record player (old fashioned!). I guess it makes you happy.

Love,

Abigail (your favorite daughter!)

He called home, hoping to speak with his favorite daughter, but it was Margaret who answered. "She's not here. Somewhere in the neighborhood with Maddie. You'll just have to settle for speaking with me."

"I am always happy to speak with my favorite wife, but I've only been gone a few hours."

"Actually," said Margaret, "I have some news since you left. I talked to my Mom right after I got home from school, and she told me she has decided to come to the assembly."

"Gretchen's coming to Tulsa? Is Walt ..."

Margaret laughed. "No, you don't have to worry. She's coming alone. Said it would be a chance to learn about this church you forced me to join ... and to support you. I'm proud of her, traveling there by herself. Although I'm sure she'll make Dad drive her to the airport in St. Louis."

"That's very nice of her," said Matthew. "Please tell her I appreciate that support. I really do." He paused. "We may still be able to get her a room in the DoubleTree ... "

"I just checked. It's sold out, but I'll find her a room. According to the information I've seen, there will be shuttle buses from several of the hotels to the convention center, so it won't matter if she's a little farther away."

Since there was still time before his evening meeting, Matthew also made a quick call to his father. Frank was back in Oak Grove, so depressed that he hardly spoke for the first few minutes. But after Matthew derided the White Sox for finishing eight games behind the Twins, his father began to sound more like himself, ranting about the collapse of his no-good team in its fancy new stadium, and then about the silly medical restrictions he was going to ignore. Matthew hung up sensing that Frank was on the road to recovery. Yes, things were beginning to feel different.

He also felt different, a change reflected in the meetings. He decided to drop the set presentation, to dispense with Aylett Raines and the rest of the lecture altogether. Instead, he spoke without notes, standing no more than six feet from the front row. If they are going to say insulting things, he told himself, then they will have to say them to my face, up close and personal.

Beyond that, there was a different tone to his remarks which he, at least, could detect, exemplified by a gathering in Topeka. The evening opened with his now-impromptu remarks, followed by a couple of supportive, softball questions. Then a middle-aged woman took the microphone. "I just don't know," she said, "why we had to have all this trouble in our church. You say that you aren't a homosexual, so what possessed you to make such an issue out of it?" Her voice was plaintive, almost whiny, and for some reason Matthew found it particularly irritating.

"As I recall," he said, using his most professorial tone, "the Apostle Paul wasn't a Gentile. But he didn't leave it for Titus and other Gentiles to fight that battle alone, did he? Because he knew that when one person is excluded it affects all of us. What's at stake is the kind of church we want to be, and I want to be part of a church that doesn't put people down just because they happen to be gay or female ... "

"I don't feel put down," she said somewhat timidly, "except maybe now."

Matthew decided to ignore the last part of her comment. "Good for you, but a lot of women over the years have, and I think it's time we stopped acting like that's acceptable." He could sense the energy, the edginess, in the room.

As the microphone was being passed to the next person, his growling stomach reminded him that he hadn't eaten that evening, and that brought to mind his most recent lunch at The Sizzling Griddle. "What questions are you getting at these church affairs?" Edgar had asked him, as he ate his glorious piece of warm pecan pie with ice cream. Matthew had listed a few, including, "How can practicing homosexuals be defended by someone who says he takes the Bible seriously?" "Man," said Edgar, shaking his head, "they got it backwards. Bible readers don't have to explain including people. If they want to exclude people and say they're following Jesus, they're the ones have to do the explaining."

Matthew felt fortified by this memory for whatever question might come. Still, he was caught off guard when the next speaker, an older man, charged him with being a Marxist because of his ties to the World Council of Churches.

"I see you've been reading *Reader's Digest.*"

"It's true, isn't it? We don't need our church money going to finance terrorists in South America."

Matthew smiled. Suggesting that *Reader's Digest* was his source was giving him too much credit. The man was misreading from a script, probably prepared by DBW. "And you," the man added, "from everything I hear, are part of this world council business."

What could he say, not to this person—his mind was made up, his convictions impervious to facts—but to others in the sanctuary? Matthew took two steps toward the man, looking directly at him.

"Check your notes from Disciples for Biblical Witness. The place you meant to name is South Africa. The World Council of Churches gave money, through its Special Fund to Combat Racism, to groups opposed to the apartheid regime in that country. That's why Nelson Mandela, when he was released from prison last year, said that the World Council of Churches had saved a whole generation of Africans for Christianity. Is that what you're against? Does that sound like Marxism? You know, sometimes Christians need to take a stand even when it isn't popular. The Council stood for justice—just like the Old Testament prophets, just like Jesus—and I, for one, am honored to be associated with such a stance."

He paused, now looking intently around the completely silent room. "I was going to tell you," he said, his voice softer, "that I'm not involved in the 'political' work of the World Council, that my main role is studying things like baptism and church unity … and that's true. But, to be honest, all of it goes together. If Christians understood the meaning of baptism, they wouldn't support racist governments. They would realize that because of their baptism Nelson Mandela is their brother in Christ. So, I would like to think that I am involved in a small way in the South African struggle. And I hope you want to be as well."

Matthew was mentally replaying this exchange the next day as he boarded a flight from Kansas City to Billings. The man had been a too-easy target, and Matthew was sure he had turned some people off by responding to him so sharply. On the other hand, some things, he reassured himself, just shouldn't pass unchallenged. Besides, there were others who told him, outside the church, that it was about time somebody stood up forcefully to such nonsense. Maybe, until now, he had been treading too lightly.

This particular trip was the result of his decision to go anywhere he was invited, regardless of whether the place was "politically important" for his nomination. The whole of Montana had—was it eighteen? seventeen?—Disciples congregations. The principle was right, but this was a long way to go, he mentally acknowledged, for not much payoff.

He was in the middle of such thoughts when a man about his age in the seat next to him said, "Good morning," and, as part of the usual airplane banter—"Where you headed?" "You from there?"—asked what kind of work he was in. Matthew started to say *I'm a theologian,* a response that was proven to stop all conversation, but this time he answered, "I'm a minister."

"Oh," said his neighbor, "what church?" Matthew told him, offering a little explanation that the Disciples is a mainline Protestant denomination, but the man was more informed than he had expected. "I think I read somewhere," he said, "about a big fight in your church over gays and lesbians. I'm United Methodist myself. Glad we don't have any fights over such things in *our* church." They both smiled.

Matthew felt a bit duplicitous for not revealing that, yes, he knew about this fight first-hand. But he wanted to know: "What's your reaction to all that?"

"I should be asking you."

"I'm a little too close to it," said Matthew. "I'd like to know how it seems to someone from another church."

"I don't go to church as regularly as I'd like, what with visits to the relatives and plain, old laziness. Maybe twice a month—something like that— so I may not be typical. If you ask me, however, I think it's all pretty silly. The church of one generation always seems ready to fight the battles of the previous one."

They were quiet for a minute while the crew made an announcement, and then he added, "I have a nephew, I'm pretty close to him, who is gay. Nicest young man you'd ever want to meet ... normal guy, good job right out of college. I don't really know if he has a partner in his life, but I hope he does. If there's a God ... " He looked directly at Matthew and smiled. "Of course you believe there is. Sometimes I'm not sure, but if there is a God, and I usually believe there is, then Ted, my nephew, is part of His creation."

Matthew was still buoyed by this conversation—an unexpected gift, he thought of it—when he stood that evening before an overflow crowd at Spruce Street Christian Church in Billings. He had decided in advance not to recount the conversation he'd had on the plane, but changed his mind part-way through the time for questions and comments. There were a few nods, maybe a few shakes of the head, and then a big man, deeply tanned and wearing a western-style shirt, stood to speak.

"I doubt," he started, "that anyone here agrees with you."

"About what?" asked Matthew. "I bet we agree that Jesus is the Christ. I bet we agree that God is love. I bet ... "

"Yeah, okay, we probably agree on a bunch of things, but I mean about this, accepting homosexuals as normal."

"*I* agree with him," shouted a young woman on the other side of the sanctuary. She stood up, chin raised, while several others said "me too," a few of them very loudly, and the audience buzzed.

"All right, all right, I stand corrected. The point I am trying to get at here, if you all will let me get it out," he gestured at the crowd, "is that even if *most* of us here in Montana don't agree with you on *that*, we still respect a man who says what he thinks and comes right here to talk about it."

As the meeting was drawing to a close, Matthew was surprised to see one of his good friends from their student days in New Haven, sitting by herself in a back corner of the sanctuary. He waved so his friend, Lydia, would know he'd seen her, and once the crowd had cleared made his way to where she was now standing.

"I heard you were going to be here from a friend who goes to this church," she told him after a welcoming hug. "Do you have time for a drink? I would invite you to our place, but Brian and I live aways out of town, and you're probably exhausted."

Matthew started to say that it might be better if they just talked there in the sanctuary, but then thought: *Oh, to hell with that! Let Ross put it in another report.* "Yes, let's go somewhere that doesn't look, sound, or smell like a church."

They talked about children and spouses while Lydia drove to a nearby Italian restaurant. He tried to describe Abigail, who was born just after he'd finished graduate school, but couldn't quite find the words to capture how special she was without sounding like he was bragging. Although, what was wrong with that? At the restaurant, they started to order wine by the glass but then changed their minds and ordered a bottle. Matthew even loosened his tie.

They talked about their mutual love of opera. "Bozeman has a good, little company," Lydia told him, "or else Brian and I go to Denver and make a weekend of it, which makes it all the more special." Matthew silently acknowledged that he and Margaret could use a few special weekends.

They talked about their course together with Professor Richter, in which Matthew wrote an extra twenty-page paper because he got interested in Niebuhr's understanding of sin. "You always were more ambitious than I cared to be," she said smiling. "No, 'ambitious' can sound negative. You always had loftier goals."

Is that true? Matthew wondered. He didn't think of himself as particularly ambitious. Like now, he hadn't campaigned to be the nominee ... had he? Someone had recently pointed out that, if he served two terms as GMP, he would still only be fifty. What did he plan to do then? The question, Matthew realized, was one he almost never considered.

They talked about the latest publications in theology, Lydia raving about a new volume on mission by a South African scholar named Bosch. Matthew admitted he hadn't even heard about the book and mentally resolved not to forget that he, too, was a scholar.

They talked about their love of teaching. "Can you believe it?" said Lydia. "This is my tenth year at Rocky Mountain College. I didn't know if I'd like an undergraduate school this small, but it's been a really good fit for me. It's a church-based college, so we have a few religious studies majors and enough students in our general courses to keep the dean happy." They smiled and clinked glasses as she toasted "to deans everywhere." Matthew silently resolved not to forget, either as dean or GMP, that he was, first and foremost, a teacher.

And they talked about the joys of living in Montana, such as taking the kids to the Little Big Horn and Red Lodge and the Yellowstone Wildlife Sanctuary. Matthew meant to talk about the good parts of living in Kentucky, such as Cumberland Falls, but instead he found himself giving thanks that his travels around the church allowed him to reconnect with friends. It was an unexpected benefit. He resolved to speak with Margaret about taking a trip with the kids out west.

Lydia insisted on paying since he was a guest in her city, and while she rummaged in her purse for her wallet, Matthew said, "This has been just what I needed, a normal evening not focused on this crazy nomination. It's easy to forget how abnormal this whole process is."

"I wouldn't want to do it," said Lydia. "But from what I saw tonight, it suits you. And I'll feel a damn sight better about churches if people like you lead them."

The next day Matthew was on his way from Montana to New Mexico. He tried to stay awake, hoping for another serendipitous conversation like the one with the Methodist man, but, in fact, he slept all the way on the plane and still was bone tired when he disembarked. How in the world do presidential candidates do it? he wondered. Any candidates, for that matter. Thanks be to God, this was practically the end of his travels through the length and breadth of the church. And yet, he was feeling better about this process than he had at any time since it began.

Since his plane had landed early and his ride hadn't arrived, Matthew decided to call Duane from a phone in the airport, catching him as he was leaving the office. Nothing was wrong, Matthew assured him. "I just wanted to say thanks for persuading me to stay the course."

"All I did," said Duane with obvious emotion, "was remind you of what you already knew. Ever since we met, ever since, I've known you were going to be a leader in the church. No question. My role has just been to give a little boost now and then." He laughed. "The whole church needs to take a breather. I bet last spring most Disciples couldn't have named the GMP or said what I did in this role. Now, suddenly, people are acting like it's the most important position in the western world! You've handled all of this just fine."

"Thanks, Duane. I just called to say I'm in a much better frame of mind, thanks to you." He paused. "Since we can speak honestly to each other, there is one thing I've never asked you that I would like to know." Duane started to respond, but Matthew forged ahead. "Do you wish that last spring you'd made a stronger statement against the war?"

There was silence before Duane chuckled softly. "Of course. Of course. I was trying to do justice to all the voices I was hearing, as if that's ever possible." He paused before adding, "That's the story of the church, isn't it? Showing up at the scene when it's too late to make a difference."

Duane, Lydia, Margaret, the man in Montana, the man on the airplane—they were all on his mind that evening as he stood before the hundred or so people gathered in the sanctuary of Carlsbad Christian Church. On the spur of the moment, he started by asking, "Do you mind if I take off my jacket and tie?"

"It's New Mexico," said a man near the front. "No one wears a suit here if he can help it." There was general laughter, and even applause, as he took them off.

The atmosphere changed, however, when a woman admitted—boasted, in fact—that she had written one of the hostile letters he'd received. Maybe, he thought to himself while she was speaking, it was one of the letters in Lucinda's packet. "I'm sure," she concluded, "that I'm not the only one who has given you a piece of their mind."

Perhaps because the audience included lots of obvious supporters, or because he was getting better at all this, the words seemed to flow.

"Yes, I have received a number of letters about the 'problem' of gays and lesbians, some of them pretty insulting, to tell you the truth. But let me tell you what I haven't received. I haven't received any letters about starvation in Sudan or AIDS in Zambia or the civil war in Sri Lanka or the cyclone in Bangladesh. Why is that, do you think? I haven't received any letters about racism in our society, no letters about domestic violence, no letters about drug abuse. What does that say about our church? I haven't received any letters about new church development or Christian education or enlisting young persons for ministry. Why is that?!" His voice grew louder with each of the last three words. "I have an African friend who thinks America has messed up priorities, and my mailbox tells me he's absolutely right."

The next few questions were positive and brief, probably, he reflected with some chagrin, because his aggressiveness had intimidated the naysayers. But then an elderly man in the front row, who had to be helped to his feet by a younger companion, said without introduction and in a raspy voice, "I can't think of anything more disgusting than a man having sex with a man."

Matthew felt his jaw clench. He had been standing beside a chair set there for him if he wanted to use it. He now moved the chair slightly until it lined up perfectly with others near it. The silence in the sanctuary was palpable as he closed his eyes, took a deep breath, and stepped toward the front of the chancel.

"Children dying of starvation when there's more than enough food to feed them, napalm that burns through a person's skin and there's no way to get it off"—his voice getting louder—"land mines that blow off a child's arm when she reaches for what looks like a toy, child pornography and sex trafficking. Stop me when I get to something that might be disgusting enough for you! How about ... " He could sense the unease growing in the sanctuary, could see people leaning over to whisper to their neighbors.

"I am sorry, friends," he said, moving his eyes across the gathering. "But, really, sometimes this just gets too absurd."

He turned directly to the elderly man in the front row. "I understand, sir, that homosexuality is outside your comfort zone"— no, that wouldn't communicate—"is foreign to your experience. And, for what it's worth, that's true for me as well. I can't imagine myself having sex with a man. But that's the point. That's not how I'm wired, not how you are apparently wired. Other people, however, are wired differently."

Suddenly, what he had said to Abigail about God also loving people like this man echoed in his head. Did his empathy only go one way? Could he really not imagine the life experiences, the cultural influences, that led this man of a different generation to make such a statement? He took a step in the man's direction. "

I shouldn't get so caustic. I apologize, Mister ... what's your name?" It was then he realized that the man—although sitting forward in the pew, hand cupped behind his ear—might not have heard a word he said.

There was no meeting the next day, but the regional minister had arranged for him to be on a radio talk show, a call-in format on KBIM in Roswell. The host, a woman named Stephanie, struck Matthew as being incredibly young for such a position. Was that an indication that he was feeling older? he wondered. Was that how he seemed to the senior ministers in the church?

Once their headphones were in place and the light turned green, Stephanie began by saying, "My guest today is the Reverend Doctor Matthew McAvoy, a professor of theology who is a candidate for the top leadership position in the Disciples of Christ, a denomination that has several congregations here in New Mexico, including one in Carlsbad where Dr. McAvoy spoke last night. He is a well-published author whose liberal social stances have led to considerable controversy among Disciples. The vote on Dr. McAvoy will take place at the Disciples General Assembly in Tulsa later this month. Welcome, Dr. McAvoy, or do you prefer Reverend?"

"Thank you, Stephanie. And Reverend is fine ... or just Matthew. I'm happy to be on the program, but I need to amend the introduction. I am not a 'candidate' for this position. That makes it sound like a political election. I am the person, the one person, nominated by the church's Executive Committee. So, I'm the nominee. I am not running for office."

"Then why all the meetings in the churches? I understand you have been to a number of places in the last—what is it?—two months."

Matthew smiled. Had it only been two months? "You can think of this as a 'get to know the nominee' tour. It's a chance for people to speak with me and, hopefully, a chance for the church to talk about serious issues. That's the idea, although we don't always do it very well."

He smiled again, and she returned it.

"But that brings me back to your introduction," he said. "I don't necessarily think of myself as a liberal. As I see it, we need a moratorium in the church on adjectives like 'liberal' and 'conservative.' I am a big advocate for teaching the Bible in the church. Is that a 'liberal' position?"

"But the things you talk about ... " Stephanie said. "I'm looking here at excerpts from a questionnaire that was sent, apparently, to every Disciples congregation—the things you talk about like 'full acceptance of gay and lesbian persons in the life of the church' are associated with a liberal agenda."

Matthew found—strangely, unexpectedly—that he wasn't sure what he wanted to say. No, he didn't like labels, had said so repeatedly during the past six months; but, yes, he was, by most people's definition, a liberal. Why did he spend so much time distancing himself from that?

"That's true," he said after a short pause. "But I'm also convinced it's a biblical agenda. What I am talking about is 'welcoming one another, just as Christ has welcomed us.' That's from Paul's letter to the Romans, not some liberal manifesto."

"I take it, however, that you were a supporter of gay causes before you were the candidate … sorry, nominee."

Matthew took a drink from the glass in front of him. "That's my other amendment to the introduction," he said after swallowing. "I am embarrassed to say it, but, to be really honest, 'social activist' isn't a very accurate label. The way I've come to see it is that God smoked me out, made me publicly accountable for things I believed but hadn't acted on, until this nomination."

"It sounds," said Stephanie, "as if you have learned interesting things about yourself through this process. What else would you say you've learned?"

Matthew paused, apparently too long for radio, so she rephrased the question: "It sounds like you've had quite an ordeal, lots of pretty vocal opposition. What have you learned from it all?"

"I have seen firsthand," he said finally, "that many places, many local Christians, feel out of touch with the national church. I don't always like how they express it, but it's important for me to hear if I am to be the General Minister and President of the whole denomination."

That was true, he reflected, but he had been saying things like that back in April. What had he *learned*?

"I've also been encouraged by the number of people who care about justice, not just for 'their group.' And by the number who seem to want leadership that challenges them to think as Christians and doesn't just go along with socially acceptable forms of discrimination." Did that sound too canned? He paused before adding, "Of course, we hear a lot from those whose minds are already made up. But I believe, I want to believe, that most persons came to the meetings we've held in Missouri and Indiana and Texas and

New Mexico, throughout the church, because they wanted to hear what I and others have to say. That's pretty healthy, if you ask me."

He paused, and this time she didn't jump in to fill the silence. "More negatively, I have learned—I guess I knew it, but now see more clearly—how great a gap there is between the way ministers, in our church at least, read scripture, and the way many lay people read it. Otherwise highly educated folks have been left with a second-grade religious education because ministers are too intimidated to teach what they know is true about the Bible's historical context, about how to read it without setting aside all we learn from science or history."

He was pleased, although he wasn't sure why, to see that Stephanie was nodding and looking impressed. She glanced at the typed sheet in front of her. "I guess you've already answered this somewhat, but how has your mind changed, how have you changed, over the past few months?"

Yes, this was the question: not just what had he learned but how was he different. He still believed in the importance of Christian unity, still saw himself as a reconciler. But now such affirmations needed footnotes. For some reason, in that moment he remembered the time in Little League when his good friend, Rudy, hit his first and only home run of the season, just inside the left field foul pole, and the umpire, who was the uncle or something of a kid on the other team, ruled that it was a foul ball because, he said, third base wasn't in line with the pole. Sitting there in the studio, Matthew could hear his father saying, "That just isn't right. There are no two ways about it, *that* just isn't *right!*"

"I now realize," he said at last, "that being a reconciler doesn't mean you refrain from drawing lines when justice seems to demand it. I'm also more aware, however, that life is messy, very messy."

Stephanie started to speak, but Matthew continued. "I don't feel comfortable with anger any more than most people, but I see now that anger is sometimes necessary when people are getting hurt." Is that what he wanted to say? After all, wasn't it a problem that people had been angry at him?

Stephanie interrupted his thoughts. "Are you talking about a kind of 'righteous anger'?"

"I don't know if it's righteous. I just know that I used to spend a lot of time walking on egg shells, trying not to offend when I should have said things more directly, even been angry at times. The trick is knowing when to do what."

Stephanie started to speak, but Matthew added a final sentence. "I guess what I've learned, if you boil it all down, is that there are worse things than conflict."

While Matthew was wondering if any of that made sense, Stephanie opened the phone lines for callers. As expected, some were off the wall, such as the woman who wondered if homosexuals might have arrived on earth in the flying saucer everyone knows landed near Roswell. "After all, we didn't hear much about all this until … " Stephanie had the engineer pull the plug.

Then there was the woman who asked him if Clarence Thomas was a Christian. Matthew said yes, as far as he knew, then asked why she wanted to know. When she didn't answer, he started to talk about the conference call with the other church leaders before deciding that this was too complicated to explain on the radio. Besides, his stand seemed less defensible, even to him, in light of Anita Hill's recent testimony. There were so many things to consider when it came to qualifications for a position like that. And, in any case, that wasn't what the woman had asked. By the time he had gone through these mental gyrations, the caller was off the line, and Stephanie was looking strained.

Perhaps to strike a lighter note, she said, "I understand from a local minister that you're a runner."

"Every morning, if the schedule allows."

"This same minister told me you're famous for never being late … in fact, for always being early. Is there a story behind that?"

And maybe because he welcomed the change of topic, Matthew told her. "My mother died of cancer when I was nine." He took a deep breath. "On her last day, the hospital called my father to tell him she was failing rapidly, and, since I was due home from school, he waited to take me with him. But I had stopped off at a friend's house, was late getting home, and by the time he found me and we got to the hospital, she had died."

Stephanie looked stricken. "I am very sorry … "

"I don't tell that often and, to be honest, I'm not sure why I did now." He took a sip of water. "But as my wife, Margaret, would say, it may help explain one of my maddening habits. And whenever I get exasperated with other people's quirks, I try to remember that there may be a story like this behind them."

The show took a different turn when the next caller, a man, asked about Matthew's views on gun regulations. The topic was certainly timely, the caller reminded them, because only the day before a man named Hennard had driven his pickup through the front window of a cafeteria in Killeen, Texas, and killed twenty-three patrons with two automatic pistols.

Matthew thanked the man for raising an issue that should concern every Christian, every citizen, and then railed against the number of weapons in private hands. He quoted statistics regarding gun deaths in the United States versus other industrialized countries. He expressed sympathy for people who felt afraid and wanted protection, but stressed that guns weren't the answer. He expressed support for hunters, but stressed that no one hunted animals with a military-style weapon or a semi-automatic handgun. He talked, in some detail, about the biblical call to peacemaking. This was the kind of question he had hoped for, had initially expected, throughout the nomination.

The next caller, of course, disagreed. There was a woman in the cafeteria, he pointed out, who had a revolver in her purse that she left in her car. If she'd had it with her, said the caller, so many people wouldn't have died. "We need more weapons in the hands of honest citizens, not fewer. That would take care of bastards like what's-his-name in Texas."

Stephanie intervened to say this may underscore the "messiness" Matthew had talked about.

Yet another caller talked about a Christian college where a deranged former employee shot a student worker, and the entire campus responded by praying for the shooter, as well as the victim. "That's a school that lives by Christian principles," said the caller. "No gay lifestyle allowed there, that's for sure."

"Let's stop right there," said Matthew. "Don't you see that demeaning or excluding gay persons is also a form of violence? I'm glad they prayed for the shooter. Every Christian should do the same. But that's not enough. I'm glad the campus is united. But that's not enough if it's only a unity of 'their kind' of people." He felt like he was now on a roll.

And then came the call.

From the first words, Matthew sensed the voice was eerily familiar. "You are so articulate on lots of things, aren't you?" The voice was cool, slightly ironic. "Gays. Guns. But what about the day when *you* will need a gun?"

"You're the one who threatened me before," said Matthew, surprised at how calm he sounded. "I know your voice."

Stephanie started to signal for the audio engineer to end the call, but Matthew waved her off. "What makes you think you can threaten people with impunity? There are laws ... "

"What about God's laws? What makes you think you can flaunt God's laws and get away with it? People who rewrite the Word of God and boast about it, who revel in it, who go around the country spreading their blasphemy, have to pay the price. And you *will* pay. You talk about people being afraid. Maybe you don't yet know what you're talking about."

They phoned the local police, who said there was no way to trace the call. The authorities seemed unequipped, thought Matthew, to handle anything like this. What had the consultant said? They were out of their league. Stephanie confirmed that, since KBIM only broadcast to southeastern New Mexico, nearly all of their calls were local. Was the man following Matthew around the country? Could he have been in the audience the previous evening?

He felt an obligation to call Duane, who said in a very high voice that they needed to cancel the remainder of the nominee's tour, until Matthew reminded him that only one more meeting had been scheduled. In a way, that's too bad, Matthew reflected. While the prospect of being General Minister and President still worried him, he was finally getting the hang of being the nominee.

CHAPTER ELEVEN

After the radio show, the national headquarters ramped up its plans for security at the General Assembly, which began on October 25. The Tulsa police were notified and arrangements made for plainclothes personnel to follow Matthew throughout what was certain to be one of the largest assemblies in Disciples history: more than five thousand voting representatives and an even greater number of visitors.

Matthew wasn't entirely comfortable with these developments. Once the phone call was not immediate in his memory, he began to downplay it in his conversations with Margaret. "This guy's intent seems to be to stoke fear. It's highly unlikely he would do anything at an assembly with thousands of people around."

"You need to stop treating things like this as ambiguous," she told him. "That's how they get away with doing it. I've agreed you need to go through with the nomination, but don't be stupid about it." At her urging, they even discussed leaving the kids at home, but finally agreed that would be hard to explain and might, itself, cause alarm. Besides, said Matthew, it just wasn't right; they should be part of this experience. And he could only begin to imagine Abigail's objections.

Because the assembly had sold out the two largest hotels in downtown Tulsa, the church was given their top-floor suites. Matthew and family were assigned the Presidential Suite in the DoubleTree, and Zachary was enthralled. Three full bathrooms, with a telephone and television in each one! Abigail, who had been out of sorts on the flight to Tulsa, took one look at the space and decided it was perfect for a Halloween party, which she set about planning.

When to hold it? The assembly began on Friday evening ... the weekends were always packed ... they left on Wednesday ... and the big vote was Tuesday. So Matthew suggested she have her party on

Monday, October 28. There were dinners he had to attend every evening, so the party had to be following the evening session. This meant a very late night, especially for Zachary, who had suddenly become Abigail's biggest cheerleader. Assemblies, Abigail pointed out, don't come every day or even every year. "Sometimes," she said, "the rules just have to be waived." Where, he wondered, had she learned that word?

On Friday morning, Margaret and the kids went shopping for decorations while Matthew tried to find places to store the expensive, breakable vases that graced the Presidential Suite. He knew from experience that Abigail did not go in for smiling pumpkins and puffy, benign ghosts. She liked lots of fake cobwebs and spiders and skulls and severed arms. Where did that come from?

When the shoppers returned with the makings of a haunted house, Matthew learned that Abigail already had a guest list, which she called a "ghost list" to make Zachary laugh. She knew several kids her age from the children's programs of previous assemblies, so they were on the list—assuming, of course, they were in Tulsa. She would give out invitations to them, and any new friends at the children's program, over the weekend. Then there were Beth and other students from the seminary. She would certainly invite them. And she included Duane.

"That's nice of you," said Matthew, "but it isn't necessary, even though he did bring you those things from Australia."

"You've been spending a lot of time with him," Abigail replied, "and maybe he needs a break."

Matthew decided she probably didn't mean that the way it sounded, although who knew with Abigail? He delivered the invitation personally when he and Duane met that afternoon for a pre-assembly huddle of church leaders, and Duane immediately accepted. "I can see the DBW headline now," he told the group. "'Gay-Loving Intellectual Hosts Devil Worship in Hotel Suite'!"

Naturally, Grandma Gretchen was invited. "I'll help your mother serve things at the party," she told Abigail. "It will be good to have something to do."

"Okay," said the mistress of ceremonies, "but you still have to wear a mask."

Another person on Abigail's list was Grandpa Frank, who had insisted on coming to the assembly even though it was little more than a month since his heart attack. Matthew had argued against it for health—and other—reasons, but Frank said he wouldn't miss this for the world. He had arranged to ride with Bernie and his wife from church, and they would stop a lot, maybe even stay somewhere overnight, on the drive from southern Iowa to Oklahoma. Thanks to a cancellation, Matthew managed to reserve a room for him two floors below the Presidential Suite.

Once the assembly began, things got more problematic. Matthew hosted a breakfast early Saturday morning for international guests at which the head of the Disciples community in Zaire, instead of bringing a normal greeting, used his time to denounce homosexuality, calling it an "abomination." Matthew had been prepared to present the man with a certificate of appreciation, but, after hearing the presentation, he kept it in his briefcase.

When the breakfast was finally over, he met Frank as planned in the Overseas Ministries display area. "There's a guy out there, right in front of the convention center," his father fumed, "with a sign says 'Keep the Bible in the Church—Vote No on McAvoy,' or some garbage like that. He's telling every idiot who'll listen that you don't believe this and you don't believe that. Next time I see him, I'm gonna punch his nose to the back of his head!"

"Dad! Remember what Karen said about not getting so worked up. Besides, that's not the message I'm trying to get across," although he admitted to himself that punching the Zaire church leader sounded appealing.

"No? Well, that's a message he'll understand, the son of a bitch! And that's what I told that reporter when she asked me."

"What reporter?!" Frank didn't answer. "Dad, look, I told you you might not like it at the assembly. People are going to say things, that's just the way it is. Maybe you ought to stay in the hotel until Tuesday."

"I'm going to stay there tonight," said Frank, "that's for sure. Whoever heard of scheduling a church thing right on top of the World Series? And what a Series! If it goes seven games, I'm staying there tomorrow night too."

"Good," said Matthew. "You watch and tell me what happens."

His father's mind, however, was back on the assembly. "There's another bastard out there with a sign says 'Beware of False Prophets.' Meaning you, I guess. What I want to know is why only the crazies have signs. Huh? Why's that? Where are the members of this group you joined? Why aren't they out there with some decent signs?"

Matthew started to say, "That's a good point," but Frank had already shifted gears. "Of course, a lot of people saw my badge and asked if I was related to you. I said no, he's related to *me*," and laughed at his own joke. "Nice people. Said they admired you, at least until I told 'em you're a Cubs fan."

They were quiet for a minute, sipping the coffee Matthew had picked up for them. While Frank stared at the crowd, Matthew looked closely at him. Sometimes it pained him to see his father's features in his own mirror: large ears, broad forehead, prominent Adam's apple. But now, standing there in the swirl of assembly goers, he just saw a man who seemed to have aged too quickly.

"So what about you?" Matthew said at last. He wanted to ask, *Do you admire what I'm doing?*, but what came out was more indirect. "You've never told me, Dad, whether you support me. I mean, whether you agree with what I've been saying about welcoming gays and lesbians."

"Look at those jackasses on the other side. I sure as hell wouldn't support them."

"Dad, please tell me straight out. Do you support what I'm trying to say or not?"

"Yeah, sure," said Frank. He took a large drink from his coffee. "Those people who say all these stupid things about homosexuals, they never knew Jeffrey."

Matthew had little to do with planning for the assembly, but he did tell the committee responsible for it that he needed—deserved—an opportunity to speak in a plenary session prior to the vote. The committee agreed, scheduling his presentation for the end of business on Saturday morning. His speech was basically written before he got to Tulsa, he had shared parts of it with Margaret over the past couple of weeks, but misconceptions he encountered during the first hours of the assembly led him to consider adding to what he had written.

"Maybe you can't order, God forbid, that homosexuals be ordained," said one woman who was clearly not a fan, "but you can appoint them to all kinds of positions." Should he remind the assembly that, in actuality, the GMP was a rather toothless office? But what if this woman's complaint, and others like it, were really signs that the church was hungry for stronger leadership? He remembered a line from Margaret: "In the Catholic Church, for all of its problems, you at least know who's in charge." Is that what Disciples were now wanting?

Another woman who stopped him after the program on Friday night was far more supportive. "You have been a rock!" she exclaimed. "It's an inspiration to see how you haven't changed since this whole ordeal started." But Matthew knew that wasn't true. How, he asked himself, could the change that seemed so monumental to him be so apparently invisible to others? Should he speak honestly to the assembly about how the nomination had affected him, about what he had learned and how he had changed?

Not surprisingly, homosexuality was the dominant topic of hallway conversations … until he wanted to scream! Should he try to shift the focus, perhaps by reminding the assembly of the massacre on Black Wall Street, right here in Tulsa? *In the midst of everything else, don't lose sight of the need to stamp out racism!* would be an important message, including for those who were in his corner.

Many people stopped him for photographs or to ask him to sign one of his books. Matthew knew that what Duane called his "celebrity status" was, in large part, related to what he'd gone through during the nomination. "Thanks for standing up for the faith, even when it cost you a lot," was the way one person put it. Should he assure the assembly goers that he was fine, and point their attention to the ones who had really suffered in the history of this church? Or was this an indication that he should be more personally revealing? The idea made him cringe, but he did consider telling about a trip to Chicago when he discovered that Abigail had packed his baseball glove, along with a note: "In case you have time to play catch. It's a great way to meet people you know!" Humor was good, although that felt like exploiting his children.

The most interesting of these chance conversations was with a college student who asked Matthew how he thought the church would look in twenty or twenty-five years. "Do you think we'll still be fighting these same battles? Is it possible for the church to change?"

"Of course the church can change," Matthew told him, trying to muster enthusiasm appropriate to the words. "Don't ever underestimate what the Holy Spirit can accomplish. Who knows, in twenty-five years gay marriage may be legal across the country, and we will be wondering why all of this seemed so difficult. And you may be GMP." They both smiled at the thought, but it left Matthew wondering: Should he offer the assembly a vision of what the church, God willing, could become in the next generation?

Then there was the man who said, "I'll bet you wish this affair had been held someplace else."

Matthew asked, "Why is that?" but of course he knew. Raymond and other national leaders had talked about it *ad nauseam*.

"Come on," said the man, "you must've heard that congregations across Texas and Oklahoma are planning to bus people in for the vote. And you know how they'll vote. If this get-together had been in Portland or Columbus, you'd be home free."

Matthew shook his head. "That's just a rumor. Every congregation is entitled to two voting representatives, and I would like to see every church represented, no matter where they're from." But that sounded so bureaucratic he wondered if it could possibly be true. Should he say what he really thought about those who might come to the assembly for a single political purpose?

In the end, he stayed with his prepared address, much of which was originally scribbled in motels late at night, while thoughts from that evening's church meeting were still fresh in his mind. "Several moments," he told the assembly, "stand out in my memory. I recall, for example, the father who asked me how he was to raise his two small sons in an age when family values and structures seem to be fast eroding. As I have tried to see through his eyes, this father has become for me a bearer of grace.

"I remember the ministers, and there were several, from small towns in places like the panhandle of Texas and rural Pennsylvania, who spoke of their sense of isolation and their frustration that no one is listening. As I have tried to see through their eyes, these colleagues have become for me bearers of grace.

"I remember the parents, and there were a number of them, who dared to speak with me, proudly and lovingly, of their sons and daughters who happen to be gay or lesbian. As I have tried to see through their eyes, these parents have become for me bearers of grace." There was a wave of applause—at first scattered, then swelling—but he continued without breaking rhythm.

"I also remember the man at one of our church meetings who referred to our gay and lesbian neighbors as 'scum.'" He paused to let this sink in. "Although I find it hard to see through his eyes, he, too, has become for me a bearer of grace. Because of him, I have come to understand that there are some things the church cannot accept—*must not* accept—and still be the church.

"'Welcome one another,' Paul wrote to the Romans, 'just as Christ has welcomed you, for the glory of God.' If our welcome is to mean anything, then it must include saying 'No!' to attitudes and actions that are unwelcoming ... like calling someone 'scum.'"

Was this, he wondered, too abstract? Too edgy? Did it matter? He looked around the vast hall, seats filling the level space in front of him, more seats climbing up the walls to his right and left. Out of the corner of his eyes, he could see the large video screens and the close-up of him at the podium.

"Some of you may be familiar with Disciples for Biblical Witness." This time it was laughter that rippled through the assembly. "In the most recent DBW newsletter, the editors declare that 'homosexuality is the defining issue of our age.' Over the past few months, I have come to see that, on this at least, they are surely correct. I used to think that giving so much emphasis to sexual orientation was causing us to take our eyes off the gospel, but I now see that all this controversy has actually been an opportunity to define again, in this generation, the meaning and practice of God's welcoming grace. Our biblical forebears faced this challenge over the question of Gentiles and circumcision. Our nineteenth-century ancestors faced it over slavery. Our parents and grandparents have faced it over questions of racial justice and the role of women. And now, it is our turn to welcome others as God has welcomed us. Now it is our turn to decide what kind of church we are called to be.

"I did not set out to be a champion of gay rights. To be painfully honest, I hadn't paid much attention to the issue until God forced me, forced all of us, to confront it through this nomination. Please hear me. I don't want Disciples to be known as a church that defends homosexuality. I want Disciples to be known as a church that proclaims God's gracious welcome to all of God's children, and as a church that has the guts to stand up and say 'No!' whenever that welcome is denied." The applause was loud, but were those boos interspersed with it?

He cleared his throat. "There may be some of you who feel that my time in this presentation would be better spent outlining future programs or discussing problems in our structures. But to use a medical metaphor, our problems are cardiac, not orthopedic. We don't need new structural bones, we need a renewed heart for the gospel of God's amazing grace."

Matthew had hoped for even louder applause at this point, but he could sense real attentiveness in the assembly hall. Few people moved in the aisles, at least that he could see with the lights in his eyes, and there was no low buzz of conversation from the hallways beyond.

"Over the past several months, I have heard people refer to the 'decline' of our church because of all the conflict we have experienced. I know as well as anyone that such conflict can be painful. But, friends, it signals decline only if you think the church we have been in the past is the church God calls us to be. Sometimes pain, even death, is necessary for new life to appear. I *hope* we are witnessing the death of a church dominated by white males. I *hope* we are witnessing the death of a denomination that draws sharp boundaries between itself and others who claim the name of Christ. And, yes, I *hope* we are witnessing the death of a church that echoes the prejudices of the culture around it. Tuesday's vote isn't just to choose a General Minister and President. It's a vote on the kind of church we hope to be." He sensed both passionate applause and passionate silence. Or was this simply his projection?

"Scripture repeatedly affirms that times of weakness—and, yes, conflict—are times of great opportunity, because they open spaces for the Spirit to move, for minds to be changed. Think of Isaiah: It is in exile that the community learns its true calling as a light to the nations. Think of Pentecost: It is in a moment of utter confusion that the Holy Spirit is experienced in all its power."

He spread his arms wide and closed his eyes. "Spare us, dear God, from those times when we think we have everything under control. Because those are the times when we rely on our strength rather than trusting in yours. May this assembly be a moment when we truly look for your guidance, when we truly act like disciples of Christ."

Even Frank acknowledged that he liked the speech, and other people mobbed Matthew afterward as he walked with Margaret through the vast array (it seemed to him like acres) of booths and displays. They made a point of stopping by the seminary's booth—where several students were hanging out, eager to congratulate their dean—and were surprised to find Gretchen there, talking with Heather and Lisa. "I wish Walt could have heard your speech," she told her son-in-law. "These wonderful young women said I can probably get a tape of it, so I may do that and make him listen. It wouldn't hurt him to learn a thing or two, like I have."

As the three of them were leaving the display area, a man shouted, "You call that leadership? Tiptoed all around the can of worms you've opened up." But others shouted at *him*, and Matthew found he had no energy—or desire—to intervene.

On Sunday, he preached twice to overflow congregations in local Disciples churches. Since the theme of the assembly was, "In Remembrance of Me," he talked about the Lord's Table as the place where Christians experience their deepest unity, their communion with Christ and one another, but also as the place from which they are sent as agents of God's justice. Holding those together, he told the congregations, is the biggest challenge facing the church, and it is possible only if we truly remember the One we call Lord.

Controversy had, indeed, brought out the press, and Sunday afternoon was, for Matthew, one long series of media interviews. Some newspaper reporters simply cornered him in the hallways of the convention center, but two television interviews had been arranged in advance, and these were conducted in what was called the Green Room, a windowless chamber behind the stage, where people waited before speaking or performing. Among the first questions in every interview: "Is it true that there is extra security at this assembly because you have received threats?" Two interviewers, he noticed, asked nothing at all about his background or qualifications for the position.

By that evening, Matthew was so exhausted he nearly fell asleep while a speaker was holding forth during the post-dinner program—a sign, he decided, that the extra security did make him feel secure. He roused himself enough, however, to stop by his father's room and found that the game was still on. Frank was beside himself. "Can you believe this? Puckett wins game six with a walk-off home run in the eleventh, and now this one's a nail-biter. Never seen a Series like it!" They watched the final three innings like friends in a bar, even sharing a couple of beers Frank had stashed in the room's little refrigerator, until the Twins won 1–0 in the tenth. Matthew was pleased that, for an hour, he had forgotten the assembly. Frank was ecstatic since, being a White Sox fan, the American League was his extended tribe. And, besides, Minneapolis wasn't that far from Oak Grove.

Despite his fatigue, Matthew asked, "Wasn't Mom born in Minneapolis?"

"Yeah, although she didn't go back there much once her mother died. You probably don't even remember being in their home."

They sat silently for a minute before Matthew said, "It's funny. Not funny ... strange. I can't quite see her. The images I have are the pictures you've got around the house. Like that picture of women in the church kitchen. I have that image of her, but I can't picture her reading or praying or doing something in worship."

"Well, that's because your mother wasn't like that. She was a hard worker, for sure, but she was a worrier, always thinking that she should've done this or that. Wouldn't surprise me if being so worried all the time didn't have something to do with her cancer." He took a drink of beer. "It didn't keep her from doing things, she just worried about 'em later. Being up front in church, that would have worried her to death, really would have."

The question seemed to slip out: "Why didn't you talk about her more after she died?"

Frank turned to face him, leaning forward on the edge of the chair, Matthew's words hanging between them. "Maybe I did, and you just didn't want to listen."

"Are you kidding? I had a million questions, but it seemed like you wanted to get on with other things, as if our life was normal."

"Well, what's wrong with that? Sometimes you have to keep going even when you don't feel like it. You weren't the only one living in that house, you know. I had Karen to think about, a business to run. If my mother hadn't been able to step in, live with us for a while, I don't know what we would've done. I really don't."

Frank settled back in his chair and took a deep breath. "They told me she had cancer, and then five months later she's gone. Who's ever prepared for something like that? Who's got a playbook for what to do when life throws a curveball like that at you? You just keep on doin' and hope it's good enough."

Monday was the day of the Halloween party, and Abigail was in full bossy preparation mode when Matthew left for an obligatory breakfast. What was this one? Disciples for Peace? The Asian American caucus? "You will need a mask," she reminded him loudly at the door.

"You will have to get it for me," he said, "or make me one. Just don't make me a monster. It would fulfill too many expectations," a remark that was lost on his daughter, precocious as she was.

The party itself was a hit. Abigail's friends were there in force, their parents in tow, most of them in masks, which they wore on and off. Beetlejuice seemed to be a favorite with the young crowd, but there was a Chuckie and a Freddy Krueger. Abigail had painted blood dripping down the side of her head, which briefly upset Zachary. Margaret and Gretchen had soft drinks for the kids and wine for the older creatures, along with trays of snacks provided by the hotel. Frank was there in a Lone Ranger mask, which Abigail got for him and made him wear. Duane came in part way through, with a mask of the Incredible Hulk. Matthew told him he looked more authoritative than usual, but immediately felt that hit too close to home and wanted to take it back. Was one of the security persons there? he wondered. It was hard to tell, especially since he hadn't previously met all the parents of Abigail's assembly friends. And who was the man in the Phantom of the Opera half mask who seemed to be alone and left soon after Matthew entered the large common room? Margaret didn't know either, so he asked one of his friends whom he had seen talking to the man. "I don't think he said his name," his friend told him. "Said he was waiting for his wife and daughter, but I guess they never showed up."

It was after eleven before everyone was gone, Duane offering to see Gretchen back to her hotel. They started to clean up, but then Matthew suggested to Margaret that it could wait—or, better, they could just leave it for the hotel. Tomorrow was the big day, and he would rather they spend some time praying together. But, in the middle of their prayer, Zachary knocked over a chair, Abigail screamed at him for pulling down the cobwebs she had attached to it, and Margaret told her to knock it off. So the prayer petered out more than ended.

They got the kids back in bed and then, sharing a glass of wine, sat together on a couch in front of a window that overlooked the city. "I expect you've noticed," said Margaret, "that when she isn't doing something she wants to do, like planning this party, our daughter has been a royal pain in the ass."

Matthew nodded his agreement. In the hotel, Abigail had insisted on wearing one of Margaret's sweaters, often swinging its arms like limp clubs at Zachary. Matthew was usually pleased to show her off in public settings, although he denied this intent. But after the first day at the assembly, when Abigail slouched sullenly during the Pension Fund dinner, he was ready to have her dropped at the children's program. "What's that about, do you suppose?"

"Oh, I think a General Minister and President can figure that out," said Margaret, as she poured them a bit more wine. Matthew put his arm around her, and they sat in silence for several minutes.

"There's something I've been meaning to tell you," he said.

She turned to look at him and raised her eyebrows, but her look was gentle, encouraging. "After one of the meetings in God knows where—no, I do remember, it was Amarillo—I agreed to have a drink with a woman who, it turned out, had been to several of these affairs ... events. And the consultant I told you about put this in a report he compiled on my 'performance' as the nominee, as if it were worth reporting on. That's probably why I never showed you the report. Anyway, he had this conspiracy theory that she was a set up courtesy of DBW. And I guess I thought you ought to know in case, once I'm GMP, they begin circulating rumors that I go places with strange women."

Margaret simply smiled and shook her head as she leaned back against his arm. Perhaps she could feel his heart beating faster as she said, "If you want to know whether I ever worry about you traveling all over the church, surrounded by female fans who think you are charming and intelligent and handsome in your suits, the answer is 'of course not.' I've been worried about a lot of things, but not that." She paused for a minute before adding, "I know you." He pulled her closer, and they sat again in silence, looking at the city lights.

"Did I ever tell you how I tell people on airplanes that I'm a theologian so they'll leave me alone?" Margaret laughed, as she straightened her legs that had been tucked beneath her. "I think," he said, "you have a much more important job than I do."

"You're also a teacher."

"Yes, but I sometimes wonder what good is it to be a teacher of theology … a theologian. I have as much advanced education as a surgeon, but I'm not sure it does anybody any good."

"You're too hard on yourself," said Margaret. "There is a lot of bad religion around, God knows, and maybe your job is to help the church avoid it. Think of yourself as a surgeon who cuts out bad religion." They both smiled, and she took his hand.

Again they looked out the window in silence, until Matthew said, "The best outcome tomorrow might be if I lose by a whisker, just under two-thirds. Then the anti-gay crowd can't claim victory, but it won't split the church."

"And you won't have the headache of actually being GMP." More smiles.

"It's true," he said, after a sip of wine. "I think I have been better as a nominee than I probably will be, might be, as the General Minister."

"I don't know about the last part," said Margaret, "but it seems to me you've been a great nominee, and I'm proud to be married to you. It's been hard, really hard, including on the kids, but I'm glad you've done it." He kissed her, and when he tried to speak, the words stuck in his throat.

CHAPTER TWELVE

On Tuesday, the day of the vote, they were all up early, weaving their way through the mess in the Presidential Suite. Beth was coming by to pick up Zachary and Abigail and take them to their respective programs, so Margaret and Matthew could enjoy their one breakfast together at the hotel. Abigail, who seemed in a much better mood after the success of her party, loudly expressed her mock disbelief when she heard these plans. "Dad isn't going to the assembly early? I'm going to report this to the newspaper. Read all about it! For once, Dad isn't the first person at the assembly." Matthew laughed along, but he was relieved when Abigail and Zachary finally left ... until he discovered next to his regular coffee mug in the kitchenette another letter from his daughter, attached to three pages stapled together.

Dear Dad!

You will do great on the election! I even bet you were a great shortstop! And Mom and Zachary and me will be there if you need any help although Zachary is NOT any help that's for sure. And I still am not happy about moving.

Love!

Abigail

P.S. Here is my report on Abby Kelly Foster because you might want to see it.

Love again!

Abigail

Matthew smiled as he scanned the report, and then stuck it and the letter in his assembly bag, feeling fortified for what he now was sure would be a fine day.

Matthew and Margaret lingered over pancakes and scrambled eggs, even had a third cup of coffee. Margaret complimented him on his choice of a Save the Children tie with bold, primary colors. Matthew said how much he appreciated their conversation last evening, how beautiful she looked this morning, and how much he looked forward to time alone with her once they got back to Lexington. Maybe they could have that romantic weekend they talked about way back in April. And how about a trip with the kids out west? He had a friend who could find them a good place to stay in Montana.

As Matthew was signing the bill, Margaret said, "I feel a little guilty not inviting your father to join us for breakfast since he's right here in the hotel."

"I don't! I've spent some time with him, and we needed this." He reached across the table and squeezed her hand. "Dad said he had something he planned to do this morning at the convention center—he didn't say what—and would meet us later. The one I feel guilty about is your mother. She worked during the whole party and would have been there half the night cleaning up if she was staying in this hotel."

"Oh, she's fine," said Margaret. "She likes being busy. She told me not to bother sitting with her this morning, that you and I have enough to think about. She said she'll find us after the vote."

After they both used the lobby restrooms (too much coffee), Matthew stopped by the front desk, where he picked up a stack of cards and notes—left for him by well-wishers, he hoped—that he stuffed in his canvas assembly bag. One of the buses shuttling people to the assembly was approaching as they left the hotel; but since the DoubleTree is fairly near the convention center and the day was pleasant, Matthew and Margaret decided to walk—stroll, actually—Margaret taking his arm once they were outside. Several assembly goers stopped to shake hands and assure him of their support. "We met you up at Cane Ridge," one couple told him. "From Cincinnati, remember? Our group took a picture with you that's still on the church bulletin board, by the way." Another woman informed Matthew that she had been there the night a man said he was going to pin Matthew's ears back. "You know, he's not even part of our church as far as we can tell. A bunch of us talked about it afterward, and no one had ever seen him before ... or since, for that matter."

Matthew and Margaret were standing near one of the entrances to the convention center, listening to a woman they hadn't previously met tell of the "good butterflies" in her stomach as she anticipated the vote, when a uniformed police officer appeared at their side and asked them to follow him.

"We'll be there in a second," Matthew told him.

"Reverend, you and your wife need to come *now*."

Was this, Matthew wondered, part of the security protocol? They were led at a fast clip to the rear of the stage where Marvin, the deputy GMP, was explaining something to another officer and two security guards. He looked more agitated than Matthew had ever seen him. "Like I said," Marvin was telling them, "I forgot to get the number of the bus, and now I can't remember who gave it to me. There were lots of people saying things to me at the same time."

"What's going on?" Matthew asked. He could feel his stomach starting to knot up.

Marvin turned toward the couple. "Just what you need, something else to worry about." He started to say more and then stopped.

"We're workin' on it right now," said one of the officers, "so everyone can stay calm."

"What?" Matthew asked, too loudly. "Stay calm about what?" Margaret, he noticed, was holding tightly to his arm.

"Someone apparently found this on a bus that's shuttlin' people to the convention center," said the officer, holding up a small, empty cardboard box. Matthew's mind registered the word "ammunition," along with "9mm."

It was Margaret who reacted first. "Zachary, Abigail. We've got to get them *right now*! Matthew ..."

"We've got your son," the officer cut in. "A student—I think her name is Beth—helped us pick him up from the preschool program. They're already in what they call the Green Room, over there where we got a guard." Margaret put her hand to her mouth and started to cry. "And, Ma'am, we got security people out lookin' for your daughter." He turned to Matthew. "Seems she didn't go to the kids' program because she and your father—this according to Beth—had some plan to collect things off the tables in the exhibit hall."

"I'm going to look for them," said Margaret with authority, but the officer put out his arm.

"No, Ma'am, you need to stay with your son back here in the Green Room. We got plenty of people in there who know what they look like. Beth tells us she's wearin' a Cubs baseball cap."

Matthew had thought a lot about the threats, even talked about them to some people, but until now he hadn't really felt threatened. It had seemed, somehow, abstract. A crazy person trying to scare him, but not ... "So you think there might actually be someone with a gun here in the convention center?" he asked the officer who seemed to be in charge. It felt to him like a fatuous question as soon as he asked it.

"Obviously we don't know anything for sure," said the officer, moving them all toward the guarded room. "But no one wants to take any chances. From what the Reverend here tells me," pointing toward Marvin, "you've had threats in recent weeks." Matthew nodded, but it was Margaret who spoke. "My mother is in the building, somewhere. You need to find her too."

"I kind of doubt she's in danger," said the officer, but then took down a description of Gretchen: mid-sixties, slightly overweight, curly hair turning gray. "What's she wearing?"

"I have no idea! We haven't seen her this morning, but she should be on one of those buses. Have someone meet the buses picking up people at the Days Inn." Margaret's exasperation was palpable. "Or can't you page them?! Surely there is some way of announcing things."

The officer shook his head. "Afraid not. We asked about that, but it seems this center's too old to have that kind of system. Just a fire alarm, no intercom."

And so they waited. At first, they said reassuring words to one another: This was just like Abigail to talk her grandfather into this little excursion. Frank wouldn't let Abigail out of his sight; the police were just being extra cautious. Nothing bad can happen to her in the midst of all these Disciples, many of whom know her by sight. Beth reported how good Zachary had been when she told him he needed to leave his friends right when they had started to do finger painting. Zachary had pulled his chair next to Beth's, and he now put his head in her lap.

After fifteen minutes, Matthew found he was jiggling one leg, then the other, and his jaw was beginning to ache. Someone had left magazines on a coffee table, and he began to arrange them so that all the edges were even, until Margaret put her hand on his arm. "Why don't you look at some of those notes you picked up after breakfast," she suggested. "Or whatever Harold gave you."

Harold had clearly been waiting for Matthew outside the hotel that morning, although he probably hadn't counted on seeing Margaret as well. As the couple approached him, Harold tried to greet Margaret, who scowled at him and turned away. "I think," he said, addressing Matthew, "that I've helped make you a hero."

"I don't know about that, but I do know you've helped stir up some pretty ugly stuff."

"I don't feel good about that," said Harold. "I hope you know I really don't. But ... anyway ... this is just a word from me"—holding out a hotel stationery envelope. "You might read it, if you have a chance, before the vote ... or sometime."

Sitting there in the Green Room, Matthew pulled the envelope from his jacket pocket and read: "Things have happened in my family that give me a better idea what you've been talking about. You have my support, whatever happens. Your friend in Christ, Harold."

Life hinges on certain moments, he reflected. If Harold had agreed to send the letter to the church, written that evening in the home of Barbara and Phil, it's likely they wouldn't be sitting anxiously in this room right now. Of course, some good things had happened because of Harold, but at the moment it was hard to think of him with anything but irritation. He tore the note in half and stuffed the pieces in his assembly bag.

After twenty-five minutes, it was Margaret who was becoming increasingly agitated. "She ... she and Frank can't be that hard to find!"

Matthew tried to take her hand. "Maybe we should pray."

"What do you think I've been doing?" she asked, biting off the words.

Silence. Why, he wondered, had prayer not been his first instinct? Well, he would do it now. But all that kept running through his head was the same one-line petition: *Dear God, don't let anything happen to Abigail!* This was not how he spoke of God in the classroom, where he disparaged the popular image of One who rushes to meet our every need: "Dear God, help me find my keys." "Dear God, take away Aunt Helen's cancer." But sitting in this suffocating room, tension hanging in the air, it was clear to him that there are times when you just need to pray beyond your theology. *Dear God, please protect our little girl!*

The prayer did nothing to dampen his growing exasperation. Why didn't they have a sofa in here instead of these awful chairs, so he could sit close to Margaret and put his arm around her? Why wasn't there at least one window? He paced the length of the room and back, then did it again, the sense of claustrophobia swelling. What was going on?!

After forty minutes, Margaret stood up abruptly. "I think," she said briskly, her eyes on Matthew, "we need to go help look for her. I certainly need to, and staying in this room isn't good for you either."

"I have strict orders to make sure you don't leave the room," said the policeman, looking uncomfortable. "Please don't make me call my lieutenant. He'll just tell you they're looking as fast as they can." Margaret started to protest, but then sat down, and Matthew followed.

Not knowing what else to do, he rummaged through his assembly bag for the notes and cards they had picked up—was it only an hour and a half ago?—at the hotel. One from the minister in Carlsbad. One from church women in Lynchburg. And then he saw one with an embossed name on the envelope flap: "Leonard Fletcher." He opened it quickly and read: "Matthew, I'm sorry we haven't had a chance to speak directly. Remember Psalm 37:1–8. Leo." Why, he wondered, did he not carry a Bible with him?

Without warning the door opened, but it was only Raymond, who tried to offer comforting words while looking anything but comforted. To let him off the hook, Matthew asked, "Is Ross at the assembly?"

"Nah. He did his job, and that was the end of it." Raymond seemed as nervous as the rest of them, which Matthew, for some reason, appreciated.

"I never heard any more from him after our meeting in Indianapolis. Didn't see him in any of the churches. Was there any follow up on his report?"

Raymond shook his head. "He may have known his business, but I decided maybe he didn't know Disciples, didn't know us. That's what Duane thought, I know that for sure." He paused for a few seconds. "And then we started hearing from other people that you were knocking it out of the park in Topeka and Billings and Carlsbad. So there didn't seem much need for what Ross had to offer. He did his job, maybe it did some good, changed a few things, and that was the end of it."

After fidgeting for another minute, Raymond said he had to leave, apologizing to everyone for doing so, then inadvertently slamming the door as he went out. Zachary began to whine, before his mother told him there was nothing to be afraid of, and he plopped his head back on Beth's lap.

Margaret's words led Matthew to think about fear. Had he been afraid, really afraid, after the phone calls? He had felt a shiver, a tightening of his stomach, but the voice was disembodied and somehow remote. He certainly wasn't worried enough to stop his travels around the church. Now, however, it was different. Had he done enough to protect his family? Should he have been more afraid for their sake? His mind drifted back to the pivotal phone call with Duane. Maybe he should have insisted more forcefully on withdrawing his name. Margaret had said she agreed with Duane about staying the course, but he wouldn't have dared ask her about that now.

There was a knock on the door, loud enough that everyone jumped, and in came Duane. Margaret stood up quickly, her eyes mirroring her words: "They've found her?"

Duane gave a slight shake of his head and ran his tongue over his lips. "Not yet," his voice very high, "but it shouldn't ..."

"What's taking so long?!" Margaret was nearly shouting. "Christ, what is taking so *long*?!"

Duane looked as stressed as Matthew had ever seen him. "There is just a lot of territory to cover. We thought they were in the display areas, but they could have stepped into the restrooms or maybe outside … " He seemed to realize that this was not a good idea to plant in people's minds, but it was soon reinforced when two new policemen entered the room with questions for the parents: Could their daughter and her grandfather have left the convention center for some reason? Perhaps gone back to the hotel?

Now Margaret was definitely shouting. "You're the ones who are supposed to be finding her! For God's sake, send your people to the hotel and look!"

Zachary was now sitting up, head nestled against Beth, wide eyes on his mother. "Where is Abigail?" his voice almost a whisper.

Margaret pointed to a phone on a small table near the door. "This work?" Without waiting for an answer, she picked it up and, after getting an outside line, dialed the DoubleTree. Frank wasn't in his room, and there was no response to a page in the lobby and restaurant. Since she was holding the phone, Margaret also called the Days Inn, and, when the reception desk dialed her room, Gretchen answered.

"Mom, what are you doing there?! We thought you were coming to the assembly."

"It was just going to be too much stress," said her mother, "like waiting to see if there's white smoke." Her tone changed. "Is everything okay, honey?"

"Yes … things are … they're fine. I'll tell you about it later. Just stay there until I call you."

As the minutes ticked by, Matthew registered things around him, as if looking through a microscope: Margaret's face like a mask, lips pinched; the elbow Zachary must have scraped while chasing his sister around the hotel rooms; the armpit stains on the shirt of the security guard; Beth's eyes, tired and sad. He looked back at his son, remembering those anguished minutes when he and Abigail searched for Zachary in the park. This was worse because they couldn't do anything but wait. He straightened the magazines on the coffee table for the third time. He started to loosen his tie, then simply made sure the knot was perfect. He poured a glass of water for Margaret and Beth, then one for himself, which he drank while pacing the length of the room … three times … four.

When the door opened again and a policewoman entered, no one bothered to stand or speak, until she said simply, "They're bringing her now." Then there she was, rushing into their midst, Frank in her wake. After her parents, and even her brother, had hugged her, Abigail asked, her voice quivering, "Why did the police come to get us? Did something happen? Is something going to happen?" She looked at her father, and Matthew could see she was close to tears.

"We're fine," Margaret told her. "The police are just being careful, and we didn't know where you were"—this last said while glaring at Frank.

"We may have looked right past her," said the police officer who had come in after them. "We were told she was wearing a baseball cap, but I guess she took it off." Abigail held up her cap, filled with new treasures from the display tables. "And then, several buses—out of towners, it looked like—pulled up just as we were starting to look, and the place got real crowded."

"So we cleared out for a while," said Frank. "Went down to a drugstore, but they didn't even have a *Sporting News*."

Abigail picked up the story, sounding a little more like her usual self. When they got back to the convention center, they went to the food court to get her an apple juice, and then were going back to the display area (she had seen great stuff on the tables that have signs about going to other countries) when the police officer ...

Matthew interrupted. "Abigail, we want to hear about it, but I need to ask you something first. Do you remember the man you were talking to when you and I went to Canc Ridge, the old church with the balcony? I asked you who he was and ..."

"Yes," she said brightly, "I saw him here."

"You did!" Matthew realized, when Margaret put her hand on his arm, that his voice was far too loud. "Do you remember what he looks like?" he asked in a less frantic tone, but he could see the anxiety now clouding Abigail's face.

"Maybe it wasn't him," she said, looking to her mother.

"Did he talk to you this time?"

"No." She paused. "But it was like he was looking at me, so I almost said 'Hi,' but then he was gone."

"What did he look like, sweetheart?" Margaret asked.

"I don't know. About as old as Dad, I guess. No, maybe older. I don't know!" She was growing increasingly agitated, and Matthew could almost see her mind making connections. "Has he done something bad? Is he the one who's mad at Dad?"

Margaret held Abigail, stroking her hair, while Matthew turned his attention to his father who, he discovered, was remarkably calm. Frank did rail briefly about nuts with guns and what kind of country have we become until Margaret nodded sharply toward the kids.

Duane came back in still looking quite strung out. He managed to smile at Abigail and pat her on the shoulder before announcing in a high voice that "everyone" had agreed there was no need to alert the assembly, and they had therefore proceeded with the vote. It was surprising, thought Matthew, how he had practically forgotten that the assembly was voting.

Duane left again to ask that coffee and soft drinks be brought in. He returned shortly, letting them know he had also ordered lunch, although no one was hungry. Apparently not knowing what else to say, he asked, "So, you all holding up okay?"

"We've been in here a long time," said Matthew, "and it feels strange just to be sitting in this room. Are you sure we still need to be here?" The security man and police officer both nodded, so Matthew asked Duane, "What's going on out there?"

"It's strange there too. Marvin, I guess it was Marvin, decided it would be good for a church group to play some music, but it was way too upbeat for what people are feeling. How long ago was that?" He glanced at this watch. "They're probably beginning to count the ballots now." Matthew started to ask if they really called them "ballots," but decided it didn't matter, and Duane continued. "Anyway, now it's pretty quiet in the hall. Very quiet, to tell the truth, for eleven thousand people. A little eerie, like the air before a thunderstorm. You know that woman from Indiana on the General Board who's always knitting during the meetings?"—this said looking at Matthew. "I saw her, and she was just sitting there doing nothing. I've never seen that before."

After a while, the food was brought in. Margaret, clearly not hungry, went to the restroom, accompanied by an officer. While Frank and Duane picked at their food and tried half-heartedly to talk about the Series, Abigail filled her father in on her adventure. She also began to show him what she had collected, including a postcard from Cane Ridge.

"I don't know where this came from," she told him. "I guess I sat my hat down, maybe while I was looking at these dolls they had from Costa something, and somebody, I guess, put this card in it." She handed it to Matthew who read silently, "Thinking of you—and your father." He handed it to a policeman with a brief, whispered explanation and a request to say nothing about it in front of Margaret. It might not be anything, he told himself, but it still left him feeling even more unsettled?

He could hear Duane and Frank now talking about the nomination, all the places Matthew had traveled, and he tried to focus his mind on the church. Not the "election," which felt almost anticlimactic, but the church as he had experienced it over these last two and half months. Like all the people he had met who without knowing it had helped him learn things about himself. Were they really agents of God's grace in his life? He had said that to the assembly. Did he believe it?

This threatener, he told himself, whoever the hell he is, isn't the church. Like the pinning-ears man, he may have nothing to do with the Disciples. And even if he does, he doesn't define us. *I won't let him define us!* The church is the pastor in Huntsville who picked up the microphone and the young woman in Billings who had the wherewithal to stand up and shout. The church is Margaret going faithfully to meeting after meeting about a minor change in the order of worship, when Protestant worship, of any sort, was still for her a stretch. He had allowed the threats and the negatives to wear on him, and with Abigail sitting safely near him, he resolved never to do that again.

In a curious way, he told himself, this could all be for the good. One of the hardest things about being a church leader is that people look to you to validate their faith, to model what it means to be a Christian or a Disciple, when, in fact, you have all the same doubts and questions they have. But if he could just rise above this moment of conflict, of threat, it might actually be inspiring to the church. It might mean that people would overlook some of the times when, as GMP, he didn't stand the test.

Duane left "to check on things," and no doubt to get out of the room, which was not only tense but increasingly stuffy. The security man had long ago taken off his jacket, but Matthew, true to form, had left his on. He checked the two inside pockets for his speeches—left side if he won, right side if he lost—and, for some reason, took out the one in the right pocket and read silently:

"I must begin by thanking you for the privilege of being your nominee, for the chance to serve as faithfully as I knew how during the recent months of discussion and reflection."

Yes, that was true.

"I know there are many disappointed people in this arena. Please hear me. I am no less excited about the future of this church, and no less committed to being part of that future, than I was an hour or a month or a year ago. And you must not be either."

Yes, if it came to that, he would still be excited, wouldn't he? And in any case, it would be important to rally the troops.

"We, Disciples, have done something significant in the way we carried out a church-wide conversation about what it means to be a church that values both unity and justice."

Yes, although as he told others, the trick is knowing when to risk division for the sake of justice, and to risk full justice for the sake of unity. You couldn't learn that in seminary.

"And now, all Disciples of good will, conservative and liberal, must show the world that 'still more excellent way' by attempting together to follow the leading of God's Spirit."

That sounded like something he would have said in April, but it was still true, wasn't it? And in the meantime, he had learned to distinguish disagreement, even strident opposition, from genuine evil. You couldn't learn that in seminary either.

He decided that, rather than reading through the rest of this speech, short as it was, he would glance over the other one, when Duane reentered the room. But this time he looked as if he had been crying. The assembly had not yet heard the results, but he knew them: 3602 in favor, 1827 against. It took a minute for this to compute.

"I just can't believe it." Duane's voice was not only high but cracking. Abigail stared at her father and then, without speaking, came to sit next to him, one hand under his coat with her finger through his belt loop.

Disappointment, yes, but was this also relief he was feeling? People later spoke of his "defeat," but at that moment he didn't feel defeated. A little shocked, a little deflated, but not defeated.

He glanced at Margaret who had her hand on his shoulder, rubbing back and forth, but was staring at the floor. He looked toward his father, but it was his mother who appeared before his mind's eye. What would she have said about all this? How would she have felt about him? Matthew cleared his throat.

"Thanks, Duane. ... You've been great through all of this. A tremendous friend." He would have stood to embrace the older man, but he didn't want Abigail to move. "Well," he said, "I need to speak to the assembly."

"I have been talking with the security people about that," said Duane, his voice high and soft, "and they don't think it's a good idea."

Now Matthew did stand up. "Duane, you know what I need to do. This is the one moment when for sure I'll have everyone's attention." In his peripheral vision, he could see Margaret shaking her head.

"Why don't we bring the police lieutenant in here," said Duane softly, "and he ... "

"Look, I didn't put myself in front of the church for the last two months just to be holed up in a guarded room when it all comes to a head."

The room was silent for several seconds before Duane said, "Well, I guess it's your call. I told them you'd probably say that." He smiled faintly. "They won't like it, but. ... Actually, they don't think anyone would try something in front of ten thousand people, especially since you won't be the GMP, although I mentioned to them the man in ..."

Matthew cut him off. "I won't talk for long." He now looked at Margaret, who breathed in deeply and let it out slowly.

"If you're going, I should go with you," she said, smoothing her skirt as she got up from the chair.

"Me too," said Abigail.

Matthew shook his head. "Beth can take you and Zachary backstage where you can see us"—he looked at the officer who nodded—"but I want you to stay there ... Abby."

She was ready to protest, but then smiled, adjusted her baseball cap, and took Zachary's hand. "Look at it this way, Dad. You won't have to spend so much time with knuckleheads! Well, except Zachary, and he'll grow out of it." Zachary gave her a shove, and they headed out the door with Beth and the officer.

The vote had just been announced as Matthew and Margaret walked up the steps to the stage and heard the swell of sound. She took his arm, and he bent his elbow to hold her hand close. For the first time in what seemed like months, a prayer came unbidden: "God, work through your servant, even though he doesn't understand your ways, even when he forgets to say thanks."

In the front rows of standing, applauding Disciples, he could see many he knew by name, most of them in tears. He knew he should feel tense—what with guards on either side of the stage, scanning the crowd—but, instead, an incredible sense of warmth arose in his chest, not unlike what he had felt waiting for Margaret to come down the aisle, that almost made *him* cry. He stepped back from the microphone and the applause increased, like a wave cresting through the arena. Margaret had his right hand, and he squeezed hers tightly. It took real nerve for her to be here, he thought. And real graciousness. This had been hardest on her. He leaned over and kissed her on the cheek. The applause crested again.

Matthew cleared his throat, raised his hands, and gradually, as the clapping subsided, particular faces came into focus: Barbara and Phil. The regional minister from Tennessee. Was that Robert and Greg? Margaret said she had met them at the Halloween party, but he hadn't seen them until now. Could that be Reena next to them?

Other faces appeared to him in the still-standing crowd: Gerald, his supportive friend from the UCC. Marvin and Isabel standing next to Raymond. Was that the rancher from Montana? There was Harold, though he could barely make him out. And right in front of him was the man—where was he from?—who had asked him if he wouldn't rather be part of a more liberal, more urban denomination. But that, of course, would be missing the point. You didn't get to choose your relatives. You may fight with them because some things are worth the battle, but, at the end of the day, your life has to take them in.

He had the right-pocket speech in his hand, but now, following instinct, he set it on the podium face down. He squeezed Margaret's hand again and took a deep breath. "Sisters and brothers in Jesus Christ ... "

AUTHOR'S NOTE

Much, if not most, fiction starts with an autobiographical kernel. Since in the case of *The Nominee* it is more than a kernel, a word of explanation seems appropriate.

Like Matthew in the novel, I was the nominee to become General Minister and President of the Christian Church (Disciples of Christ) denomination in 1991. As in the plot of the novel, my nomination was narrowly rejected in the church's General Assembly because, in large measure, of my support for the LGBTQ community; and this support did lead to a good deal of opposition, including hateful letters and phone calls. There are also other ways in which my life parallels that of the fictional Matthew. For example, I was, at the time of the nomination, dean of a Disciples seminary, and was involved with the World Council of Churches.

The Nominee, however, is still very much a work of fiction. Matthew's particular thoughts and actions should not be construed as mine; we bear resemblance, but we are not the same. The other characters, including Margaret and Abigail, are entirely creations of my imagination, with one exception: Duane is modeled on the Rev. John O. Humbert, who, as readers will note, is a hero of the story.

I did speak to dozens of local gatherings of Disciples during the nomination, but the encounters described in the novel are invented, as are all of the dialogues. The plot, while broadly based on my experience, was shaped with the intention of evoking certain thoughts and emotions, of highlighting specific themes. The particular scenes of the novel, while in some cases inspired by actual events, are fictional creations. It should go without saying that I do not, and never did, speak for the Disciples of Christ denomination.

Having said all of that, I want to stress that animosity toward lesbian, gay, and transgendered neighbors remains all too factual. To me, the real heroes of my nomination were those persons whose sexual orientation far too often led to their marginalization, or worse, in church and society. And while there has been progress since 1991, many in the majority still seem to believe that what is normal for them should be the norm for everybody else.

If this novel helps raise awareness of—and opposition to—ongoing discrimination, I will be gratified.

—Michael Kinnamon